THE DEVIL'S LAUGHTER

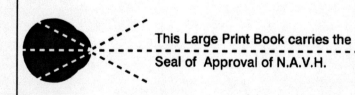

LOU PROPHET, BOUNTY HUNTER

THE DEVIL'S LAUGHTER

PETER BRANDVOLD

WHEELER PUBLISHING
A part of Gale, Cengage Learning

GALE
CENGAGE Learning·

Detroit • New York • San Francisco • New Haven, Conn • Waterville, Maine • London

LIBRARY OF CONGRESS CATALOGING-IN-PUBLICATION DATA

Brandvold, Peter.
  The devil's laughter : Lou Prophet, bounty hunter / by Peter Brandvold. — Large print ed.
    p. cm. — (Wheeler Publishing large print Western)
    ISBN 978-1-4104-5175-0 (softcover) — ISBN 1-4104-5175-5 (softcover)
  1. Prophet, Lou (Fictitious character)—Fiction. 2. Outlaws—Fiction. 3. Large type books. I. Title.
PS3552.R3236D486 2012
813'.54—dc23   2012026931

Published in 2012 by arrangement with The Berkley Publishing Group, a member of Penguin Group (USA) Inc.

Printed in the United States of America
    1 2 3 4 5   16 15 14 13 12
ED296

For all the other wanderers
of the American wastelands.

Adelante?

1

The Mexican gods had their necks in a hump.

Rain slashed nearly straight down from the night-black sky. Flooded arroyos surged. Thunder boomed like giant boulders crashing down the highest mountains in Sonora.

The wind knocked branches off the nut trees and mesquites in this broad, ridge-sheathed canyon and sent them careening toward the soaked, sandy earth. A couple bounced off the big bounty hunter's shoulders, nearly knocking off his hat, as if the gods of Mexico didn't want him here. As if they didn't want anybody here but wanted only to scour the Earth, once and for all, of all humanity.

The big dun, aptly named Mean and Ugly, didn't like the weather a bit and didn't hesitate to let his rider know he'd rather be in a warm barn with plenty of oats and a mare or two to brush noses with.

"Me, too, feller," Lou Prophet said as he and the ugly dun moved through the storm-tossed night, the collar of his yellow rain slicker raised to his unshaven jaws. "Me, too. . . ."

Lightning flashed, lighting up the heavens from one horizon to the other. Prophet put Mean and Ugly up a low hill amongst thrashing, dripping walnut trees, the rain sluicing off his funnel-brimmed Stetson. Lightning flashed again. It was like someone raising and lowering a lamp wick quickly in Heaven. Prophet jerked back on the horse's reins with one hand and lowered his Winchester with the other.

For a wink of time during that last flash, he'd seen a silhouetted figure standing amongst the walnuts and mesquites just ahead and to his right. A big man in a low-crowned sombrero and an ankle-length coat buffeted by the wind.

A small orange flame licked at Prophet from the rainy darkness. Something nudged his hat. As the gun's belch reached his ears, he drew his Winchester's hammer back with his gloved thumb and fired. He cocked the gun quickly, keeping the stock clamped against his right thigh over which the tail of his yellow rain slicker hung, and fired three more times.

During another brief lightning flash he glimpsed his assailant falling backward, tossing his own rifle away. He did not see the man hit the ground before silver-stitched darkness closed down again. There might have been a scream, but the wailing storm drowned it the same way it seemed intent on drowning everything else on this harsh night way too far south of the Mexican border.

Holding Mean and Ugly's reins taut in one hand, racking a fresh cartridge in his rifle with the other, Prophet looked around, slitting his eyes against the rain reaching under his hat to pepper his eyes. When no more bullets screeched toward him, he stepped down from Mean's back and looped the reins over a low branch of a bending pecan tree. He grabbed his sawed-off, double-barrel ten-gauge off his saddle horn and slung the leather lanyard over his neck and shoulder, letting the handy gut shredder, invaluable for close-up work, hang down his back.

"In Dixie Land where I was born in," he sang softly to ease his nerves drawn taut as coiled snakes between his broad shoulders, tramping over the wet ground to where the dead man lay — a black mound in the darkness. "Early on one frosty mornin' — Look

9

away! Look away!"

He looked around carefully, then returned his slitted gaze to the dead man. Lightning flashed. It glittered along the dead man's black leather coat and breeches and shone in his white teeth revealed by stretched-back, mustache-mantled lips. His hat had tumbled down his back when he'd fallen. The top of his head was bald as a baby's ass, but long black hair curled down both sides of it to dangle in wet tangles in the mud around his shoulders.

"Look away! Dixie Land!" Prophet sang, lifting his head to peer into the rain-slashed darkness before him, through the jostling trees.

Weaving amongst the trees, he strode forward, thumbing fresh cartridges from his shell belt and sliding them through his Winchester's loading gate. He continued forward until he came to an arroyo through which muddy water eddied, running from his right to his left.

Looking around for a way across the arroyo, he spied movement in the corner of his right eye and turned to see a man and horse lunge up out of the wash. Lightning flashed, showing the water glistening off the man's duster and dripping off the brim of his low-crowned straw sombrero.

As the horse set its feet atop the bank and set itself to shake off the muddy water, the man swung his head toward Prophet. He was merely a silhouette now, ambient light winking off his horse's bit and his saddle trimmings as well as the rifle in his hands. Prophet crouched, raised the Winchester, and drew the off-cocked hammer back until it clicked.

Lightning flashed.

Thunder clapped, causing the Earth to leap.

At the same time, Prophet triggered his rifle and saw the flash of the rider's own carbine. The reports of both guns were drowned by the thunderclap, but Prophet heard the thud of the other man's bullet striking a tree behind him. In the darkness following the lightning flash, he saw the dark shadow of the man's big steeldust lunge toward him and then veer away, its saddle empty, stirrups flapping against its sides.

Something moved in the flooded arroyo. Prophet stepped closer to see a large oblong object, which another lightning flash revealed to be the man he'd just shot floating on his back, arms and legs akimbo. Bobbing and turning, he was carried past Prophet and out of sight downstream.

Prophet dropped to one knee and looked

11

around, quietly singing, "Old Missus married Will the Weaver; Will was a gay deceiver, Look away . . . !" Deciding no other threats were near, he rose and walked along the edge of the arroyo, finding a freshly downed tree sprawled across it. "Look away! Look away! Dixie Land!" he sang, tightroping the tree and throwing his arms out for balance so he wouldn't fall in the flashing stream.

He strode through the rocky, wet desert, swinging his head from right to left and back again, holding his rifle up high across chest in both hands. While the rain continued to slash at him, running like an open irrigation pipe from the funneled trough of his hat so that it was like looking through a mini waterfall, he climbed a low ridge and dropped to a knee, resting his rifle on his shoulder.

On another, higher slope that climbed to a velvet black mountain wall, several vertical and horizontal rectangles of yellow light shone. Lightning flashes revealed the dim image of a sprawling hacienda beneath a peaked roof tiled in red sandstone.

The casa sat behind a pale adobe wall. Between the wall and the house was a gap of fifty or sixty yards and what appeared to be a veritable jungle of storm-lashed shrubs and trees. Large verandas with broad archways on both the first and second floors fronted the building. Beyond the casa, the ridge wall loomed tall and formidable, several hundred feet above the valley floor. The ridge and the stormy night fairly swallowed the structure clinging to it like a small jewel hidden in the folds of a large, black sofa.

Cigarette smoke touched Prophet's nostrils.

Instinctively, he pulled the rifle off his shoulder and crouched low, looking around. Below on his left, about halfway down the other side of the low ridge he was on, stood a gnarled tree. A lean-to had been erected in front of the tree, slanting downslope from it. Lightning revealed the wind- and rain-buffeted tarpaulin lashed to the ground with ropes and wooden spikes. Beneath the tarpaulin, a man crouched, facing downslope and toward the casa sprawled on the next rise.

In front of the crouched figure, a pinprick of orange light glowed dully, then faded. The man's right arm came down, and during another flash of lightning Prophet saw the ghostly cloud of cigarette smoke blown out into the storm. Prophet began to lift his Winchester's stock toward his shoulder, then checked the motion.

No point in wasting a bullet. No telling how many he was going to need here. Besides, the shot might be heard between thunderclaps up at the casa. He had to shoot sparingly, carefully from here on in.

He moved down the slope a ways and leaned the rifle against a boulder. Inside the lean-to, the Mexican brought his cigarette to his lips once more. He froze with the end of the quirley barely touching his lower lip and frowned. Something hovered a couple of feet in front of his face. He'd just recognized the large, gloved hand and had opened his mouth to scream when the hand smashed over his nose and mouth, brutally drawing his head back and up, exposing his bearded neck above the knotted blue bandanna.

He screamed into the hand, kicked as he felt the cold slash of the big knife across his throat. He convulsed as the hot blood spurted from the severed arteries.

Prophet held the man's head back taut until the blood gradually stopped geysering. Then he removed his hand, let the Mexican flop back against the gnarled tree, dead but still jerking, and tramped back to retrieve his rifle. He held the gun in one hand as he carefully made his way down the slope, weaving amongst the rocks and hunkering behind shrubs or boulders when lightning flashed, afraid he'd be silhouetted against the slope.

He made his gradual way toward a black gap in the adobe wall over which vines grew like slithering black snakes. Tree branches hung low over the wall, some scraping against it. Nothing around had been taken care of in a while. Likely, the hacienda had been abandoned by its hacendado for whatever reason — perhaps Mojaves had pushed him out — and was now the regular hideout of the gang of thieves and coldblooded killers lead by Antonio Lazzaro and Red Snake Corbin. All had been wanted for several years in nearly every western territory north of the border, and their hideout had been a well-kept secret.

Until Prophet had uncovered its location by tracking the gang here after they'd robbed a bank in Nogales and hightailed it across the border like a pack of calf-killing wolves. He'd been summoned to Nogales from where he'd been holed up in San Antonio, with a telegraph in the customarily cryptic language of his sometimes partner and lover, Louisa Bonaventure:

BE IN NOGALES BY AUGUST 15TH.

He'd ridden hard, but he'd reached Nogales a day late. The Lazzaro gang had

15

hit the bank the day before.

Apparently, Louisa had infiltrated the gang, though Prophet had not known this beforehand. She could be damn secretive at times, Louisa could. She'd likely thought she could take them all down herself, but this bunch must have been too much for even the Vengeance Queen, as Louisa was known far and wide across the frontier. She hadn't been able to stop them from leaving seven dead in the street outside the Bank of Nogales, including two peasant boys who'd been playing around the bank with stick guns.

That must have been damn hard on her, Prophet thought. Louisa could not abide the killing of innocents, especially innocent women and children. She must have realized too late that she'd had the tiger by the tail, and she'd needed Prophet's help. He just hoped he'd gotten here in time. He'd lost the trail several days ago and had taken several more days in picking it up again.

Because of the gang's especially cold-blooded reputation, the Nogales lawman had been unable to form a posse. The lawman and his two deputies had gotten discouraged by a hail of lead flung their way by a couple of Lazzaro's rear trail riders and had turned back to Nogales twenty miles south of the border.

Prophet had tracked the lawmen, keeping his distance, as bounty hunters were treated like chicken-killing dogs by most badge toters. When the Mexican lawmen had headed back north, Prophet had drifted onto the killers' trail and began dusting it slowly, with the casual expertise and caution of a stalking puma. Still, Lazzaro was a sneaky son of a bitch. He'd covered his trail well and had taken several detours to throw off shadowers, and such tactics had worked even on Prophet.

Now a wagon trail angled out from the rocky desert to curve through a gap in the adobe wall before him. Both ruts were virtual rain-pelted streams. The wings of a wooden gate were thrown back against the wall, both hanging from rotting posts. Prophet ran crouching across the trail and dropped to a knee about two feet from the wall, on the left side of the gap.

He was about to rise and bolt through the gap when he saw the silhouette of a man sitting against the inside of the wall, on the gap's right side. The guard was hunkered beneath his sombrero, facing the casa. He was sitting on the inside of the wall because the rain was slashing from the opposite side.

Obviously, the gang hadn't suspected they'd been followed down from the border. They'd grown fat, lazy, and careless.

Prophet grinned beneath his dripping hat brim.

He tensed when the guard swung his head toward him. He started to raise the rifle but checked the move. The guard's lips were moving and Prophet heard him speaking in Spanish. To a man on the other side of the gap and whose back was likely just on the other side of the wall from Prophet.

Again, the bounty hunter grinned. He raised his rifle but before he could click the hammer back, something carved a hot line across the back of his neck before hammering the wall in front of him. Bizarre laughter cackled as though from down a long tunnel, muffled by the rain and thunder.

"Preparese para bailar con El Diablo, Senor Prophet!"

2

"Prepare to shake hands with the Devil, Senor Prophet!" echoed in the bounty hunter's ears as, instead of swinging around toward the trail, which was the direction that the crazy laughter and the warning had come from, Prophet bolted off his heels and ran toward the gap, firing his Winchester.

The guard who'd been hunkered down inside the wall on the gap's right side had been gaining his feet and bringing up a Spencer carbine when Prophet's first two rounds hammered through him.

As he flew backward, triggering a shot in the air one-handed, Prophet dove forward to land in the spot where the guard had been slumped. The rifle behind him roared three, four times, slinging mud and gravel every which way, one shot kissing the end of the bounty hunter's left boot heel. Prophet twisted around, saw the second gate guard hastily gaining his feet and reaching for a pistol holstered on his left hip. He was having trouble getting the pistol up above the flap of his leather duster and, knowing he was about to die, screamed horrifically as Prophet slung two rounds between two large, silver circles sewn into the duster's front.

The guard flew back against the wall, dropping the pistol in the mud, and then slid down the side of the wall before piling up belly down at its base.

Prophet ejected the last spent cartridge and seated fresh as he pushed up onto his knees and fired at the tall figure running across the trail toward the wall. A rifle flashed twice from the figure's middle. Both rounds screeched over Prophet's head.

The bounty hunter fired twice. Through the wafting powder smoke and the slashing rain he watched the running figure jerk and twist as he dove toward the wall.

There was a scream and a squishing, splashing sound as the man hit the ground at the base of the wall and lay still.

Prophet glanced at the dark, slumped figure and said, "I believe you have me at a disadvantage, amigo," as he thumbed fresh shells through his Winchester's loading gate, hoping all the rain and mud didn't foul the action. All he needed was a jammed rifle.

He hadn't recognized the dead man's voice. Likely someone he'd hunted before. He was always a little surprised by how well known he'd become in the long years since the war, when he'd started hunting men for a living.

Maybe notorious was a better word.

There was still plenty of thunder but not enough, probably, to have covered the recent gunfire. He looked through the dripping, thrashing foliage toward the big house with its windows lit.

That someone inside had heard the fusillade was confirmed when the big paneled door on the first story burst open and a lean man with a long, mustached face and wearing a short charro jacket and string tie burst out, holding a pistol in his right hand. Another, bigger man emerged from the opening behind him, holding a sawed-off shotgun in both hands across his chest.

Then two more came out behind the bigger man, and the smaller man, the man whom Prophet recognized as Hector Foran, a former Federale captain from Sonora who'd been riding with the Lazzaro bunch for several years, shouted orders while he waved his pistol around.

Prophet, still on one knee, pressed his Winchester's stock against his shoulder, aimed carefully across the fifty-foot distance between him and the casa, and fired once, twice, three, then four times, watching the big man with the shotgun and two other men go down howling on the veranda's elevated floor.

Hector Foran leaped back, wide-eyed and rattled, then triggered his pistol twice. He probably couldn't see much due to the light emanating from the house behind him. Prophet triggered one more round, but the bullet merely plowed into the casa's front wall as Foran bolted back into the house, yelling and leaving the stout oak doors standing wide behind him.

Bringing his own sawed-off ten-gauge around to his front, Prophet ran forward, one hand on the jostling barn blaster, the other holding his rifle. He looked around at the sprawling, dilapidated building before him, hearing shots fired from the second story, and leaped onto the veranda and rushed between the open doors.

He was in a bland, gray hall with a steel-banded oak barrel on his right. Stairs coming up from below lay to his left, and just now he heard the clacks of heels on the steps and saw two hatless heads rising up out of the casa's bowels. The lead man turned at the top of the stairs, eyes blazing, mouth forming a perfect circle when he saw

Prophet bearing down on him with his double-barreled ten-gauge. The brigand lifted a big, pearl-gripped LeMat in his left hand and a Colt Navy in his right.

Prophet tripped the coach gut shredder's first trigger.

Ka-boooom!

The blast rocked the cracked flagstones beneath his boots. It lifted the two-pistoled hombre two feet off the floor and hurled him straight back over a wooden table, howling and blowing off the pointed toe of his right black boot with the shotgun shell in his pearl-gripped LeMat.

The second man on the stairs had a change of heart when he saw his partner shaking and bleeding his life out on the other side of the table. Wheeling, he ran back down the stairs. Prophet ran to the head of the stairs and aimed down into the dingy well.

"You don't turn around, you'll get it in the back, friend."

The man stopped. He was tall and thick, with red pants and high black boots. He wore an eye patch. When Prophet saw the good eye, he said with a shrug, "Don't make no difference to me, just thought it might make you feel better."

The man showed his teeth and yelled as

he raised a short-barreled Smith & Wesson. The gut shredder roared again and blew the one-eyed man on down the stairs and into the dingy shadows below.

Quickly, the bounty hunter breeched the smoking gut shredder, plucked out the spent loads, shoved fresh ones into the barrels, and snapped the gun closed. In the ceiling he could hear the thumps of pounding boots and the explosions of wild gunfire amidst shouts and yells of frantic men.

Prophet smiled as he hummed softly, "In Dixie Land where I was born, early on one frosty mornin' . . ."

He turned to walk on down the hall lit by a tar-soaked torch bracketed to the wall in a steel cage, stopping when boots sounded on the stone stairs straight ahead of him, just beyond a broad kitchen with a large, black cookstove and a long, heavy wooden table littered with tin plates and food scraps and many pots and wooden cups. A couple of pots on the range sputtered and dribbled juices down their sides.

The spicy smells were enticing, but Prophet didn't have time to think about his empty belly. Three men were descending the stone steps before him. Both barrels of the gut shredder, triggered one after the other, were enough to send all three tumbling and rolling and painting the stones around them dark red. Prophet reloaded the shotgun — "Look away! Look away! Look away! Dixie land!" — and continued walking past the stairs, stepping over one of the dead men. He paused at a half-open doorway on his left.

Inside, a lamp burned on a broad mahogany desk covered in cloth-bound ledgers and rolled maps. Prophet nudged the door open slowly with the shotgun's stock. The hinges squawked.

The widening doorway revealed a broad office with more heavy furniture and bookcases, most of them empty. A fire danced in a fieldstone hearth under a gaudy painting of a naked, full-breasted brunette sprawled on a red velvet settee on a veranda trimmed with many potted plants.

There were maps of most of the American southwestern territories and the northern Mexican provinces on the walls, some with flags pinned to them, likely indicating targets the gang had yet to hone in on — probably towns or ranch headquarters with blooded horses or well-stocked bank vaults. Lazzaro was also known for smuggling diamonds across the border, so some of the flags likely indicated diamond caches, as well.

Prophet had just moved away from the door when a gun clicked in his right ear. The hard, cold barrel of the gun was pressed to his head behind his ear.

"Drop the Greener, *mi* amigo," said a low, resonate voice. Prophet could smell the man's leather clothes and the sickly sweet cologne as well as the faint stench of tequila and cigar smoke.

Prophet lifted the shotgun's lanyard from around his neck and dropped the gun on the floor a few feet in front of him.

"Now the rifle and your sidearm."

Prophet did as he was told, cold chicken flesh spreading out between his shoulder blades at the low, menacing voice of the gun-wielding hombre behind him. He glanced over his right shoulder to see the dandified Mexican in the short charro jacket sweating, keeping the cocked Colt aimed at Prophet's head.

"How many more of you are there, Senor Prophet?" asked Hector Foran, beads of sweat running down his cheeks and into his carefully trimmed beard.

Some said that Foran had become the brains of the outfit, setting up their jobs. That would explain the fancy digs complete with territorial maps and books that were probably chock-full of the timetables of enticing train and stage coach targets.

"Hell," Prophet said, "you're surround—!"

He wheeled, slashing upward with his right arm. Foran's Colt roared on the heels of another thunderclap, the bullet thumping into the ceiling. Prophet closed his fingers around the man's gun hand, wrapped his other hand around the man's throat, and shoved him hard against the wall.

Boots thumped behind him. There'd been other men in the room, and they were bounding toward him. Prophet felt a stone drop in his belly when he heard a hammer click.

Foran, red-faced and wild-eyed, turned his head to the side and yelled, "Don't kill him!"

Something hard as a pistol butt slammed against the back of Prophet's head. It was a glancing blow, his shoulder taking much of it. It still made birds twitter and chirp in Prophet's head and caused Foran's red-faced visage to become two bleary pictures as the floor came up to slam against Prophet's knees.

He stared down at Foran's high-topped, black, copper-tipped boots, shaking his head to clear it.

"I'm going to ask you once more, Senor

Prophet," Foran said, bending down and glowering at the woozy bounty hunter, "how many more in your party?"

"There's gotta be several upstairs," said one of the men behind Prophet. There were two, maybe three other men in the room with Foran.

"Like I said — you're surrounded. Posse, Rurales, cavalry boys . . ." Best to let them think they were badly outgunned. Nervous men were distracted men, and easier to kill.

Prophet heaved himself up off his knees. He twisted his six-foot-four-inch, two-hundred-and-thirty-pound frame around and lunged at one of the three figures standing behind him, in a semicircle between him and the desk.

He glimpsed a gun held taut in a brown hand and grabbed it as the man shouted. The others lurched back. Prophet slammed his big body into the man whose gun he now had. While he and the man hit the floor, Prophet snaked the pistol up and fired.

He'd been moving and firing at the same time and managed to only clip the ear of the man he'd been aiming at — a Yanqui redhead whose freckled face he recognized as the American outlaw Red Barker. Barker triggered his own pistol as he cursed and showed his teeth and clamped a hand over his bloody ear. He recocked the pistol as he swung it toward Prophet, crouching and extending his gun hand as he continued to curse.

Prophet tried to raise his own gun again but the man he'd fallen on — a fat Mex who smelled like a cantina — swatted Prophet's wrist just as Prophet squeezed the trigger. The bullet slammed into the door as another gun belched.

Prophet jerked, winced, and cast his horrified gaze at Barker, whose extended arm went suddenly limp. The redhead's freckled, blue-eyed face acquired a confused expression.

No smoke curled from the barrel of the silver-chased Remington in his hand. Surprisingly, no bullet had hammered into Prophet's large person — at least, none that he could feel at the moment. Smoke wafted in the doorway behind the now-sagging Barker — pale, weblike fingers gently waving this way and that, dimly illuminated by the several lit candles and lamps in the office and a burning oil pot in the hall.

Foran leaped back toward the desk, cursing in Spanish, and raising his own Colt toward the door in which a dusky figure now appeared, jostling shadows obscuring it, though light from the hall shone briefly on two clear, hazel eyes as the gun in the shooter's hand lapped flames into the room, roaring between thunderclaps outside.

The man nearest Barker took the second bullet and flew backward into the room's shadows while the third bullet slammed with a hollow crunching sound into the head of the fat Mex struggling with Prophet. His head hit the floor with a hard thud.

Prophet stared at the figure in the door, saw the pistol leap in the shooter's hand twice more, throwing Foran across a low table while triggering his pistol into the ceiling. The brains of the outfit hit the floor on the table's other side, screaming, "*Mierda*! Spare me — *por favor*. Oh, god — please spare me!"

The dusky figure clad in deerskins and wearing a red sash around its trim waist stepped fluidly into the room, rocking the silver-chased Colt in and aiming again at Foran cowering against the back wall flanking the desk. "To give you the information you were seeking from my partner, in a none-too-polite way, I'll tell you that there is only one more assailant, Senor Foran."

Prophet hauled himself to his feet and looked back at Foran, who was clutching his right, bloody shoulder and staring at the person who'd just entered the smoky, shadowy room. His pointed chin jutted as he dropped his lower jaw, his brown eyes white-ringed with befuddlement. *"You, Senorita Batista?"*

"The name's not Leona Batista, amigo. The name's Bonaventure." She glanced at Prophet. "I ride with this big, ugly lummox . . . when I'm in the mood for suffering his poor hygiene and bad jokes."

Foran looked from Prophet to the hazel-eyed blond in the straw sombrero and deerskin charro outfit complete with red bandanna and red sash, and hardened his jaws. *"Traidor!"* he shouted.

"Si." The blond's Colt roared.

The .45 slug blew a quarter-sized hole in the middle of Foran's forehead, jerking his head back as though he'd been punched in the chin. He gurgled down deep in his throat, and his eyes rolled back in his head, the lids staying open. He sagged back against the wall that was dripping with the man's own blood and brains and dropped his chin to his chest as though in prayer.

Red Barker made a noise near Louisa's brown boots, and she casually angled her Colt toward the man and shot him through his right eye, giving the pistoleer a Louisa Bonaventure–style finishing touch.

31

3

Louisa had barely even looked at the red-head before she'd shot him. That's how cool and confident she was with her own shooting prowess. It was maddening sometimes, Prophet thought — this need of hers to show off.

And some women appreciated his jokes. . . .

Now she twirled her Colt on her finger with a characteristic flourish and dropped the piece in the holster thonged low on her right thigh. Another pearl-gripped Colt jutted from a second holster on her left thigh. Two cartridge belts crisscrossed her slender waist, beneath the sash. Her leggings were fringed, as were the sleeves of her short, hickory tan charro jacket.

Prophet studied the girl, who was all of twenty-one but whose clear, hard, hazel eyes were a good fifty years older, and gave a wry chuff. "Good Lord, girl — you look like

Bill Cody!"

"That's how they dress down here, Lou. You'd want me to look like one of 'em, wouldn't you?"

Prophet studied the girl once more. He was more accustomed to seeing her in a simple riding skirt and blouse, maybe with a loose sweater beneath which she concealed her smoke wagons. He had to admit, though, that she wore the stylish Mexican garb right well. The deerskin clung nicely to her five-foot-four-inch and hundred-and-ten-pound frame. The sombrero shaded her face mysteriously. Her silky blond hair fluttered down over her shoulders in loose sausage curls.

A faint flush rose in her cheeks, and she looked down at the outfit before raising her eyes to his once more. Her lips shaped a smile, and her eyes flashed alluringly as she strode over to him, stopped a foot away, and stared up at him. "You like, amigo?"

"Some women think my jokes are right funny."

"Only the whores you pay to listen."

Prophet appraised her outfit again and curled his upper lip. "I like what's under all that a whole lot better than the get-up itself."

She showed her white teeth as she rose up

33

on the toes of her boots and pressed her lips to his. When she pulled away, he glanced at the dead men around him and then at the open door to the hallway, noting that the big house was silent now except for the thunder creaking its stout ceiling beams and the rain rattling its windows.

"I do appreciate your coming . . . finally."

"You heard my arrival, I take it?

"You can't go anywhere without causing a commotion, Lou."

Prophet glanced at the ceiling over her pretty head. "You sure they're all dead?"

"Oh, they're all dead. I surprised them right well. Don't think a one of them suspected me of . . . *being a traitor*, as Senor Foran so aptly put it."

Prophet frowned, vaguely surprised by the girl's droll tone. She almost sounded as though she partly regretted the ruse she'd pulled on Lazzaro's bunch of cold-blooded killers.

"The Nogales loot?"

Louisa grimaced then strode around behind the big desk and sagged back in the leather bullhorn chair. She crossed her fancily stitched cowhide boots on the edge of the desk, giving one of the large-roweled copper spurs a singing spin.

"We got a little problem," she said, tossing

her big sombrero onto the desk in front of her and scrubbing her gloved hands through her hair so that it stuck up in long, silky, sexy tufts all over her head.

Prophet kicked over the big, dead Mexican and glanced over his shoulder at Louisa. "I don't like problems, girl. You know that."

"Well, you got one now. Or . . . four of them to be exact."

Prophet leaned down to scoop his Peacemaker off the floor where the Mex had lain on it. Now he grabbed his Winchester and shotgun, lay both across the desk, then kicked a ladder-back chair over in front of the desk and slacked into it. He looked at Louisa, the blond *bandita*, sitting across from him, her hair pleasingly tousled.

"Tell me."

"Lazzaro and Red Snake Corbin lit out with the loot. Sometime this afternoon, when the rest of the men . . . and I . . . were enjoying siesta. They and two others had a double cross on."

Prophet's broad, broken-nosed face colored up and turned as weathery as the night outside the office's large, shuttered windows. "You mean, we got more to go after? How'd that happen?"

Louisa gave back as good as she got. "It happened because there were twenty, nearly

35

thirty men around here, and a woman, and I had one helluva time keeping track of them all." She pursed her lips and sighed. "And I reckon they hornswoggled me, just like the others. I had no idea Lazzaro and Sugar and two other men were gonna pull foot."

"Who's Sugar?"

"Sugar Delphi. She's blind."

"Say that again?"

"She's blind — sure enough. And she's . . ." Louisa looked uncertain, a little perplexed. "She's Lazzaro's woman. He's her eyes, I reckon." She hiked a shoulder noncommittally.

She dropped her boots to the floor, leaned forward, and grabbed one of the two cut-glass decanters off the table's left side. "She may be blind, but she's a tough nut. She drugged me. That's why I didn't know they were taking off with the loot until they'd gone. I reckon the others still didn't know about it. Lazzaro, Sugar, Red Snake Corbin, and Roy Kiljoy headed out while the others were asleep, ahead of the storm."

"*Drugged* you?"

"Left me asleep upstairs where we roomed together. We sort of looked out for each other, Sugar and me. Despite that she's been blind from birth." Louisa filled a goblet with what looked like brandy and slid it across the desk to Prophet. She filled the second goblet, and Prophet arched a brow at his partner whom he'd known to drink nothing stronger than the occasional ginger beer or cherry sarsaparilla.

"Hold on, there — what're you doin'?"

Louisa lifted the goblet and tipped back a goodly portion. She swallowed, smacked her bee-stung, ruby red lips, and ran the back of her hand across her mouth. "A girl's gotta do more than just dress the part to fit in around here. These fellas and Sugar drank damn near all day and all night. It would have looked a mite suspicious if I hadn't joined in on the fun."

"You picked up a blue tongue, too." Prophet clucked in reproof and stared at her, genuinely surprised by her transformation.

Normally, she didn't cuss — only a muttered "shucks" or "shoot" or, at the most, a "gosh dang" or two. She'd been raised by God-fearin' folks up Nebraska way — before they were all slaughtered by the Handsome Dave Duvall gang, that was. "I'm gonna have to get you out of here before you try to cut in on my deal with the Devil."

She sat back in her chair and arched a

brow with her own brand of cool admonishment. "I'd never go that far, Lou."

"Looks like you're halfway there." Prophet threw back the entire shot of brandy in two short swallows, enjoying the warm flush throughout his soaked, chilled, bullet-burned, and head-bruised body, and refilled the glass. "You mean to tell me that Foran and the others weren't onto 'em?"

"Nope. Surprised even me. They were a tight bunch, or so I figured. They headed out early afternoon, siesta time. The days don't really start around here until after nine o'clock at night. Then . . ." Louisa lifted her glass to her lips once more and tossed back the rest of the brandy. "The Devil takes the hindmost."

Prophet cursed and reached inside his rain slicker, pulled a soggy chamois sack from his shirt pocket. He tossed the pouch onto the desk with another curse. "I need some dry tobacco."

Louisa opened and closed a few desk drawers before tossing three long cigars onto the desk in front of Prophet. "There you go — have a cigar on Foran."

"Don't mind if I do." Prophet bit the end off one of the cigars and touched the end to the mantle of the lamp on the desk, puffing smoke as he rolled the cylinder between his lips. "Which way they head?"

"I scouted around a little before the rain came, saw four sets of shod hoofprints heading southwest."

"How'd they get past the scouts? I had a helluva time!"

"Scouts don't get posted until dark. You must've done a good job of trackin' us out from Nogales, Lou. Lazzaro and Red Snake had no idea you were behind us."

The bounty hunter only grunted at this to mask his chagrin.

She lifted her chin at him. "You're bleeding."

Prophet swiped his hand to his shoulder, felt the blood running down from the bullet burn across the back of his neck. "A little tattoo to commemorate the day. Don't recollect we ever took down this many all at once before."

"The Becker twins up in Dakota — remember? Two years ago." Louisa heaved herself out of her chair, leaned down to remove the silk neckerchief sticking up out of the breast pocket of Foran's short jacket, and walked around behind Prophet. "There were thirty of them."

"Ah, yeah," Prophet said, sipping the brandy. "But we used dynamite we stole from those drunken soldiers — remember?"

"We made a nice haul. I think you must have stomped with your tail up for two months after we collected those bounties." Louisa dampened the silk hanky from the brandy bottle, lifted Prophet's neckerchief so she could get at the burn, then lightly ran the brandy-soaked cloth along the length of the graze.

Prophet winced as the brandy hit the open cut, but let a devilish smile lift his mouth corners and narrow his pale blue eyes. "That's what I'm here for. Easy money and fast women. Yes, Ole Scratch lived up to his end of the bargain up there in Dakota."

"I'd just as soon not hear about it," Louisa said, rubbing the handkerchief a little too hard across the cut.

Prophet sucked a sharp breath, chuckled, reached behind him to grab her arm, and pulled her onto his lap. "I ain't had the pleasure of your blankets for a while." She felt warm and supple in his lap. "You oughta write more often." He stared down at her smooth, tan cleavage showing behind her vest and above her low-buttoned calico blouse.

She laughed and wrapped her arms around his neck.

"How'd you know to find me in El Paso?" he asked her, holding her tight against him.

"Harry Morgan out of Tulsa told me you'd cleaned up a gang on the panhandle and said you were heading that way. Knowing how hard you like to work when you don't have to, I figured you'd be there for the winter."

"Woulda been." He kissed her, and she returned the kiss for a time, her lips as silky smooth and as tasty as he remembered them, her tongue darting playfully against his.

Then she pulled away. "I don't know about you," she said, squirming up off his lap. "But all this shootin' and killin' makes a girl hungry. Come on — I'll rustle us up something in the kitchen."

She grabbed the brandy decanter off the desk and strode out of the room, the whang strings on her coat sleeves and deerskin breeches jostling and adding to the shadows tossed to and fro by the torches and the lamp. Prophet frowned at her.

She seemed different, somehow. And it wasn't just her change of clothes or her barn talk, either. Usually, when they'd been apart for a while she couldn't keep her hands off of him. He chuckled, remembering.

Oh, well. Mexico had a strange pull on folks. She'd likely be back sipping sarsaparilla just as soon as they were north of the

41

border again. He heaved his wet, weary body out of the chair, gathered up his guns, and followed her out of the room and down the hall.

He'd just passed the stairs angling down from the second story when someone groaned. Boots thumped on the stairs, spurs ringing.

Prophet wheeled, pumping and raising his rifle. A man was moving down the stone steps — slowly, heavily, boot heels catching on the steps. Prophet saw his lime green slacks above the black boots. Curlicues of white stitching ran up the sides of the slacks.

As he kept descending the stairs, Prophet saw the twin red-leather holsters strapped to his thighs, below a billowy blouse the same green as the slacks. Both the man's hands were clamped over his bulging belly as he kept stumbling down the stairs. He was hatless, and he wore a thin beard. His dark eyes were pain-racked as, halfway down the stairs, he stopped, stared at Prophet for a moment, then lifted his chin and wailed, *"Estoy viniendo ensamblarle en cielo, mi hermano!"*

Prophet chuckled. "If you got a brother in Heaven, *mi* amigo, you sure as hell ain't seein' him anytime soon!"

Prophet lowered the barn blaster, raised

42

his Colt, and put the green-clad hombre out of his misery. He'd turned away and continued on down the hall before the man had piled up at the bottom of the stairs.

"You leave anymore alive up there?" he asked Louisa, who had turned sideways toward him at the entrance to the kitchen.

"If I did, they're in no better condition than he is."

Prophet looked out the open door. The rain hung like a gray curtain beyond the veranda, water sluicing in straight streams from the edge of the roof and splashing in the growing puddles in the yard. He hoped he hadn't left any scouts alive out there. Likely not or they'd have made their presence known by now. Despite the thunder, the gunfire had likely carried a good distance.

He turned to Louisa, who was setting a couple of plates on the cluttered table on which she'd also set the brandy decanter, which glittered brightly in the light of the several lanterns placed here and there about the cavernous but crudely furnished room.

"I'm gonna fetch my horse, girl."

"The barn's in the back."

Prophet steeled himself against the onslaught, closed his slicker, pulled his hat brim low over his forehead, and jogged out in to the rainy night, boots splashing. It took him nearly a half hour to find Mean and Ugly where he'd left him. The horse was as mad as an old wet hen at having been left alone in the storm. When he saw Prophet he reared, whinnied angrily, shook his head, and when Prophet reached for his reins, he moved up and tried to take a nip out of the bounty hunter's shoulder.

Prophet had had too many shoulder seams ripped out of his shirts to give his back to the horse for long. Sensing the nip coming, he whipped around and slammed his elbow against the ugly beast's head. Mean lurched back, snorting and stretching his leathery lips back from his thick, yellow teeth.

"Goddamnit, Mean — I'm trying to get you to a warm barn, you mean, ugly bastard!"

The horse pitched his head and flicked his ears notched by numerous fights with other horses in livery barns and corrals throughout the frontier. Prophet poked his rifle down into its sheath, swung the sawed-off shotgun down his back, and stepped wearily into the leather.

He put the horse across the flooded arroyo and up the other side, and swung around behind the massive hacienda to a barn that sat hunched amongst several corrals and other outbuildings in the overgrown foliage.

The Lazzaro gang took good care of their horses; he'd give them that. Despite the storm, the fifteen or so mounts stood relatively calmly in their stables, with plenty of oats, water, and hay. Prophet took his time unrigging Mean and Ugly, rubbing down the crotchety beast, then stabling him with a nice surrounding of oats and fresh green hay that smelled like the springtime in Georgia. He put Mean between two mares so he couldn't fight with the other geldings and two nickering stallions, then went out and closed the heavy wooden doors behind him.

A snort sounded off to his right. He turned sharply, cocking and leveling his rifle straight out from his right hip but eased the pressure on the trigger when he saw the coyote staring at him from around the barn's far front corner.

The lightning wasn't as bright as before, as the storm seemed to be winding down. But the intermittent blue flashes shone in the animal's anxious eyes and on the wet tip of its hanging tongue. The animal was no threat to the horses, so Prophet depressed the Winchester's hammer and lowered the weapon.

"Nice night, eh, feller?"

He glanced at the gray black sky and began tramping back to the casa, casting several frustrated glances toward the southwest, where fifteen thousand dollars' worth of Mexican coins and greenbacks and four notorious killers, including some blind woman named Sugar, were heading.

And where he'd be heading soon with a partner not herself.

4

"How was it?" Prophet asked, as he hungrily ate the dead outlaws' supper — beans and carne seca with a small pile of corn tortillas. Whoever had done the cooking hadn't been half bad; the grub was padding out the bounty hunter's belly right well. "I mean," he said, "any problems aside from losing the loot?"

He gave a wry grunt.

"Twenty against one is long odds even for me."

"Don't get your panties in a twist. I was worried when I rode into Nogales and learned you was ridin' with Lazzaro's bunch. Or figured you was, anyways. I remember, in case you don't, what happened last time we were down in Mexico."

"Another time," she said, shrugging her shoulder as she took a bite of beans and followed it up with a sip of brandy from a dented tin cup. "And I was another person.

I'm tougher now."

Prophet looked at her over his steaming forkful of food. "Don't get too tough."

Louisa said after a pensive moment, "Sugar . . ." Her train of thought appeared to get cloudy. Just then, more thunder rumbled and lightning flashed, throwing a blue white light through the recessed windows behind her. She shook her head and continued, frowning down at her brandy cup. "She's a strange woman, Lou. Don't know quite what to make of her."

"She's a killer," Prophet said, shrugging, as if that said it all.

"A blind killer who started riding with Lazzaro about five years ago, and she's been in on most of the jobs they've pulled. Even blind, she somehow manages to pile up her share of the bodies. Don't ask me how."

Louisa paused as she ate for a while, then continued:

"Her family sent her to a convent. That's where she met Lazzaro. He was holed up there wounded for a time, on the run from Rurales. The nuns gave him sanctuary, tended his wounds. When he left, he took Sugar with him. First thing she did was to ride back to her family's ranch in Texas and kill her parents — both her ma as well as her pa and an uncle. With Lazzaro's help, though I see now how she likely didn't need it."

"You sayin' she might not be as blind as she lets on?"

Louisa shook her head. "No, she can't see with her eyes. I know that. But I think she can see with some other . . . sense. That's why she drugged me. She had a bad sense about me, though I played it pretty damn close to the vest and gave her no reason to suspect anything under the table."

Prophet stopped chewing the load of food in his mouth to scowl across the table at his blond partner. "Why didn't she kill you, you think?"

Louisa glanced sidelong at him, sharply, as though annoyed. "How do I know? I don't know how she thinks."

"All right, all right." Prophet forked more food into his mouth. "Maybe we'll find that out when we catch up to her."

Louisa sighed and splashed more brandy into each of their cups. "Sorry, Lou. Not just for being snappy but . . . because I let 'em get away. Had the wool pulled over my eyes by a blind woman."

Broodingly, Prophet listened to another stretch of belching thunder as the storm drifted off to the east. "Should have been me, wrigglin' my way on in here."

49

"Don't be stupid, bucko. Half the gang knows you."

"Yeah?" Prophet grinned at her, trying to lighten the mood despite the frustration of four of the main gang members absconding with the loot and the weather that had soaked and chilled him bone deep. "I reckon I couldn't wear that deerskin half as good as you, neither."

"Don't get fresh."

Prophet sighed and finished his meal. He polished off the last of the brandy, then slid his chair back from the table, digging in his shirt pocket for one of Foran's cigars.

"You need to get out of those duds, Lou," she said. "Hang 'em by the fire."

"Don't get fresh, Miss Bonnyventure."

Prophet winked at her and strode over to the door. He'd like nothing better than to get out of his wet clothes, but they weren't as wet as before, and he'd hung his rain slicker to dry. Besides, he didn't feel much like sitting around in his birthday suit in a known outlaw lair, even if all the outlaws were dead. There were plenty of outlaws in Mexico to grieve him plenty, and he'd as soon be dressed for more trouble that might visit him this night.

"It's Bonaventure," Louisa corrected him, still sitting at the table, sliding her uneaten food around on her plate. It was all part of their routine exchange — something they did to kill the boredom of long rides after curly wolves. "There's no *y* in it. Never has been."

The old joke made Prophet feel better.

He walked out onto the broad veranda, stepping over a couple of dead men. He lit the cheroot and stood smoking as he stared out at the storm that had relented considerably though the night was as black as before. After a time, he spied a long wicker divan abutting the casa's front wall and slacked into it with a tired groan. He lay down, resting his head against the arm farthest from the door, and leisurely smoked the cigar.

He heard the clack of boot heels and then he saw Louisa standing in the doorway, staring out across the veranda and into the deep night, past the water still dripping over the edge of the tiled roof. The drops glittered like diamonds in the less frequent and far less violent lightning flashes. It lit up the whites of the girl's eyes.

Her strangely pensive eyes. More pensive, more brooding than usual, Prophet thought. Something had happened here that had stirred her somehow. He drew deep on the cigar, blew the smoke out in the fragrant, humid night, obscuring Louisa's blond

51

silhouette half-concealed by the doorway.

Probably something about the blind woman's history aligning somewhat with her own. Some kind of madness had likely gotten into Sugar Delphi, a killer blind woman, in the same way a certain, lesser madness had climbed over the otherwise cool, stalwart barricades of Miss Louisa Bonaventure. After she'd witnessed her family slaughtered by the Handsome Dave Duvall gang. And after she'd taught herself to ride and shoot and kill hungrily and then had ridden the gang down, with Prophet's help, to send them all howling back to the merciless hell they'd hailed from.

That was probably it, Prophet thought, studying the pale oval of her face in profile. She'd learned of the misery lurking inside Miss Delphi, and it had recalled her own, maybe reminded her how different her life would have been had Handsome Dave Duvall not come riding into her family's farmyard along the shores of Sand Creek, Nebraska, that fateful afternoon nearly five long years ago.

He brought the cigar to his lips once more but held it there, at the edge of his mouth, as Louisa came out onto the veranda and walked over to him.

"Get out of those clothes or you're going

to catch your death of cold."

He drew on the cigar and blew the smoke out across the veranda. "You first."

She stepped back and kicked out of her boots, one after another, kicking them both under the wicker divan. She unbuttoned the jacket, shucked out of it. Then the shirt and camisole.

Pert breasts jostling, she peeled off her deerskin trousers and socks and pink lace panties, and stood before him, thrusting her shoulders back, arms straight down at her sides. He couldn't see her face well in the night's murky shadows, but she appeared to have a grave, almost anxious expression. Her naked breasts, swathed in chicken flesh, rose and fell deeply as she breathed.

Prophet sat up, flicked the cigar into the wet yard where it landed with a sizzle. Staring up at the pretty, naked, wild, crazy-assed blond before him, feeling his loins warm and hot blood churn through his veins — no one could arouse him like Louisa could though he made no bones of tying himself to a single woman — he unbuttoned his shirt, jerked it down off his shoulders, and tossed it on the floor.

Louisa knelt to help him with the rest — cartridge belt, pants, and then his long-handles, rolling the underwear down his long, muscular legs until his erect member jutted toward her. She closed her hand around it. Prophet groaned and sank back against the divan. She lowered her head, and he sighed again, groaned, ground his heels into the veranda's scarred wooden floor.

They made love twice, the second time as wild and frantic as the first, Louisa squirming and grunting around on top of him as well as under him, mewling and clutching with arms and legs, like an enraged wildcat. He'd gotten used to the uninhibited, desperate way the girl always made love with him, as if it were the first and last time she'd ever enjoy the act, so it didn't startle him as it had the first time up in Dakota Territory, when they'd been on the trail of Handsome Dave Duvall.

He made light of it now, not wanting to attract attention to the bizarreness, however it thrilled him, of her way of coupling, as though she were fighting to keep her head above a storm-tossed sea. "Damn, you did miss ole Lou," he said, sliding her hair away from her face with the back of his big, brown hand.

"I missed you, Lou." She sandwiched his face in her hands, kissed him hard, tugging on his bottom lip with her teeth until it almost hurt, then rose and gathered up their clothes.

"Where you goin'?"

"I'm going to throw your wet duds over chairs in the kitchen, near the stove. Then I'm gonna find us a blanket."

She trotted off, and he turned his head to admire her taut, round bottom before she scampered through the hacienda's open door.

She returned a while later with his blanket roll and saddle. She set the saddle at the head of the divan for a pillow, then lay down beside him and drew the wool blankets of the bedroll over them both. She curled her cool, smooth, willowy body against him, hooking a leg over his, and went to sleep.

He stared out at the night for a time, the coolness of the mist angling in on him occasionally and feeling good after the heat of their coupling. Then he followed her into sleep for what must have been an hour before he felt her stir and heard her dress and stride quietly into the casa, where it was warm. The night had turned cool. Prophet fell back asleep for another couple of hours before a cool breeze woke him.

He dressed in his now-dry duds, gathered his weapons, and strolled around the hacienda, eyes and ears alert. The mist had lifted, and a few stars shone above high, thin, pancake clouds. When he'd checked on the horses, finding them all resting peacefully, he returned to the divan onto which he slumped once more, fully dressed, only kicking off his boots, and slept again until something woke him.

He opened his eyes to a clear blue, milky dawn and reached for the Winchester leaning against the veranda rail two feet away. Cocking the rifle, he swung his feet to the floor and looked around. The yard fronting the hacienda was revealed by the pearl light washing through the untended trees and shrubs, showing a cracked flagstone walk angling toward the gate where the two guards lay sprawled in the bloody mud.

He heard the soft thuds of oncoming riders punctuated with frequent splashes of hooves in puddles. Over the wall left of the gate, bobbing heads appeared — heads donning straw sombreros with an insignia of some kind in the crown.

From his vantage he could see the bobbing shoulders of several riders all clad in gray, and he cursed. The insignia in the hat crowns was doubtless the eagle emblem of the Mexican Rurales.

Prophet rose, stomped quietly into his boots, set the rifle down, and wrapped his shell belt and Colt around his waist. As he did, he cast his gaze toward the open gate in the adobe wall and saw the Rurales stop just outside the gap while the leader, a lean man with a mustache and spade beard, looked down at the dead men sprawled around him.

The lead Rurale lifted his head to peer toward Prophet, then clucked to his horse, a roan Arab cross, and came on inside the gate, followed by a shaggy string of five other Rurales, all swinging their heads around to inspect the carnage.

Boots thudded inside the hacienda's open door. "Company?" Louisa asked, stopping in the doorway and holding her Winchester carbine across her chest.

"I reckon you best put the coffee on, Ma," Prophet dryly quipped as he donned his hat and, setting the Winchester on his shoulder, stood atop the veranda steps to stare at the men clomping toward him. "I'll scrounge us up some eggs from the chicken coop."

The lead rider wore captain's bars on his sun-faded, mud-flecked gray tunic. His long, angular face with pointed chin and broad, heavy mouth was dark and leathery, with several short, knotted white scars. Fresh mud caked his horse's cannons and belly. The mud had splashed up over the captain's dark blue, yellow-striped uniform slacks.

"Look what the cat dragged in," Prophet growled, yawning and raking a hand down his face bristling with three-day-old beard stubble.

"Cat?" The captain feigned a puzzled expression, glancing around. "I see no cat. I see plenty of dead men, though, Lou. You know, the old saying is true — the trail of the evil dead leads to hell."

"Mere superstition." Prophet glowered. "Didn't figure you were this far north, Chacin."

"I am everywhere, Prophet. Where I am not, I have men watching and listening on my behalf. Back in Tres Leones, I heard that a big gringo with a devilish little cannon purchased food and supplies, and had — how do you say? — *cooled his heels* for a day while his horse rested before heading out on the same trail that the Lazzaro gang took when they came storming down from the border." The captain grinned, showing fang-like yellow eyeteeth. "You enjoyed a couple of the senoritas, I hear."

Louisa drawled, "So worried about me that you had to distract yourself, eh, Lou?"

Prophet shrugged.

Chacin looked at the two dead men on

the porch. "Did you kill them all, Lou? You and the gringa?" Chacin's eyes burned a little when they found Louisa standing in the broad, open doorway, in front of the two dead banditos.

"No, but a goodly portion. How nice you rode in just in time to offer assistance."

"I was certain that you and the Vengeance Queen — *si*, I know you by reputation, *chiquita*, and I am delighted to see that you are every bit as lovely as your legend claims — I was certain that you, *mi* amigo Prophet, could handle yourselves even against twenty of the vilest desperadoes to haunt northern Mexico for the past five years, somehow managing to stay one step ahead of me."

"Two steps, more like," Louisa said. Her reputation had stretched far and wide, and so had Prophet's. Even Ned Buntline had written about her and the ex-Confederate man hunter who, after all the horrors he'd witnessed from the Wilderness to Chickamauga, had sold his soul to the Devil in return for all the hoof-stomping, hog-killing good times he could wring from the years he had left, funded by the bounties on the heads of badmen.

Ignoring Louisa's comment, Chacin sat back in his saddle and studied the hacienda. "Damned impressive hideout. I figured they were holed up in the mountains farther south. Maybe the Sierra Madre." He sighed fatefully, making a dramatic show of it, inflating then deflating his chest and rounding his broad shoulders. "Oh, well . . . gone but not forgotten. Now, if you will just hand over the loot they stole from the Nogales bank, my men and I will be on our way."

"How do you know this Sonoran lizard, Lou?" Louisa asked, strolling out onto the veranda and pulling up on his left, spreading her boots a little more than shoulder-width apart.

"Now, now," Prophet said, grinning at Chacin scowling at Louisa. "Me and Jorge go way back . . . to about five, six years ago now. Run into each other from time to time, when business calls me down here south of the border."

Chacin said through a nostril-flared sneer, "This lizard, as you so rudely call me, senorita, once had a deal with Senor Prophet. We would split any bounty money he acquires down here in my beloved Mejico fifty-fifty. Half for me, half for him."

"Now, you know that wasn't the agreement, Jorge."

"But it was the agreement, Lou."

Prophet shook his head. "The agreement was eighty-twenty in my favor if I run 'em

60

down and you don't get your hands dirty. That's the toll charge for crossin' back over the border with my bounty in the form of the entire person or just his head, you see."

He glanced at Louisa, sneering now himself, his own nostrils flaring and the cords standing out in his stout, sun-leathered neck. "Only the lizard here, as you so aptly called *mi* amigo Captain Chacin of the illustrious Rurales, reneged on the deal. Tried to whipsaw me between two contingents of these gray-bellied bastards and force me to take only twenty percent . . . though his hands were as clean as the day the bastard was born, and I'd damn near popped all my caps!"

"That was a long time ago, Lou." Chacin waved a gauntlet-gloved hand in front of his nose as though brushing away a fly. "I forget the details."

"Quit beatin' the Devil around the stump and admit you're a double-crossin' son of a bitch."

Chacin dipped his chin and blinked his cold, gray brown eyes once. "The last few times you have been down here, Lou, you failed to look up your partner, Chacin, and turn over to the Rurales our fifty percent cut of your dinero. You see, I have many pairs of eyes and ears, and those eyes and ears are always on the lookout for the big man with the crooked nose who rides an ugly, angry lineback dun who *deserves a bullet in his head as much as his rider does!*"

Prophet leaned forward at the waist, veins bulging in his brick red forehead. "Don't you dare insult my hoss, you son of a bitch. Backwater!"

"Boys, boys," Louisa said, dropping down the veranda steps, holding her hands up, palms out. "I sense there's some bad blood between you, as there often is between even the most honorable businessmen. But I'm sure, since you both are honorable as well as sensible — I mean, no one wants a lead swap here, right? — I'm quite confident we can come to some sort of agreement."

"There's nothin' to agree on," Prophet said, snarling at Chacin while his five other men looked edgily on. Those with scanty English looked confused. "The loot's gone, Jorge. I got here too late. Lazzaro hauled freight. Headed straight south — probably toward the Sierra Madre, just like you said."

"Huh? What?" Chacin looked incredulous, and then he grinned wolfishly. "You always get your man, Lou. And the loot!"

"Not this time," Louisa said. "They lit out before Lou got here."

Chacin glanced at the short, stocky Rurale wearing sergeant's chevrons on his sleeves sitting a dirty cream mare behind and to Chacin's right. The sergeant had thick, curly brown hair puffing down from his sombrero, and a mustache that looked ridiculously large on his small, moon-shaped face. He pursed his lips inside his mustache and shook his head.

Chacin looked at Prophet, the wolf grin still bright on his face. "You have horn-swoggled me one too many times, Lou." He lifted a finger up close to his face and waggled it. "You will not hornswoggle me again." He said *hornswoggle* as though he were so fond of the English expression that he tried to work it into conversations whenever he could. He glanced at the sergeant. "Sergeant Frieri, pat them both down. If there is money, surely they will have stuffed their pockets with some of it."

Frieri stepped down from his horse, tossed his reins to a young corporal behind him, and grinned lustily at Louisa. "May I start with the *rubia, el Capitan?*" He winked as he strode toward Louisa — a bandy-legged little man with an enormous gut pooching out his uniform tunic.

"Si," said the captain, showing his fang-like eyeteeth again.

Frieri slowed as he approached the blond

63

bounty hunter, grinning and holding his hands up, palms out, inching them toward Louisa's chest. Louisa stared at the short man blandly and didn't move a muscle until he was two feet away.

Then her right boot shot up in blur of sudden action.

"Whaoffff!" Sergeant Frieri jackknifed forward and crossed his little, thick hands over his balls.

Louisa lowered the boot she'd just impaled the Rurale's oysters with and stepped backward, holding her hands over the pearl grips of her matched Colts. To a man, the Rurales raised their rifles while checking their startled horses down with taut hands on the reins. A corporal who must have fancied himself a pistoleer clawed a Russian .44 from the crossdraw holster on his right hip.

Prophet brought up his own Colt and fired.

Bam!

The corporal screamed and dropped the Russian as he was about to cock it and clutched the hole in the yellow stripe running down the outside of his left thigh. His horse reared and lurched sharply to the right.

The groaning corporal flew off the left

side of his saddle and hit the muddy yard with a yowl. His horse wheeled and ran back out the open gate, trampling and rolling one of the dead banditos over.

Prophet recocked the Colt as Louisa drew both of hers and waited for hell to pop.

5

Captain Chacin kept his own carbine on his saddlebow as he shouted, swinging his head around, *"¡Parada! ¡Parada! ¡Lleve a cabo su fuego!"*

Stop! Stop! Hold your fire!

All the horses were fidgety now, stomping, and the Rurales all had to keep them in check with a taut hand on the reins. The corporal whom Prophet had wounded lay in the mud, writhing and clutching his bloody thigh. When the other Rurales had lowered their rifles, Chacin gave Prophet a hard sidelong look then rode over to the wounded corporal, shook his head, then extended his Winchester carbine one-handed. The corporal's dark eyes doubled in size when he saw the rifle aimed at his head.

"No, *el Capitan!*"

Chacin's carbine belched. The corporal had raised a hand as though to shield his head from the bullet. The bullet tore a hole through the open hand before plowing through the man's brain plate then exiting his right ear and splashing into a mud puddle, instantly turning the puddle a milky red. The corporal flopped onto his back, shaking, while the other Rurales looked in horror from their captain to the dead man.

Chacin set his Winchester back atop his saddlebow and looked at Prophet in disgust. "See what you make me do?"

Prophet wasn't at all surprised that Chacin had put the man down like a rabid dog. A wounded rider would have complicated his life, and life was complicated enough on the Mexican frontier.

"You want me to say I'm sorry?" Prophet asked, keeping his cocked Colt raised and waving it around slightly at the Rurales astraddle their agitated horses.

Louisa held both her cocked pistols on the short, fat, curly-headed sergeant groaning on the ground before her, grimacing up at her and muttering Spanish curses through his teeth. Tightly, out the corner of her mouth, she said, "Let's kill them all, Lou. Starting with this one here."

The sergeant's eyes widened. He glanced over his shoulder at Captain Chacin, who smiled with only his mouth, showing those fangs again. "All right, all right — perhaps it is time for us all to calm down and discuss the situation like reasonable men . . . and, uh, women."

"I don't think so," Prophet said, aiming the Colt at Chacin now. "We got nothin' to discuss. I've gone into business with you for the last time, Jorge. I don't give a shit how many men you got up here in old Sonory. There's only five of you now, and me and my partner here got the drop on you. If you don't take this ragtag bunch and ride out the same way you came in, pronto, we'll do it her way."

Chacin stared back at Prophet for a long time. Save for the blowing and occasional stomping of the horses and the chirping of the morning birds, a tense silence fell over the group. Frieri kept both hands on his crotch, scowling warily over his shoulder at Chacin, knowing that in his defenseless condition, if the lead started flying, he'd surely be first to have his wick trimmed.

The captain's chin jutted. His leathery cheeks dimpled above his mustache and goatee, and his face turned a darker red as he neck-reined his Arabian cross around. Without saying anything, he put the steel to the Arab's flanks and galloped out of the yard. The other Rurales looked from

68

Prophet to Louisa to the dead man on the ground, their faces hard but wary under their sombreros' wide brims.

They reined around and followed the stiff-backed captain out of the yard. Frieri muttered something shrilly, then, casting his fearful gaze at Prophet and the Vengeance Queen, gained his feet, wincing, and ran over to the steeldust stallion ground-tied but prancing around behind him. Cursing and grunting, he hauled himself awkwardly into the saddle. Keeping one hand on his bruised oysters, and slouched forward on the steeldust's back, he trotted out of the yard, swinging left, to follow the others in the direction from which they'd come.

"We got the bulge on 'em for now," Prophet said, holstering the Colt. "But it won't last long. They got us outnumbered, and I know Chacin well enough to know he ain't gonna be happy till he's got the loot and we've both taken it in the neck."

He strode back into the hacienda.

As he gathered up his gear, Louisa gathered up her bedroll and saddlebags, and they met at the back door before tramping quickly outside and making a beeline for the barn. Prophet saddled his feisty dun while Louisa saddled the brown-and-white pinto she'd never given a name because, knowing the horse could take a bullet meant for her at any time or that she might have to run it into the ground to save her own skin, she didn't want to get too attached. She knew the risk of attachments.

They led the horses into the puddle-dimpled yard growing light now as the sun climbed, the humidity rising like pale snakes from the warming earth, and mounted up. They both looked around, Prophet slipping his Colt from its holster and replacing the cartridge he'd capped on the dead corporal.

"How far you think they rode?" Louisa said, letting her gaze settle on the shadowy eastern plain stippled with Spanish bayonet and sage and rising toward steep ridges silhouetted against the rising sun.

"Not far," Prophet said. "Likely, he'll try to get around us, cut us off, so keep your eyes skinned."

He booted Mean west from the barn. Louisa put her pinto up beside him as they angled across the yard to the wagon road that curved along its southern edge.

"Southwest, you say?"

"That's the direction they took when they left here. That doesn't mean it's the direction they stuck to."

"If they weren't haulin' so damn much gold, I'd let 'em go," Prophet said.

"You've wanted Lazzaro for a long time, Lou. As have I." Louisa specialized in tracking men who'd killed women and children, and Lazzaro was notorious for taking women and children hostage to help him get out of the towns he'd plundered, usually leaving his hostages dead in the desert when he was sure he'd outrun any posses fogging his back trail. He hadn't pulled that stunt in Nogales, however. Likely because he knew the law didn't have the balls to be a threat.

"I know," Prophet said. "But we could wait and get him when he heads back north. Chacin'll never run him down on his own — not with that raggedy-heeled band of muchachos and old men he's ridin' with."

"I reckon that's possible," Louisa said as they kicked their mounts into trots, the hooves making soft thuds on the wet ground and splashing through puddles, "but with that much money we likely won't see him again for a long, long time. He might even decide to stay down here. In that case, we might never see him and Sugar and the two others again."

Prophet glanced at his partner, whose blond hair streamed back behind her shoulders as she rode, the sun-bleached strands glistening in the intensifying, golden morning sunshine. The girl had always owned a strange, oblique edge — an edge that Prophet had only seen in men, particular pistoleers like Clay Allison, Ben Thompson, and John Wesley Hardin, but rarely in women.

"This blind pistolera," Prophet said. "This Sugar Delphi . . ."

Louisa looked at him.

"What's she like?"

Louisa blinked, let a moment pass as they continued riding west. "Just like I told you. She can't see. Aside from that, she's just like the others." Her eyes narrowed slightly. "A cold-blooded killer."

At the same time but eight miles southwest, Sugar Delphi jerked back on her cream-dappled black's reins, shook a thick lock of her rust red hair back from her pale face set with clear blue, blind eyes, and yelled, "Halt!"

The three male riders, gang leader Antonio Lazzaro, Red Snake Corbin, and Roy Kiljoy all brought their loping mounts to grinding halts on the south side of the flooded arroyo that they'd been following since breaking camp at the first blush of dawn. Lazzaro was carrying the saddlebags stuffed with fifteen thousand dollars of stolen Mexican coins and greenbacks, and he jerked a look behind him now to make sure the bags had not fallen off his horse.

Satisfied, he turned to Sugar, scowling. "What the hell's the matter?"

She sat her blowing, dappled black gelding, swinging her head around as though she could actually see something of this broad desert valley carpeted in little but rocks and the occasional tuft of yucca and greasewood and surrounded by low escarpments of ancient, black volcanic rock. Thin troughs muttered with runoff from the recent deluge, and the air was damn near as humid as the Mexican lowlands surrounding the Gulf.

Sugar turned to him, looked right through him with those cobalt blues of hers. "Can't you smell it?"

"Smell what?"

"Death."

Lazzaro looked around, fighting impatience. He'd ridden with the blind woman for nearly four years and knew that she had the senses — aside from sight, that was — of a wild puma cat. He sniffed the air and continued to scan the low, sandy mounds around him before turning back to her once more, his own deep-set eyes crinkling deeply at the corners.

"Sugar, all I can smell is the whiskey I'm

gonna drink at the Colorado Gulch Station. Death? What's that mean — *death*?"

He looked at the other three men. Red Snake — long and lean and hawk-faced — sat the saddle of his copperbottom dun, looking around cautiously, his brass-cased Henry repeater in his right hand. The two red snakes tattooed on both his exposed, lightly haired forearms coiled downward past his thin wrists, their heads resting against the backs of his hands, forked tongues slithering hungrily across his bulging knuckles and into his two middle fingers.

He jerked his bright-eyed, incredulous gaze to Lazzaro. He never spoke directly to Sugar, for some reason. Maybe he was repelled by her blindness, or, having been raised in the superstition-stitched hills of West Virginia, he thought her a witch who might put a hex on him if he were to speak to her directly and possibly offend her.

"Could she be a little more specific?" he asked Lazzaro, trying to keep his impatience out of his slightly high-pitched voice.

Of course, Lazzaro didn't need to answer for Sugar, as the woman was only blind, not deaf.

"Human remains," she said, staring off the right side of the trail. "One, maybe one and a half days dead. Chewed on by coyotes early this morning, after the rains stopped." She touched spurs to her black.

Horse and rider galloped off the trail and into the desert, the dappled black gelding picking its way for the blind woman on her back. The black and Sugar Delphi always rode as one, the horse's eyes for all intents and purposes becoming the redhead's eyes.

Lazzaro scowled after the woman then gigged his own horse after Sugar. Red Snake shared a skeptical glance with the fourth rider in the group — Roy Kiljoy, who, at five feet three inches tall, made up in viciousness and cruelty what he lacked in height. He also made up for it by his breadth, for he was as wide as a door.

He wore greasy, smoke-stained trail garb with a broad sombrero. His blond mustache drooped down over both sides of his narrow mouth that always hung open a little. His light-blue eyes seemed to have a pale film over them; they were shallow and pitiless and poison mean.

He did not care for Sugar Delphi, and he had made his views very clear to the other men of the gang, including Lazzaro, who considered Sugar his woman. The gang leader did not hold the sentiment against the short, thick border tough from Missouri — at least not to the point that he'd ever

considered cutting him loose or killing him
— for everyone who'd ever met Kiljoy accepted his hideous nature as one would ac-
cept that of a maverick longhorn or coiled
diamondback.

All that Lazzaro cared about was that Kiljoy lived up to his last name. The stubby
brigand indeed seemed to take great pleasure in killing, and such a talent was a great
asset for a gang leader like Lazzaro, a
sadistic killer in his own right.

Kiljoy said nothing, just sat scowling after
the redhead and Lazzaro, slowly shaking his
head obliquely, as though wondering what
in hell the ghoulish albeit beautiful woman
was up to now. That was Red Snake's sentiment, as well.

"I don't know about you, Roy," he said to
Kiljoy, "but I wanna see what she's seein'.
Or smellin'."

"Lots o' death out here," said Kiljoy, looking around at the low, rocky hills. "If we
don't keep movin', we're likely gonna smell
a little whiffy on the lee side ourselves." He
kept sliding his dark gaze around. "Bounty
hunters, lawmen, regulators, banditos, Injuns . . . hell, a man who don't keep movin'
sets his own trap out here."

"Yeah, well . . . just the same, I'm gonna
kill the cat!" Red Snake whipped his rein

ends against his dun's left hip and galloped
off between the hills.

6

"Death," said Sugar. "I told you I smelled it."

Antonio Lazzaro and Red Snake Corbin rode up beside the woman to stare down at the overturned wagon and the man lying slumped in the rocks beyond it.

The wagon lay twisted between two boulders and a slender mesquite tree, which it had broken like a matchstick when it had run off the trail. Or been run off the trail. Various foodstuffs and camping supplies as well as rusted picks and shovels were strewn about the wagon and boulders, where they'd tumbled during the crash. Deep gouges in the form of unshod hoofprints scored the ground all around the wagon, rocks, and dead man even in the wake of the previous night's deluge.

The man lay spread eagle and staked to the ground. There wasn't enough left of him after the Mojaves had had their fun with him — likely seeing how loud they could get him to scream — to judge his age, much less his facial features. He'd been cut up badly, and then the coyotes or wildcats had eaten him, burrowing into all orifices. Only a few tufts of curly gray hair remained atop his blood-crusted skull.

Lazzaro looked at Sugar, who stood staring straight out across the desert beyond the dead man, who'd probably been a prospector seeking color in the local ranges and washes. The blind woman's lush red hair hung to her shoulders. Some of it was twisted into small braids, and these hung down the sides of her head, trimmed with colored wooden beads.

"Mojave?" he asked.

She nodded.

Red Snake turned to Lazzaro and whispered, "How in the hell can she tell if it's Mojave as opposed to, say, Chiricowys or Coyotero? All three bands been known to run in these parts."

Lazzaro had just started to shrug when Sugar jerked her head toward them as she reined her dappled black around. "I suggest we light a shuck, gentlemen. The Mojaves who did this are still near . . . and they're hungry for white blood!"

She ground her spurs into the dappled

black's flanks. The horse whinnied, swept past the dumbly staring Lazzaro and Red Snake Corbin, and galloped back out toward the trail where Roy Kiljoy sat his Appaloosa, gravely glancing around at the starkly forbidding ridges turning more golden now as the sun rose a third of the way toward its zenith.

A minute later, the three men were back on the trail, galloping twenty yards behind Sugar, who rode with the sun streaking her blowing, copper red hair, her black sombrero dangling by a rawhide thong down her back, over her black-and-red leather jacket stitched with small, silver horses.

As he rode crouched in his own saddle, Red Snake glanced to the right, then shouted at Lazzaro riding half a length ahead and a little right of him, then tossed his head to indicate the white smoke puffs rising from one of the highest northern ridges. Lazzaro turned his head toward the smoke puffs, then jerked his head toward the left.

Red Snake followed his gaze past Kiljoy to see another series of charcoal-colored puffs rising from a lower ridge half a mile south of the trail they were following.

Kiljoy turned his big, unshaven, fair-featured but sunburned face toward Red

Snake, his blond mustache blowing in the wind. It was a dark look. Kiljoy shook his head. "I really hate 'Paches, Snake. I hate 'em worse than tooth pullers an' sky pilots."

"You can discuss that with them shortly," said Sugar, whipping her head around to stare back at the men behind her.

She lifted her chin. Kiljoy, Red Snake, and Lazzaro glanced over their shoulders. Six or seven dusky-skinned, black-haired riders galloped toward them, angling onto the trail from the north and south, leaning far forward and batting their moccasined heels against the flanks of their lunging mustang ponies painted for war.

"Ah, shit!" grouched Lazzaro.

Red Snake expressed the same sentiment.

Kiljoy whipped his rein ends against his Appy's right hip and yelled, "Hold on to your topknots and ride like hell, boys!"

Lazzaro's mount lunged hard, until it was long-striding beside Sugar's horse and gradually overtaking her. He did not wonder how the blind woman had known the Mojaves were behind them. He'd stopped wondering long ago how she sensed the things she did and now merely accepted the fact without question. It didn't even seem all that strange to him anymore. In many ways her inexplicable gift was a blessing, as it had saved his life countless times.

Hearing the Mojaves howling and yowling behind him, Lazzaro and the others climbed a low rise, and Lazzaro felt the slightest loosening of the knot in his belly. The Colorado Gulch Relay Station opened below him — a sprawl of weather-silvered wooden buildings and holding corrals in a broad horseshoe gouge in the large, black rock escarpment rising like a mess of giant dominos just north of it. To the south and west was nothing but more of the same stark terrain that Lazzaro and the others had just crossed.

Gunfire crackled amidst the Indians' eerie howls.

Lazzaro glanced behind, past the galloping horses of Red Snake and Kiljoy, and showed nearly his entire set of silver upper teeth below his ragged black mustache. The Indians were chewing up the trail and gaining on him.

Kiljoy had hipped around in his saddle, taking his reins in his teeth, and was just now racking a cartridge into his old-model Winchester rifle's breech. The gun lapped smoke and flames from its barrel, the smoke instantly torn by the wind, the report sounding like a branch broken over a knee.

The Mojaves kept coming, none of the six

so much as flinching.

"Save your lead, Roy, you crazy son of a bitch!" Lazzaro yelled. "You ain't gonna hit nothin' from the hurricane deck!"

The four outlaws were galloping into the stage station yard now.

"Oh, yeah?" Kiljoy said, glowering at Lazzaro as, reins in his teeth, he racked another shell into his rifle's breech.

He hipped around and raised the Winchester to his shoulder. The Mojaves weren't slowing up a bit as they kept coming from seventy yards away, one rider leading, four riding abreast, another lone rider bringing up the rear.

Kiljoy's rifle leaped and belched. The Mojave galloping behind and to the left of the leader jerked as though he'd been punched in the chest. Slowly, releasing his rope reins, he turned slowly in the saddle as his horse kept striding. Just as slowly he sagged down the blanket saddle, hit the ground between him and the Mojave to his left, and rolled wildly.

The rear rider's horse stumbled over the wounded Mojave, whinnied shrilly just before it buried its head in the trail, and turned a complete somersault, its dark brown tail waving like a flag, its rider disappearing somewhere beneath the Appaloosa's massive, crumpling body.

Kiljoy bellowed as he lowered the carbine, took the reins from his teeth, and hauled back on them, slowing his own Appy. "Now, that's a boss shot if I ever seen one!"

"Ah, quit blowin'!" Red Snake said, leaping off his horse in the middle of the station yard, noting guns crackling around him. One man was shooting at the Indians from behind a water barrel on the low-slung station house's front porch while another gent was triggering a rifle from behind an open barn door on the yard's opposite side.

All four outlaws were on the ground now, sliding their rifles from their saddle boots and spanking their horses away. Even Sugar grabbed her carbine out of its sheath, racked a shell, dropped to a knee, and began firing at the Mojaves. The Indians were just now slowing and curveting their mounts while triggering lead toward the outlaws and the two men shooting from the barn and station house porch.

Kiljoy blew one of the savages off his horse and, ejecting the spent brass from his Winchester's breech, glanced at Sugar. She was triggering her own rifle as fast as she could, keeping her pale right cheek pressed taut against the stock.

"For Christ's sakes, woman!" Kiljoy

snarled. "Get on inside the station before them redskins perforate your purty hide!"

All of her shots flew wild. Red Snake was half relieved to see that. A half-blind woman who could shoot a man off a galloping horse would be enough to cause him to lie awake nights. Two bullets blew up the still-damp dust in front of her, and she lowered the rifle, casting those eerie blue eyes at the short, ugly brigand.

"A rare piece of good advice from you, Roy," she said. "I believe I'll take it!"

With that, staying low and holding her carbine in her right hand, she ran up onto the porch, tripped the cabin's latch, and pushed inside, slamming the stout, halved-log, Z-frame door behind her.

Inside, Sugar dropped to her butt and pressed her back to the door. "Hello?" she called, hearing someone triggering a pistol from ahead of her and right. "I'm friendly if you are!" she yelled.

The agent of the Colorado Gulch Relay Station turned his thick-bearded face from the eastern window he was triggering a Colt Army out of. "I'm as friendly as an un-weaned pup, miss. To anyone that ain't tryin' to lift my hair, that is."

"I don't believe Mojaves normally take scalps, mister . . ."

"Hannady!" the station agent shouted above the roar of the Colt he triggered. "Fletcher Hannady. You can call me Fletch. All my friends do. And . . ." He paused to trigger another shot out the window. "What you say about the Mojaves ain't always true. Since scalp hunters been ridin' free and easy around here, they've sort of adopted the habit. Been more than one Mojave around with white men's scalps dangling from his sash!"

Hannady pulled his smoking pistol out of the window and dropped his fat bulk clad in a plaid wool shirt, suspenders, and duck trousers down against the wall. His bib beard scraped against his bulging belly.

"I'm Sugar!" the blind outlaw woman called from the door, keeping her voice raised against the din of gunfire continuing outside.

"Sugar," Hannady said, as he plucked fresh cartridges from an open shell box on the floor behind him and slipped them through the Colt's open loading gate, slowly rolling the barrel between his thumb and index finger. "You must be sweet."

He gave her a leering look, winked, then flipped the loading gate closed. He frowned and looked around the room, then slowly turned his head toward the open window

86

above him, the open shutter of which was nudged by a vagrant breeze. The rusty hinges squawked softly.

"The shooting stopped," Sugar said, still sitting in front of the door and staring wide-eyed but with her customary lack of expression straight down the length of the earthen-floored station house.

With a grunt, Hannady heaved himself up off the floor and edged a look out the window. "I'll be damned," he said softly. "They're hightailin' it. Two of 'em, anyways. I see three dead."

"Six followed us here."

"Yeah, well, there been a whole lot more than them six ridin' loco around the station. Ranches been burned, a whole gold town sacked up on the California border. There's a good twenty or so Mojaves jumped the reservation a while back. Joined up with some broncos been holin' up in the Sierra Madre, and they're all runnin' loco together, killin' every white man, woman, and child in sight." He shook his head. "That five likely peeled off from a larger war party when they seen you."

Hannady looked out the window again, still extending his pistol out in front of him. "I been alone here since my two hostlers and cook was killed two weeks ago when

87

they were out cuttin' wood. Mojaves. Fortunately, them two boys outside are U.S. marshals. They was just stoppin' for breakfast when we heard you four comin' hard, like the devil's hounds were nippin' at your heels."

Sugar had just started to rise but let her slender back fall against the door again. Slowly, she turned her fine, blind head toward Hannady, fine lines drawing taut above the bridge of her long, slender nose. "Did you say U.S. marshals, Fletch?"

"U.S. marshals — that's right. They don't wear their badges cause the Mojaves find 'em right handy targets. But they're marshals, just the same. Holmes and Butler been around the ole Mojave merry-go-round a few times. Nice to have gun-handy men around." Slowly, staring down at Sugar, Hannady walked toward her, stopped only a few feet away. His thick, suety chest rose and fell heavily behind his dirty work shirt. "Say, you're right purty."

"Mr. Hannady," Sugar said in her silky-smooth voice, looking up at him obliquely, "you smell bad."

"Say, now, that ain't nice. I was just bein' friendly."

"I don't appreciate your brand of friendliness, Mr. Hannady."

"Say . . . wait now . . . !" Hannady said as he saw her lift her carbine and press the stock against her shoulder. "You got no cause to — !"

Red flames lashed from the round muzzle. The cracking report was a thunderclap in the close-walled room, causing glasses to clink on the counter to Sugar's left, and dust to sift from the rafters. The carbine spoke two, three more times, throwing Hannady over a near, round table, overturning the table as he piled up on the floor behind it.

Smoke wafted in the air around Sugar as, gritting her teeth and staring blindly up at where Hannady had been standing a moment before, she ejected the last spent shell casing and pumped a fresh cartridge into the chamber.

Behind Sugar, the men in the yard were speaking. Boots thumped on the porch. A knock on the door followed by Lazzaro's Spanish-accented voice: "Sugar?"

Sugar ran her tongue along her lower lip. "Antonio," she said sweetly, "your two new friends are U.S. marshals."

Lazzaro said nothing. She could smell the sweat, horse, and powder smoke odor of him as he stood on the other side of the door. Other men were talking in the yard behind him. Friendly tones.

Boots thudded as Lazzaro strode back across the veranda. The other men stopped talking.

Then one man said, "Wait! Hold on!"

Lazzaro's pistol barked four times in quick succession. After a few seconds, a groaning curse was followed by one more pistol shot.

Sugar recognized Red Snake's devilish laugh.

7

Prophet wheeled from the waterhole, closing his hand around his Colt's worn walnut grips and sliding the gun out of it holster and up in a fluid motion of practiced, high-speed action.

Bam! Bam-bam!

The arrow that the Mojave had loosed from his bow at the same time Prophet's first bullet had torn through his throat ricocheted off a rock to Prophet's left and dropped into the natural stone water tank with a plop. The Mojave himself — a stocky warrior with many small, white scars on his cherry face, stretched his lips back from his teeth and sucked a sharp breath. He cupped both hands over his bloody throat and stared wide-eyed at Prophet and Louisa, moving his jaws as though he were trying to say something.

Prophet looked around at the stone ridges crowding close in nearly a complete circle, all resembling giant cracked teeth in a leering devil's grin. He and Louisa stood crouched, Colts extended. They were on the side of an escarpment about forty yards up from the base.

They both held the reins of their nickering, prancing horses whom they'd led up here to drink from the rock tank. The tank was so full after the recent deluge that the water was spilling down over its lip and running down into a natural trough before seeping into the sand around which some sparse grass and rain-beaten wildflowers grew.

Prophet had spied the Indian a few seconds before, while he'd crouched to fill his canteen. His canteen lay at his feet now, the cork hanging from the lip by a rawhide thong.

Neither he nor Louisa said anything as they tensely perused the ridges. It was midday, the sun nearly straight up, and the sun was a brassy ball, making it hard to see.

"There!" Louisa wheeled in the opposite direction from the first Mojave and triggered her Colt three times.

The slugs hammered a square boulder on a shelf of rock about fifty yards away. Prophet had glimpsed a brown face drawing back behind the boulder a half second before Louisa's first bullet had plowed into it, spraying rock dust.

Prophet saw another figure stepping between two formations at the top of the ridge to his right. He holstered his Colt and slid his Winchester from his saddle boot, dropping to a knee and raising the rifle stock to his shoulder but holding fire. That Indian — a Mojave, judging by the area and the war paint — had taken cover, too.

The tension hung like a dark cloud. The sun hammered down on them. The water lapping over the stone tank made barely audible jangling sounds.

"I thought you scouted the tank, Lou." Louisa sounded quietly edgy.

"I did scout the tank, Miss Bonnyventure. And I seen neither hide nor hair of any Mojave." Prophet spat to one side. "But then, them bein' Mojave, I like as not wouldn't."

"Mojaves, you think?"

Prophet nodded. "I thought I saw smoke talk a ways back. But when I looked again it was gone, and I thought I was just gettin' nervy, it bein' Mojaveria and all. I hadn't heard of any broncos jumping their rez of late."

"Well, it's been a while since either of us has seen a newspaper."

"Point taken." Prophet looked around,

saw a narrow path meandering up through the rocks on the other side of the tank. "Cover me."

Holding Mean's reins, he leaned his rifle against the side of the tank, then picked up his canteen and dunked it under the tepid water. It bubbled as it slid down the canteen's neck. When the vessel was full, he corked it, looped the leather lanyard over his saddle horn, and grabbed his rifle.

"Follow me," he said, leading Mean around behind the rock tank. "And be damn quick about it."

"Don't get bossy, goddamnit."

"Christ, girl — what a tongue you've grown!"

"Still wouldn't hold a candle to yours."

"Damn near as bad, and it ain't proper, you bein' a girl an' all."

Several arrows zipped through the air around him and clattered off the rocks. Prophet wheeled and fired at the shadows moving amongst the rocks around them. Louisa did the same, losing her footing as her pinto jerked warily, and stumbled over a rock.

"This doesn't look good, Lou."

"Nothin' looks good in Mojave country, *chiquita*."

He snapped three more shots, then

rammed his rifle's butt against Mean's left hip. *"Hyah, you cayuse!"* he wailed.

The hammer-headed dun didn't need any more convincing. As more arrows clattered around his prancing hooves, and as two Mojaves opened up with rifles, Mean whinnied shrilly and galloped on up the path, shaking his head angrily and trailing his reins. Prophet ran past Louisa and the pinto, and dropped to a knee, shouting, "Head on up the ridge! I'll cover you!"

Louisa pumped and triggered her Winchester, evoking at least one cry from the rocks behind them, then wheeled and ran, leading the pinto on up and over the rise. Behind her, Prophet laid down a barrage of covering fire.

The Indians were spread out in the rocks on the fire side of the tank, some high atop the surrounding ridges, some low. He wasn't sure how many, but as he fired he felt the wind of several bullets and arrows curling the air around him, heard the spangs as bullets and wooden missiles hammered the rocks.

Maybe as few as seven, possibly as many as ten. Two seemed to have rifles.

When his Winchester's hammer pinged on an empty chamber, Prophet rose, wheeled, and ran, crouching low and tracing a slightly zigzagging course up the narrow, meandering passageway up the rock-strewn slope. The two rifles cracked behind him, blowing up gravel around his heels. Arrows made soft screeching sounds, like the rush of fast birds whipping past, before they hammered the rocks, some breaking with crunching noises.

"Hurry, Lou!" Louisa shouted from between two rocks at the top of the ridge.

Prophet sawed his arms, pounded his legs. His breath raked in and out of his lungs. The wind felt like thick copper in his throat. He silently scolded himself for his tobacco habit. Weak lungs were not conducive to a safe run through Mojave country.

"I am hurryin'," he said between gasping breaths as he threw himself atop the ridge and rolled several yards down the other side as a bullet kissed the seam of his left denim pant leg. *"Ow!"*

The exclamation wasn't so much for the slight bullet burn as the sharp rocks galling his arms and legs and the rap of his left hand against the side of a boulder.

"You hit?"

"Nah, just gettin' old."

As Louisa fired from between the rocks, Prophet gained his hands and knees and crabbed back to the top of the ridge, doffing his hat and pressing his left shoulder up to a boulder to Louisa's left. Still trying to regain his wind, he slipped cartridges from the loops of his shell belt and slid them through his Winchester's loading gate.

"Goddamnit," Louisa bit out. Her rifle jerked and roared once more. "They keep comin'. How many are there, anyway?"

Prophet slipped the last shell into his rifle, racked one into the chamber, and edged a look around the side of his covering boulder.

Three Mojaves were running amongst the rocks, dodging and weaving between boulders. Beyond them, several more were skipping down a ridge that was just out of rifle range. Most appeared nearly naked except for muslin loincloths, pointed toed moccasins and red flannel bandannas or hats made of hawk feathers. They all appeared to be wearing war paint — three vermillion and blue stripes across their noses, with three shorter slanted stripes on their foreheads.

One just now running up the slope toward Prophet and Louisa wore a white lightning bolt across his forehead, above the painted stripes and just below a green flannel headband. His eyes were spruce green, and they glinted brightly in that cherry-dark face. A half-breed. He yowled now as he dove behind a small boulder, Prophet's and Louisa's lead blowing up rocks and gravel behind his fleet heels.

Several bullets and arrows winged in from behind the Mojave with the lightning blaze, barking into the rocks around Prophet and Louisa, driving them back behind their respective boulders. Prophet could hear several more now running up slope — the rasp of breaths, the clatter of rocks under moccasin-clad feet.

A shadow moved on the ground to his left. He saw it out of the corner of his left eye as he hunkered behind his boulder on that hip. He had to roll nearly completely around to face the Mojave who'd just now bolted up past Prophet's boulder, paused a moment, sweat streaking his dark face.

Prophet raised his rifle.

The Indian grinned. For a weapon he appeared to have only a war hatchet that he gripped in his big, left fist. He wore a tight necklace of porcupine quills.

Prophet had just gotten his Winchester's barrel leveled when the Indian took one quick stride forward, then lifted his right leg — a knife slash of a kick that ripped the rifle out of the bounty hunter's hands and sent it tumbling through the air behind him.

"Lou!" Louisa cried.

"Holy shit," Prophet said.

The Mojave's green eyes flashed. His face was incredibly broad. His mouth was wide and thick, his dark skin scaly as a snake's and pocked with white as though the skin had peeled from sunburn. Likely, some disease or a condition the savage had been born with.

And he was a savage, for only a savage could yowl like he yowled, causing Prophet's ears to ache, a half second before he lunged again toward the bounty hunter, jerking the feathered war hatchet out and up and then swinging with all his might toward Prophet's head. His eyes popped so wide, showing the jaundice-yellow whites around the green, that for a moment Prophet though that both the demented-looking orbs would pop out of his head.

Louisa yelled again as Prophet ducked under the blow, pistoning off his heels and ramming his head and left shoulder into the Mojave's naked, sweat-slick belly above which an awful-smelling medicine pouch swung from a rawhide sack. The Mojave wrapped the arm that had swung the hatchet around Prophet's neck, snarling like a grizzly as he held Prophet's head against his belly with that arm while hammering the bounty hunter's face with his other fist.

Meanwhile, Prophet kept his feet moving, driving the big man — he must have been as tall and heavy as Prophet himself — straight backward and up off his feet. The ground came up furiously, and the Mojave grunted loudly, the air hammered from his lungs, as his back slammed hard. For a fraction of a second, he lay slightly limp beneath Prophet.

"Get out of the way, Lou!" Louisa cried. He saw from the periphery of his vision his blond partner trying to draw a bead on the big Mojave.

Prophet had started to roll away but then he saw another Mojave rising up out of the rocks and bearing down on Louisa, an arrow nocked to his bow. The girl saw the Indian and wheeled, her hair flying as she triggered her carbine into the man's belly button from two feet away.

Prophet had the sickening feeling — one that he'd grown far too accustomed to during the war — that they were about to be overtaken. But for the moment he had his hands full with the big Mojave with the white lightning bolt painted across his forehead. No, not painted, he saw now, as he rose onto his knees and swung his right arm up and threw his fist down furiously at the man's face.

Not painted. That lightning bolt was one massive, white, hideously knotted scar carved by the point of a none-too-sharp knife.

Prophet's fist smacked the side of the Mojave's jaw. He felt the impact deep into his shoulder. It was as though he'd punched a wet sandstone wall. The Indian shook his head as though to clear the cobwebs from his brain. Then he narrowed those green eyes under heavy lids at Prophet, gritted his teeth, and slashed at Prophet's jaw with his left fist. Prophet blocked the blow with his right forearm and slammed his left fist straight down, connecting solidly with the point of the Mojave's chin.

Prophet was astonished to see the man merely smile, showing all his crooked, yellow teeth, and loose a mad, coyote-like howl. The ear-numbing yell did just what the Indian had intended — it disoriented Prophet long enough for the Indian to arch his back and sort of buck, bouncing his lower body off the ground with wicked force.

Before Prophet could reorient himself, he found himself flying over the Indian's left shoulder, turning a somersault and catching a brief glimpse of the brassy sky yawning above stony sawtooth ridges.

It was like landing in a dinosaur's mouth of jagged teeth. Prophet groaned and immediately tried to rise but felt as though a wagon were on his chest. He looked down over the toes of his boots and saw the big Indian gaining his own feet heavily just as Louisa, her rifle's hammer clicking on an empty chamber, was overtaken by two other howling Mojaves.

Louisa gave a grunt as she tried to swing her rifle like a club, but one of the Mojaves grabbed it out of her hands while the other wrapped his arms around her waist and swung her around, laughing.

8

Prophet reached for the Colt but grabbed only leather. The pistol had fallen out of the holster when he'd been airborne. It lay about ten feet away, nestled between two black rocks and partly covered with gravel.

Ah, hell . . .

The big Indian with the lightning bolt carved across his forehead staggered toward Prophet. He had a skull-sized rock in his hands. He was bringing it up over his head when a spat of rifle fire clattered.

Slugs spanged off rocks around the Mojave and the two others who had wrestled Louisa to the ground, one trying to straddle her. The Indian standing over her staggered forward suddenly, grabbing the small of his back with both hands. Dust flew up around Louisa and screamed off another rock, and then as the one straddling her swung around, eyes blazing furiously, a dark, round hole appeared in his forehead. The slug chewed out the back of his skull and spit brains, bone, and blood onto the rocks to Louisa's right, snapping his head back. Louisa gasped and turned her face away from the blood, brushing a hand across her cheek.

The gunfire continued. The other Mojaves that had been clambering up over the ridge were wheeling and heading off to the north, down the shoulder of the slope. A couple swung around to fling arrows or fire carbines or old-model Colt pistols but otherwise they were running off, eerily silent now, like cowed coyotes. A few dropped as they ran, and rolled, limbs flopping.

Prophet looked around. The big Indian was nowhere in sight. He rose to a sitting position with a groan and grabbed his Colt. Brushing the gun off quickly, he clicked the hammer back, then gained his knees, wincing as another rock gouged into him, then heaved himself to his feet.

He brushed dust and sand from his eyes and swung his head right to left and back again, still seeing the Indians dashing off through the rocks — seventy yards away, dwindling fast. Louisa was grunting disdainfully as she kicked the dead Mojave off her. Prophet walked back up toward the crest of the slope and saw five Rurales walking slowly down the ridge on his left. Chacin was surrounded by stocky Sergeant Frieri and three other Rurales, all holding their Winchester or Spencer carbines across their chests as they walked down through the rocks, swinging their heads around warily.

Prophet stared skeptically at the Rurale captain with the handlebar mustache mantling his heavy mouth, above his narrow, jutting chin. "Never thought I'd be happy to see Chacin," he muttered to Louisa, who was just now climbing to her feet, her mussed hair in her eyes.

"Say again, Lou?" Chacin stopped about forty yards away and held a hand to his ear. "I couldn't quite hear you."

"What's your play, you sneaky bastard?"

"Play?" Chacin looked grieved. "What do you mean — play? Did my men and I not just save your hides? Your ugly old hide and the *chiquita*'s *magnifico* young and voluptuous one?"

Louisa had stepped up beside Prophet, feeding fresh cartridges into her Winchester's breech. "He asked you what your play is, you arrogant son of a bitch."

Prophet glanced at her, arching one brow, still surprised to hear such barn talk being spewed from the once-prudish girl's bee-stung lips.

Chacin laughed. His men were spread out

105

in a ragged semicircle around him. "I like her, Lou. I can see why you ride with her. She is not only beautiful but she has spirit, too. A very rare thing in any country, if you ask me. But to answer your question, senorita . . ."

The Rurale captain continued strolling toward Prophet while his men remained where they'd been, looking around for more Mojaves. ". . . I know that you know where Lazzaro is heading. That much is obvious. You know the expression you can't fool an old coyote? I am that old coyote. And I also know that there is a chance I might be able to draw the information out of you, given time and the implementation of my considerable skills practiced on dozens of screaming Yaquis."

Chacin shrugged exaggeratedly and curled one end of his upswept mustache between the thumb and index finger of his gloved left hand. "But why should I waste so much time and ruin such a beautiful young body when it is so unnecessary? Why not merely join forces with you and this big, ugly bounty hunter here, when of course seven guns riding after such devils as Antonio Lazzaro and Sugar Delphi are so much better than five . . . especially when Relampago and his zealous bronco Mojaves are running off their leash?"

Prophet and Louisa followed the captain's glance toward the north, where, in the far distance, beyond a low ridge, a column of smoke rose, gently unspooling in the sunny sky.

"There is a herd of them, Lou," Chacin said darkly. "Running in about five different packs."

Louisa glanced at Prophet. *"Relampago?"*

"El Lightning," Prophet said, keeping his eyes on Chacin.

"I know as much Spanish as you do, Lou," Louisa said dryly. "I'm just wondering who in hell the hombre is."

"A very bad Injun down here, *chiquita*," Chacin said, feigning an American accent. "I chased him for nearly ten years. He alone accounted for the killing of nearly thirty Rurales. No telling how many peons he tortured and killed in his ill-founded quest to secure northwestern Sonora for his own. For over ten years, he has made everything north of the Mar de Cortes to San Diego a very dangerous place for all white men."

"He's a big, tough son of a rabid jackal," Prophet said, squeezing his throbbing jaw. "Damn near as big and tough as me."

"Si, si," Chacin said. "And he will be back,

so perhaps it is best if we all get moving, eh?"

He smiled lopsidedly and arched a cunning brow, switching his gaze between the two bounty hunters. Prophet and Louisa looked at each other. A lot was agreed upon with that fleeting look, the most important being that it appeared they were stuck with Chacin whether they liked it or not.

Prophet turned around, set his rifle on his shoulder and began walking off in the direction he'd sent his horse. "Here, Mean! Come on, boy! Don't let El Lightnin' get you!"

"All right, where we headed?" Prophet asked as he and Louisa rode along a twisting trail down the shoulder of a low ridge, the sun angling down in front of them and throwing rock and cactus shadows back toward them.

"How do I know?"

Prophet glanced back at the Rurales riding behind him and Louisa. "Chacin sure sounded convincing."

"I don't know anything about where Lazzaro and Sugar are headed. If I did, I probably would have had my throat cut instead of slipping by with a mere drugging."

Prophet glanced around. He saw no smoke

in the north, but in the south a pale column rose between two distant ridges. He stared straight ahead across as vast an expanse of eroded, washed-out, and sun-blasted badlands as he'd seen since he'd last been down here, about a hundred miles northwest of the little fishing village of Puerto Penasco, at the northern tip of the Sea of Cortez. Nothing seemed to grow out here but rocks and sky, though occasionally he spied a patch of Mormon tea or an organ pipe cactus, the rare mesquite or creosote clump. Since he and Louisa and the Rurales had left the spot of El Lightning's attack, he'd seen more Mojave green rattlers than plants, and once he'd watched a Gila monster pull its striped tail into a hole beneath a boulder.

"Well, it's purty obvious to me," he said now, fingering his aching jaw once more. El Lightning had one hell of a right haymaker. "They gotta be headed for the Dead Mountains."

"That them yonder?"

"Straight out across that flat stretch of badlands," Prophet said, narrowing his gaze against the bright sun. "These mountains we're in are the Santa Rosas. Those are the Dead Plains straight ahead — about forty miles of the hottest, driest country south of Death Valley. No water whatsoever. I know 'cause I almost died there twice, chasin' tough nuts like Lazzaro and Sugar Delphi. Never wanted to be caught down here again, but here I am, sure enough." He slapped his thigh, gave a fateful sigh, and glanced behind him. "That fifteen thousand in Mexican *dinero* they're haulin' looks a mite light to me now."

"It's not the money I'm after."

"Yeah, me, too." Prophet's voice was dubious. His main mission in life was to have enough money to enjoy his remaining postwar years in the form of tanglefoot and parlor girls. But somehow he nearly always found himself hip deep in Louisa's vendetta to rid the world of evil.

An impossible task, but there it was. And here he was, heading across one of the most forbidding badlands in North America toward the nearly equally formidable Montanas Muertas. The Dead Mountains.

Shadowing killers, trailed by Rurales, and surrounded by blood-hungry Mojaves.

Damn, things just couldn't get much worse.

He and Louisa and the dogged Rurales rode on. Captain Chacin and his four coyote-eyed lackeys followed from about twenty yards back, rolling their shoulders with the slow gaits of their horses.

Sergeant Frieri was still snarling angrily at Louisa and sitting light in his saddle, sort of hipped to one side, due to the battering the blond had given his balls. As one ragged, dusty group, they dropped down out of the rugged Santa Rosas and trailed out into the relatively flat badlands that weren't nearly as flat as they'd appeared from above.

There were low, rocky ridges and deep, narrow washes pocked with ancient, sun-bleached bones. Scrub lined the arroyos — brittle tufts of cholla, beavertail cactus, and prickly pear — and along one of these the group rode in double file. The washes offered a modicum of cover from the prying eyes of the Mojaves whom Prophet could sense, no doubt knowing exactly where his group was despite the cover of the dry water course.

Dry it was. So was the air. If the recent deluge had visited this parched land, there was no sign of it. From his few previous trips to these forbidden environs, Prophet knew of one water source, but it was likely dry now in late August, and well out of the way. If it wasn't dry, the Mojaves had probably poisoned it.

One good thing had happened when they'd entered the wash. Louisa, too, had noted the tracks of the four shod hooves leading off away from them, along the same arroyo they themselves were following. If Chacin had noticed the sign, he hadn't let on. The few times Prophet had glanced behind, the captain had been riding with his chin low, as though he were sleeping. His sombrero covered his eyes.

Sergeant Frieri rode beside his superior, looking grim, one nostril flared.

The sun turned a vibrant copper late in the afternoon. It sank fast, shedding fiery bayonets. Prophet's party stopped in a broad horseshoe of the wash where mesquites grew thick along the banks and there were plenty of boulders to offer cover if the Mojaves came calling.

That wasn't likely, because as a general rule Mojaves didn't like to fight at night, believing that if they were killed in the dark their souls would be trapped forever in darkness. But that was a rule that had been broken more than once, and Prophet's group organized a night watch — two men or one man and Louisa awake at all hours and positioned strategically around the camp.

The horses were tended, bedrolls arranged. They built no fire and ate a meager supper of jerky or whatever else they could find in their saddlebags. They drank their water sparingly, knowing they probably wouldn't find water again until the day after tomorrow, when they'd reach the Dead Mountains. There was a well at the eastern edge of the mountains — or at least a well had been there a few years ago, in a mining village called San Gezo, populated mostly by Americans though the village had originally been Mexican. If the well was dry, Prophet's group would be in a hard spot, which was always the risk when traveling in this godforsaken country.

The Rurales passed around a couple of bottles, though the tanglefoot wasn't offered to Prophet and Louisa until they'd made the Rurale rounds enough times to liberate the Mexicans' charity. The pulque burned off a good three layers of Prophet's throat before popping in his belly like an entire string of Mexican firecrackers.

He squeezed his eyes shut and wagged his head. When the initial burn had passed, he grinned and offered the bottle to Louisa.

"There you go, Calamity Jane. Have you a swig of that. You'll likely swear off firewater forever after, maybe even decide to quit cursin' a blue streak."

The blond bounty hunter took a swig of the Mexican national tanglefoot, as potent as any twice-distilled corn mash Prophet

113

had ever sampled but tasting more like grapefruit juice seasoned with diamondback venom. She tried her best to pretend it didn't faze her, but Prophet could tell by the way her eyes glazed that she was struggling to keep her panties from catching fire.

Later, when he and Chacin had drunk nearly half the second bottle themselves and were sitting around by the light of the quarter moon, playing two-handed poker over a flat rock, Chacin said, "Dishonesty seems to be a gringo trait, does it not?"

Prophet had sensed the man's mood darkening with each swig he'd taken from the clear bottle. Prophet himself was in no mood for any of the bean eater's bullshit.

"You wanna chew that up a little finer, there, Captain?"

The two Rurales who'd been sleeping nearby lifted their heads from their saddles and stared warily through the moonlit darkness at the two men glaring across the rock at each other, like two bulls in the same corral. Louisa lay against her own saddle somewhere behind Prophet.

"You know what I am talking about, Lou. I am talking about our past business arrangements, all of which you reneged on."

"That so?"

"*Si.* That is so." Chacin raised his voice

114

dangerously and dipped his chin, the moonlight flashing like silver daggers in his eyes. "And when were you going to tell me that we had cut the trail of the men and the blind *chiquita* we have been following?"

"When I was goddamn good and ready!"

Silence.

Far off, a coyote gave a mournful howl.

Both men reached for their sidearms at the same time, extending the Colts toward the other's chest and clicking the hammers back in thundering unison.

9

Prophet stared at Chacin across the flat rock in the moonlit darkness. All he could see of his eyes were two tiny, stiletto-like glints beneath the man's heavy brow. The moonlight silvered the left curl of the man's handlebar mustache and lay in a thin line atop the barrel of the Colt in the man's right hand, aimed at Prophet's heart.

Prophet slowly took up the slack in his trigger finger as raw fury throbbed in his ears. He thought he could hear Chacin increasing the tension on his own six-shooter, and the throbbing in the bounty hunter's ears grew louder.

"Boys, boys," Louisa said, "if you can't hold your booze you oughta stick to sarsaparilla."

Prophet held the Rurale captain's glowering stare for another five seconds. But the girl's calmly cajoling voice had thrust a lance through the tension that had fallen like a hot, wet blanket over the little camp in the rocky arroyo, relieving it. Chacin's lips spread, lifting the curled ends of his mustache and showing his fang-like, yellow eyeteeth. The silver stilettos in his eyes grew faintly smaller. Prophet put some slack in his trigger finger, felt the thudding in his ears slow.

He and Chacin chuckled softly at the same time and raised their pistol barrels. "Perhaps we are indeed acting a little foolish — eh, Lou?"

"Perhaps. Not that I like you any better than I did five minutes ago."

"Nor that I feel any love for you, amigo," Chacin said, twirling his Colt on his finger and returning it to the covered, black holster strapped for the cross draw on his left hip. "But perhaps there is another, less resolute way we can resolve our differences."

"Perhaps there is," Prophet said, shoving his own Colt into the holster on his right thigh, with a faint snicking of iron on leather. "You wanna fight with knives? First one to get a hand cut off has to keep his mouth shut about their differences for the rest of this blessed trek?"

"How 'bout if you leg or arm wrestle?" Louisa said wearily, still resting her head back against her saddle. "A one-handed

117

man isn't much good out here."

Prophet glanced at her, then arched a brow at Chacin. "I reckon she's got a point."

"As sensible as she is lovely."

Louisa sighed.

Chacin said, "I like the arm-wrestling suggestion. It's the manly solution." He smiled.

"Rules what I laid out? Loser goes mute for as long as we're doomed to suffer each other's company?"

"That sounds fair," Chacin said, unbuttoning the cuff of his right shirtsleeve. The two Rurales who'd been sleeping were stirring with interest. "The first one to mention our, uh . . . *differences* again has the right to shoot the other without retribution from the other's men." Chacin gave an oily smile. "Or women."

"Fine as frog hair," Prophet said, rolling up the right sleeve of his own buckskin shirt.

"Shall we up the stakes just a little?" Chacin said, staring down at his arm as he rolled the sleeve up tight against his bulging bicep.

"Why not?"

Chacin turned his head toward the men crawling up behind him, and spoke in Spanish. One of the men crawled away, grabbed one of the empty pulque bottles, scampered over to where Prophet and Chacin faced each other, and broke the neck of the bottle

118

on the flat rock between them — first on the rock's left side, then on the rock's right side. Carefully, using the side of his hand, he piled the jagged shards of broken glass into two neat piles. He sat back on his heels, grinning and blowing out an eager little puff of air.

Another Rurale, hatless, his black hair rumpled, sat beside the Rurale who brought the bottle, and both watched Chacin and Prophet anxiously. They muttered to each other, placing bets, and Louisa came up from behind Prophet to hover between him and Chacin on the other side of the rock from the two lower-ranking Rurales. The one who'd brought the bottle was young, probably not yet twenty. The other was in his thirties, with a haggard, hound-dog look.

"All right — I'll throw in."

"I thought you never gambled," Prophet said, throwing his right arm out to limber it, flexing his thick, callused fingers.

"You didn't think I cussed, either."

"I hope you're at least gonna bet on me."

Louisa spoke in halting, broken Spanish to the two Rurales. When they agreed on terms, Prophet and Chacin, grinning evilly at each other, set their elbows on the rock and clamped their palms and laced their fingers together.

"May the lovely senorita set us off?" Prophet asked the captain.

Chacin hiked a shoulder.

"Get on with it," Louisa said, setting back against a rock several feet away, crossing her ankles and folding her arms on her chest.

Prophet got the upper hand quickly and worked the captain's own right hand about a third of the way down toward the broken glass. Chacin cursed through his gritted teeth, and Prophet, grinding his own molars, watched his hand move back up and then inch knuckle-down toward the glass piled on his own side of the rock, the shards glittering like diamonds in the moonlight.

Prophet wasn't surprised by the Rurale's strength. He was as tall as Prophet, though not as broad and muscular, but his arms were long and his hands were as large as Prophet's, his forearms corded from a life — at least, an early life — of the hard work customary amongst the peons of Mexico. And Chacin had very likely been a peon, which made it hard for Prophet to hate the man completely. It was the rich in Mexico he had no truck with. Fortunately, there weren't that many rich Mexicans — at least not in the places he frequented south of the border.

Prophet pushed up with his right hand, staring at his scarred, bulging knuckles. Chacin thrust his head forward, face angled down, eyes bulging, lips stretched back from his teeth. He growled like an old dog, staring lustily at the glass shards piled near Prophet's right elbow. "My, they look sharp — don't they, Lou?" he rasped. He licked his upper lip. "Don't fret, *mi* amigo. Such a wound won't take all that long to heal in the dry desert air."

The two other Rurales, sitting cross-legged to Prophet's right, leaned forward with their elbows on their knees and snickered.

Chacin's growl rose in pitch when Prophet, pressing his right heel harder against the ground, managed to heave the captain's hand back up to their starting point and then a quarter of the way down toward Chacin's waiting pile of broken glass.

The captain's slender bicep bulged beneath the rolled shirtsleeve, a thick vein rising darkly. Prophet grunted, watched his hand drive Chacin's to within about four inches of the glass.

"Damn, them shards look sharp — don't they, Jorge?" Prophet said, sucking a breath through his own gritted teeth. "Sorta like little, razor-edged knives . . . only glass can really stick in . . ."

Chacin cursed in Spanish.

". . . There . . . !"

Prophet shoved the man's hand into the glass. He didn't want to cut him badly, because there was no reason to inhibit the man's ability to shoot. But the Mexicans wouldn't see it that way. If he didn't make it hurt as much as he could, Chacin and the other Rurales would merely think him a fool.

The two young Rurales gasped as Prophet mashed his hand down on the captain's, twisting it both directions, feeling Chacin's own hand quiver beneath him, hearing the glass grind like sand in a wheel hub, watching the blood darken it.

Chacin's hand lay like a dead fish beneath Prophet's. His rasping breaths quieted. He compressed his lips and looked dully across the rock at his opponent, who lifted his own hand, felt the old tension drop down over the camp once more.

The two Rurales both grunted and jerked their hands at the same time.

"No, no." Louisa's silver-chased Colt was out and extended in her right fist, aimed between Prophet and Chacin, at the two Rurales, who froze with their guns still in their covered holsters.

The Rurales stared at Prophet. Prophet stared across the rock at Chacin. Neither man said anything. Even the coyotes had fallen silent.

Chacin's expression remained implacable as he lifted his slack hand from the pile of glass and brushed it across his uniform pants. He smiled and glanced at Louisa's cocked silver Colt.

"I think I am in love with her, Lou."

"You and every other man she's ever hauled down on," Prophet said.

Late in the morning of the next day, Sugar Delphi set one of her black boots down in front of a scorpion. The scorpion stopped suddenly, probed the boot in front of it with its extended stinger, then turned and headed back in the opposite direction.

Sugar set her other boot down in the creature's path. The scorpion stopped. Just as it started to probe the second roadblock, Sugar squashed the creature beneath the high, undershot heel of her other boot. She ground the beast to a greasy pulp in the small sharp rocks of the arroyo she and her group had been traveling since dawn.

She hadn't looked down at the now-deceased creature. Somehow, she'd just sensed it was there and that it was something that needed killing. Behind her, Red Snake Corbin quietly cleared his throat and shared an oblique glance with Roy Kiljoy. Tony Lazzaro chuckled and leaned forward, crossing his wrists on his saddle horn.

"What is it, Sugar?" he asked the woman, who sometimes seemed his woman and sometimes no one's woman at all. "What's got your drawers in a twist? We ain't seen Mojave sign all day."

"Give me a minute." Sugar moved forward, probed the side of the wash with the same boot she'd used to squash the scorpion, then began to climb, not looking down but keeping her eyes straight ahead, crouching every now and then to push off the steep slope. Even blind and sort of groping, loosing rocks and sand in her wake, she gained the top of the bank quickly and stood pointing her head toward the east, the direction from which they'd come.

"Sugar," Lazzaro said, biting a chunk of tobacco off the braid he carried in the pocket of his black cotton shirt, under a brown cowhide vest. "We're burnin' daylight, and you know how Tony don't like burnin' daylight."

Lazzaro had been born in Mexico but he'd been sent to live with his aunt and uncle in Wyoming when he was only three, so he spoke perfect English, though he was also fluent in Spanish. Both languages served him well, since he ran his outlaw gang back and forth across the border, dealing in anything that earned him money, from simple bank and stagecoach holdups to diamond smuggling and slave trading with the mines in southern Mexico.

It had once been a much larger gang, but since he and Sugar had decided to retire to Central America, where Lazzaro owned a half interest in a sugar plantation, he'd had no use for the others and had lost no sleep over pulling foot with a choice few men, Sugar, and all the money from their last holdup.

"Someone's trailin' us, Tony," Sugar said from atop the bank, staring toward the east as though she could see what she was talking about.

" 'Paches?"

Sugar shook her head, causing the small, beaded braids to dance over her ears. "White men."

Lazzaro turned to gaze back down the wash though he couldn't see much farther than the next bend about fifty feet away. He turned to the redhead, canting his head to one side and narrowing one eye beneath his low-crowned, gray sombrero adorned with black stitching. "Sugar, dear, you did kill the *rubia*, like we agreed you would, didn't you?"

Sugar shook her head. "I wasn't sure about her." She shook her head again, frowning a little as she continued to stare east. "I guess I wanted to be sure."

"You wanted to be sure about what?" Lazzaro's voice was taut with strained patience.

Sugar started descending the slope the way she'd climbed it, haltingly, testing her footing. "I guess we'll maybe find that out."

Sitting his horse to Lazzaro's left, Red Snake loosed a caustic chuff. He glanced darkly at the gang leader, then lowered his eyes. Roy Kiljoy kept his own hard, expectant gaze on Lazzaro. Testing, probing.

The gang leader sighed. He'd given the blind woman about all the slack he could afford to give her. Her sixth and seventh senses had saved his hide more than once, in ways he could never understand, but he had his pride. He swung his right boot over his saddle horn. "Sugar, my sweet, I reckon it's time for you and me to come to an understandin'."

He dropped down to the ground and walked over to where Sugar was walking and sliding down the side of the slope, his eyes flat and mean though she couldn't see them.

"Oh, really, Tony?" she said when she stood flat-footed on the floor of the wash, aiming those cool, cobalt blue eyes at him as though they were twin pistol maws. She crossed her arms on her chest. "And what understanding is that?"

Lazzaro's right hand shot up, back, and forward so quickly that the two men sitting their horses behind him only saw him jerk. They heard the crack of his hand against Sugar's face, saw her head whip back and to the side.

She stumbled back and fell against the slope.

"That I'm the leader of this pack of curly wolves, small as it suddenly is. Not you! And, yeah, even you follow my orders or pay the price!"

10

Sugar had had her head turned away, her red hair screening her left cheek but not enough to completely hide the flush caused by the back of Lazzaro's hand. Now she turned to him, her jaws hard, a forked vein standing out in her forehead.

"Goddamn you to hell, lover!" she said, her low voice sounding like a hand run across guitar strings discordantly.

Lazzaro stepped back, a self-satisfied look on his round face with its weak chin and silver teeth showing between his thin lips mantled by a long, pencil-thin mustache.

"Hang on, now," Red Snake said as he and Kiljoy watched Sugar slide her .36 Remington from the holster on her right hip.

Lazzaro threw a waylaying arm out, staring at Sugar, who was now regaining her feet, the Remy in her hand. "Shut up. Both of you stay out of it!" He grinned at the blind woman, who held both of her hands straight down at her sides and stared unseeingly toward Lazzaro, her hair hanging in tangles about her face, nostrils flaring, and her chest rising and falling sharply behind her leather vest.

"If you're gonna pull that hogleg on me, Sugar," Lazzaro said, "you best make sure you kill me with it!"

She took one stumbling step straight out away from the bank, staring somewhere just over Lazzaro's right shoulder, and raised the Remington. "Goddamn you to hell, Tony!"

The Remington barked, stabbing smoke and flames.

Lazzaro snickered as he stepped to his right, sort of ducking and weaving his head, smirking. The bullet tore a twig from a mesquite somewhere behind him. The horses nickered and pranced.

"Come on, Sugar," Lazzaro taunted. "Let's see you put that sixth sense of yours to good use. Come on — you wanna shoot ole Tony, then shoot him!"

Knowing she'd draw a bead on his voice, he stepped back in the opposite direction, throwing his arms out and exaggeratedly stepping on the balls of his boots, trying to make as little sound as possible.

Again, Sugar's Remy popped, blowing up

dirt and stones from the arroyo bank five feet behind where Lazzaro had last been standing. The horses continued to nicker while the men held their reins taut, staring in wary amazement at the blind woman extending the pistol straight out in front of her and raking the hammer back once more.

"A blind woman," Lazzaro said, shaking his head and continuing to sneer at Sugar, "no way she should be carryin' a gun."

Pop!

The bullet blew up several strands of Lazzaro's long, thin hair. He gave a startled, bemused yelp and jerked back in the other direction, jogging several yards down the arroyo now while Sugar clicked the Remy's hammer back and tracked him, bunching her lips furiously.

"I swear, I'll kill you, Tony!"

Lazzaro stood crouching beside a wagon-sized boulder in the middle of the arroyo, one hand on it, ready to run behind it if it looked like she was going to come even closer with her next shot. "Really? You gonna kill good ole Tony, who out of the kindness of his heart rescued you from them mean old nuns at the convent?"

"That was then, you son of a bitch! This is now!"

The Remy roared. Lazzaro had just started

to lurch behind the boulder when her bullet slammed into the face of the rock, spraying shards. He jerked his head with a start and laughed, then very slowly and quietly stepped around behind the boulder to the other side, turning to the other two men who sat their horses behind Sugar now, and pressed two fingers to his grinning lips.

Then he faced the blind woman, spread his arms, and threw his shoulders and chest back, grinning so broadly that all his full set of upper silver teeth shone beneath the thin line of his mustache. He remained silent as the girl stepped forward, jerking her head and gun around, trying to get a fix on him. A bird chattered in a tree to Lazzaro's left. She swung the gun toward it and fired.

Lazzaro snickered.

She swung the gun toward him and fired again, the slug slamming into the side of another boulder about six feet to his right and behind him.

He lowered his hands and took off running across the arroyo. "One more, *chiquita!*"

Sugar screamed her fury, ran three steps forward, and fired.

Lazzaro dove behind a tree, the slug kicking up rocks about two feet behind him. He hit the ground and rolled and came up with his own long-barreled Smith & Wesson in his fist.

Bam! Bam! Bam! Bam! Bam-bam!

His bullets plowed up dirt and gravel in a semicircle about one foot in front of Sugar's copper-tipped black boots. She gave a cry and stumbled backward, tripping over a rock and dropping onto her butt about ten feet in front of Red Snake Corbin and Roy Kiljoy.

She lowered her empty gun to her side and stared down at the toes of her boots. Her eyes were wide and glassy, her cheeks flushed behind her hair. She lowered her head farther and her shoulders jerked as she sobbed. Her head dropped still lower until her chin was nearly scraping her vest. Her head and shoulders jerked as she cried.

Red Snake and Kiljoy glanced at each other, at the sobbing woman, and then at Lazzaro, who heaved himself to his feet now, his smoking Smith & Wesson in his right hand. Slowly, he walked toward Sugar, who raised her knees, set her elbows against them, and pressed her hands to her temples as she cried.

"There, there, Sugar." Lazzaro stopped before her and looked down at her with the hard eyes of a parent who'd been forced against his will to punish an unruly child.

"No need to cry. I was just tryin' to take you down a badly needed notch, that's all."

Sugar sniffed and nodded, keeping her chin down. "I know." She sniffed again. "I know you were, Tony."

Kiljoy looked at Lazzaro. "That wasn't good — all that shootin'. Every Mojave in ten miles prob'ly heard it."

Lazzaro said, "Go check. Both of you. Leave mine and Sugar's horses here."

Red Snake dropped the reins of both mounts. Then he and Kiljoy split up, each riding up an opposite bank and out onto the sunburned desert. Lazzaro slipped his Smith & Wesson into the holster on his right hip, near the second holster angled for the cross draw and containing a short-barreled Russian. He dropped to a knee beside the sobbing woman, ran his hand through his long, stringy hair with restrained affection.

"I know you like to be independent. Just like a she-coyote. The thing is, girl, you can't be. Not totally. Even with that special gift you have, you're still blind. You need ole Tony."

Sugar nodded. "I do. I do need you, Tony."

"Sometimes you forget that."

"I reckon I do."

"And what's more, Sugar girl, you need to remember who's the head honcho here.

133

Because sometimes I think you forget."

"I do forget it."

"Just like you musta forgot when I told you — after you told me you suspected that Leona girl wasn't who she said she was."

For the first time, Sugar lifted her head, showing her tear-streaked cheeks and swollen, red-rimmed eyes. "I know, Tony, but you see I didn't know who she was, and I thought I could —"

"No, no, no," Lazzaro said, wagging his finger at her. "That's where you went wrong. You took matters into your own hands. You left her alive after I told you you had to kill her or leave it to me to kill her."

Guiltily, Sugar lowered her head again and sniffed, running the back of her hand across her nose.

"You felt somethin' for her, did you?"

"I reckon I sorta did," Sugar said.

"Well, now, let that be a lesson for you. You don't need to go feelin' nothin' for nobody except ole Tony." Lazzaro placed two gloved fingers under her chin and lifted her face toward his. "Ain't I the one who sprung you from that monastery your witch of a ma sent you to? Ain't I the one that took you back home and helped you do away with all them that wronged you. Especially your pa and brother who thought that just cause you was blind they could do what they wanted to you anytime they felt like it?"

Tears welled in her eyes and dribbled down her cheeks as she remembered. Her face crumpled, and she began sobbing again in earnest. "Oh, Tony," she cried, throwing her arms around his neck. "I'm so sorry!"

"You'll never cross me again, will you, Sugar?"

"Never!"

" 'Cause you need ole Tony."

"I need you, Tony!"

Lazzaro smiled and patted her back. "There, there. No need to cry about it. Hell, it's all spilled milk, anyway, and I already done forgot all about it!"

She pulled away from him, wiped her wet face with both hands. "Thank you, Tony."

"Let's get movin'. We got a long, hot desert to cross."

Lazzaro rose to his feet. Sugar grabbed his hand. "Wait, Tony. Don't you think we oughta camp here in the shade today, travel at night?"

"Ah, shit." Lazzaro looked through the mesquites and across the desert toward where the Montanas Muertas humped, stark and gray, in the western distance. "I wanna get across this damn desert, then head south to the Gulf. I don't got time to sit here and twiddle my thumbs and wait for the sun to go down. Besides, it's a whole lot easier for you to ride in the dark than it is for me an' Red Snake and Roy."

"But . . . the Mojaves. . . ."

Lazzaro glared at her. "Now, Sugar. What'd we just get done talkin' about?"

"Okay." Sugar forced a meek smile and rose. "Okay, Tony — you're right. There I go again, second-guessing you. I'm sorry."

Lazzaro's group followed the wash for another mile. When it angled west, they climbed out of it and headed south along a jog of low mountains, some of which looked like giant mushrooms of hardened lava. The sun was high, blasting its heat onto the desert floor with a molten hammer and a molten chisel.

Lazzaro knew there was a well at the eastern edge of the Dead Mountains, in an old Mexican village that had been taken over by miners working for an American gold company, but he didn't want to ride that far west. He wanted to plow straight south toward the sea. He'd heard that San Gezo was cursed, and having holed up there once himself, he believed it. It was hot and dusty and far from anywhere. There was a well between here and Puerto Penasco. A far stretch south of his gang's current location, but they'd likely reach it in six, seven hours or so.

The horses slowed, hung their heads.

Lazzaro led the way toward the uninterrupted southern horizon. To the west and east, the mountains beckoned. He ignored them. South was his direction. South, damnit, to a free life in Central America.

"I don't know, Boss," said Roy Kiljoy, loosening his neckerchief that was mottled white with the salt of his sweat. "Might be a good idea to ride at night. Cooler, you know."

"I like to see where I'm goin'."

"Yeah, but this way it's awful hot," said Red Snake, looking around at the white-hot desert mounded with rocks and stippled with occasional cacti. "And the Mojaves can keep better track of us. Hell, I think I can feel their eyes on us."

Lazzaro glanced at Sugar riding off his horse's right hip. "You three been cahootin' against me?"

Sugar said nothing, just stared straight ahead, letting her black clomp along, occasionally kicking a rock.

Lazzaro opened his mouth to speak but only said, *"Gnahh!"* as he flew out of his saddle and hit the ground in a heap. A rifle report flatted out across the desert.

"Hellfire!" Kiljoy said, sawing back on his horse's reins and staring toward a low, long mound of sand and rocks to the east. *"Injuns!"*

"Tony?" Sugar said, hearing the gang leader groaning on the ground somewhere to her left. "Tony? Are you all right, Tony?"

Her query was answered by several more rifle cracks and the whine of several ricochets. One of the horses whinnied shrilly.

"Goddamnit!" Lazzaro barked as Red Snake and Kiljoy raised their rifles. "Goddamnit — *shoot* those goddamn savages!"

Red Snake swung down from his saddle and, holding his bridle reins, raised his Winchester and pumped three shots into the low mound of sand and rocks rising about fifty yards to the east where he'd seen rifle barrels bristling and smoke puffing. Kiljoy fired once from his saddle, then dismounted and dropped to a knee about ten yards to Red Snake's right.

He raised the rifle to his shoulder as Red Snake snapped off his fourth shot, levered another round into his Henry's breech, then held fire, staring down the barrel toward the mound.

"Where are they?" Kiljoy said as Lazzaro

groaned behind him. Sugar was down on both knees beside the gang leader, who lay propped on an elbow, clutching his hand to his lower right side, just above his cartridge belt.

"I don't see nothin'," Red Snake said, his pulse throbbing in his ears.

"Kill 'em!" Lazzaro shouted. "Kill every last one of them dry-gulchin' catamounts!"

Kiljoy started walking forward, swinging his rifle back and forth in front of him. Red Snake followed him up the low hill, both men stopping suddenly when they saw three Mojaves dashing down the other side of the rise toward three horses being held by a fourth warrior. Kiljoy triggered a shot, but all three running Mojaves were out of accurate rifle range, and the slug merely puffed dust well behind them.

He and Red Snake looked around, both men breathing hard from anxiety. "You know, Roy," Red Snake said, squeezing his rifle in his hands so that the snakes tattooed on his thin arms seemed to be trying to wrap themselves around the brass-framed Henry, "I don't mind tanglin' with Injuns up on the plains. But down here in the desert, where it's just so damn hot . . . it just ties my innards in big, tight knots. You don't think I'm yaller for sayin' so, do you?"

Kiljoy stared after the Indians, all four of whom were now mounted and galloping off through the rocks and scrub, heading east. A couple glanced back over their shoulders as their war ponies tore up the desert and loosed demonic, taunting yowls.

The squat, ugly outlaw spat to one side, wiped chaw from his long, blond mustache, and narrowed an eye at Red Snake. "Yeah. Yeah, that does make me think you're yaller." He spat again and started walking in his bull-legged way back toward Lazzaro, Sugar, and the horses. "Pull yourself together, goddamnit, Red Snake."

"Well, I'll be goddamned!" Red Snake said, exasperated. "Don't tell me you like fightin' Mojaves any more than I do, Roy!"

As the two men tramped back through the hot rocks and prickly pear, Sugar was holding her balled-up green neckerchief against the bloody hole in Lazzaro's side. "You're gonna have to hold that there, Tony. Can you hold it?"

Lazzaro was sweating like a butcher in a Tucson grocery shop and breathing hard, stretching his lips back in painful grimaces. With his shaky left hand, he held the neckerchief against the bloody wound and spat a rabid curse.

"Ten years I been runnin' loco both north

and south of the border, and this is the first time I been shot this bad. The others was only flesh wounds."

"Does it hurt bad?"

"Yeah, it hurts bad, Sugar — for chrissakes!"

"Don't die, Tony." Sugar meant it. She hadn't been lying about agreeing with all that Lazzaro had told her. She'd still be in that monastery, taking her whippings from the vile nuns, if Lazzaro hadn't holed up there two winters ago, on the run from Rurales, and taken her with him when he'd left.

After killing the cruelest of the sadistic nuns . . .

She indeed had a special sense that gave her an advantage over other blind people — an extra sense that was sometimes almost as good as seeing with her eyes — but she'd be helpless without Lazzaro, who, when all was said and done, had been admirably good and patient with her. What other man would let a blind woman ride with him, share in his spoils with him?

That special sense often made her cocky, caused her to feel more independent than she actually was, and it took a good tongue lashing from Lazzaro to realize her true and rightful place in this vast, hard world.

"Please don't die on me, Tony."

"Shut up and help get me back on my horse. Gotta keep movin'. Gotta keep movin' south."

"I don't know that you can ride, Tony," Sugar said, wrapping his left arm around her shoulders and helping the man to his feet.

Kiljoy and Red Snake had stopped ten feet from them. Kiljoy said, "I don't believe we'll be headin' south, Boss."

"Goddamnit, we're headin' for the sea!" Lazzaro barked.

"Take a look." Kiljoy jerked his chin to indicate south, where a column of smoke rose about two hundred yards away. Another interrupted column of smoke — obviously signal smoke — lifted in the east, the direction from which their bushwhackers had galloped.

Lazzaro groaned, sighed. "All right, I reckon you two and the Injuns win. We'll head west. Let's go, goddamnit. . . ." He'd barely finished that last before his eyes closed and his knees buckled. He was out before he hit the ground.

"Tony!"

11

A voice rose on the warm, still night.

Prophet, scouting ahead of Louisa and the five Rurales, drew back on Mean's reins. He looked around at the dark desert relieved by a vivid wash of lilac blue behind the black, jagged ridges looming in the northwest.

He could see little but the silhouettes of rocks and shrubs stretching around him in all directions. A vagrant breeze nudged the spindly branches of a creosote shrub. That appeared the only movement. The desert was as silent as an opera house long after the crowd has left.

The air was still hot but not as hot as before the sun had gone down a little over an hour before, where that lilac wash lingered now. That's when Prophet and Louisa and the Rurales had broken their day camp in a shaded wash, where they'd waited out the heat and headed straight out across the desert toward the Montanas Muertas.

They'd lost Lazzaro's trail on a rocky stretch of rugged terrain, but Prophet had little doubt the gang was headed west toward the Dead Mountains. There was really nowhere else for them to head, as Mojaves appeared to have the other three directions buttoned down tight as a drumhead. Trying to bust through would be running a deadly gauntlet of arrows fletched with hawk feathers and hot lead.

No telling how many Indians were out here, but their sign said plenty.

There it was again — the faint keening sound that resembled a human voice. Possibly a bobcat's whine, but Prophet didn't think so. There was a human quality in the breathy voice. It seemed to come from the north though Prophet could detect no movement that way. And no campfire. Maybe the desert floor dropped off in that direction, and he just couldn't see it from here.

Best check it out.

Prophet wrapped his right hand around his Winchester's stock and slid the rifle from his saddle boot. Tilting the barrel up, he swung down from the saddle, the squawk of the dry leather in the quiet desert night making him grit his teeth anxiously. There were no substantial shrubs around to which he could tie his horse, so he ground-tied the mount, knowing that nothing less than a mountain lion or pack of howling Mojaves could tear Mean from the rein anchor. He'd been appropriately named, but he was a loyal bastard. Prophet would give him that.

He patted the horse's right whither, then slowly, quietly pumped a cartridge into the Winchester's breech. Holding the rifle up high, he walked slowly north from the horse that craned his neck to stare after him but knew instinctively to keep quiet.

Prophet walked slowly out away from the horse for thirty yards, then dropped suddenly to one knee. He'd spied a murky wash of movement ahead and to his left — a flicker of a shadow moving amongst shadows. A hollow thud, like that of a boot clipping a stone, reached his ears from the same direction.

An Indian war party?

It would be odd for Mojaves to be out skulking around at night, but not unheard of. Anyone who depended too heavily on anything but his senses out here was a damn fool, and Prophet's senses were now alerting him to trouble.

There was someone out there in the darkness. By the sound, they were moving in his general direction.

He straightened and strode quickly but quietly ahead and right, intending to make a swing around whomever was out here. Stopping again in the shadow of a spindly saguaro, he stared northwest, pricking his ears.

Someone sighed. And sighed again. It was a raspy sound, someone breathing in and out raggedly and making small, agonized groaning sounds. Again there was the hollow thud as the walker kicked a stone.

Prophet stepped out from the saguaro's shadow and stole slowly forward. When he'd walked twenty yards and could see the dark land dropping darkly ahead of him, he aimed the Winchester straight out from his right hip and said in a voice that sounded inordinately loud in the taut silence, "Who's there?"

Knowing that a gunman would likely target his voice, he stepped to his right and dropped to a knee.

Another raspy breath. The slender shadow about thirty yards ahead of him stopped suddenly, jerking a little back and forth. "Joaquin?" a thin, pinched voice said.

"Nope." Prophet winced, awaiting a gun flash and the whistle of a bullet hurling toward him, tightening his right index finger

146

on the Winchester's trigger.

"Por favor," said the man in the darkness. "If you have any soul at all, senor, I implore you to help me. My name is Gabriel Bocangel, and I am walking around out here, a desperate hombre, looking for my son."

Prophet studied the shadow, waiting for any quick movement that would mark the man a killer. When none came, Prophet said, "Where's your son?"

"I am looking for him, senor. Joaquin. I fear he is dead, killed by Mojaves."

"You don't sound too good yourself."

"I have been better, senor."

"Come on ahead."

Prophet watched the slender shadow grow larger until it became a man of about five-four, maybe one hundred and twenty pounds, stumbling toward him. He was hatless and his black hair glistened in the moonlight. He wore patched denims and a red-and-black wool shirt with a red bandanna knotted about his thick neck. He wore a cartridge belt but no gun — at least none that Prophet could see. As he approached the bounty hunter, nearly dragging the toes of his stockmen's boots, he was holding his right arm.

He came to within ten feet of Prophet, looked up at the big bounty hunter through pain-racked eyes, and heaved a ragged sigh. He dropped to his knees.

Prophet lowered the Winchester's barrel and walked over to the man who knelt with his head down, thick black hair hanging down over his forehead. Blood glistened as it oozed through the hand the Mexican had clamped over his upper right arm. It also glistened on the broken-off arrow that protruded four inches out the back of the man's arm.

"Mojaves?"

"Si."

Prophet knelt beside the man. "What were you doin' out here — you and your son?"

"Is that important, senor?" Senor Bocangel looked up at Prophet, a raven's wing of black hair lightly streaked with silver hanging over his right brow. "If not, I would prefer not to say."

Prophet met the man's wry gaze. What an odd response. Prophet lifted the man's right arm slightly, and Bocangel groaned and sucked a sharp breath through his teeth. "What have we got here?"

He poked his hat brim off his forehead and lowered his head to get a better look at the man's arm. About half the flint arrow point was protruding out the front of the man's arm, angling toward the inside, dark

148

with fresh blood.

"I tried to pull it out, senor," Bocangel said in a faintly chagrined tone, "but I stopped when I started to faint. I thought perhaps if I fainted I would bleed to death. Or be found by the Mojaves."

"That's gotta come out. Can you stand?"

The Mexican sounded immensely tired. "Perhaps."

"Let's get you back to my horse."

Prophet wrapped the man's left arm around his neck and led him over to where Mean and Ugly stood ground-tied and regarding the newcomer with shiny-eyed wariness. He eased Bocangel down on a rock on Mean's far side.

"Ay, Cristo!"

Prophet went over to the horse and poked his hand into a saddlebag pouch, looking around warily and listening carefully for the tread of near Mojaves. "How far away did this happen?"

"A mile," the Mexican said, hanging his head. "Maybe two. I can't remember how far I walked."

Prophet tramped back over to Senor Bocangel with a whiskey bottle and a handful of torn-up rags he used for bandages. "How'd you lose track of your boy?"

"Joaquin walked away from our camp to

149

gather firewood. While he was gone, three Mojaves shot arrows into the camp. I took one here. They rode off, howling like the demon dogs they are, in the direction Joaquin had gone. I came out looking for him. I heard one shot. Once I was about to return to our camp but realized I was lost." He wagged his head sadly. "Everything looks the same out here, senor."

"Does at that." Prophet glanced at the man's cross-draw holster riding empty on his left hip. "Where's your gun?"

"I must have lost it when I fell down a hill. I did not notice until just after dark." Bocangel groaned, sniffed, swallowed. "I chose a direction and decided to walk in a straight line . . . and then I heard you."

Prophet offered the bottle. "Have a swig off that. Have a big pull. You're gonna need it here in a minute."

"Por favor." Senor Bocangel lifted the bottle to his lips and tipped his head back. His throat worked twice, loudly, and then he lowered his head and the bottle, and gave a raspy sigh. "Ah, wheesky. Eez good."

"Want somethin' to chomp down on?"

Bocangel gave a wan smile and shook his head.

Prophet wrapped his thumb and index finger around the bloody shaft. "All right —

I'll try to make this quick, but don't hold me to it."

"*Por favor*, senor . . . *ahhhhh!*"

"There we go. Came out clean." Prophet held the ten-inch bloody shaft up in front of him. "Must've just glanced off the bone."

Bocangel was panting wildly, like a dog that had run five miles in the hot sun.

"The name's Prophet," the bounty hunter said, using both hands to rip the Mexican's sleeve away from his arm, exposing both the exit and entrance wounds. "Lou Prophet. You mighta heard of me."

"I don't think so, sen . . . *ahhhhh!*"

Bocangel threw his head back, grimacing, as Prophet doused both wounds with the whiskey.

"That hurt me damn near as much as it hurt you, Senor Bocangel," Prophet said, lowering the bottle and taking up one of the bandages. "That right there's the last of my busthead."

"*Cristo!* I do not wish to be rude, Senor Prophet, but I believe I am going to pass out."

Senor Bocangel sagged to the side. Prophet grabbed him and eased him to the ground, leaning him back gently against the rock.

As the Mexican's chin dropped toward his

151

chest and he smacked his lips a few times, breathing raspily, Prophet wrapped the bandage around the man's wounded arm. Hoof thuds grew in the east. Probably Louisa and Chacin and the other Rurales, but he wasn't taking any chances. He grabbed his rifle and walked a ways from the unconscious stranger, and stood waiting, holding the rifle up high across his chest.

When the riders were near enough for him to see their outlines, he said, "Louisa?"

"Here."

Prophet lowered the rifle. "We're gonna have to slow the pace a little."

"For who?" Chacin said, riding beside Louisa, the other four Rurales following in a ragged line.

"My new friend'll be ridin' with us."

Chacin gigged his Arab up to where Senor Bocangel sat against the rock. Louisa gigged her pinto up more slowly, glancing from Prophet to the unconscious Mexican. The four other Rurales followed suit, looking down curiously.

"What happened to him, Lou?" asked the Rurale captain.

"Took a Mojave arrow through the arm." Prophet held the whiskey bottle up to the crescent moon. About a quarter remained. He uncorked it, took a shot, rammed the cork back into the lip with the heel of his hand, and stowed the bottle back in his saddlebag pouch.

"Best leave him under a tree," Chacin said. "He'll slow us down too much."

"Can't leave a man alone out here on foot, Chacin." Prophet leaned down and picked up the little Mexican in his arms. "We'll take him to that village in the mountains yonder. I was through there once, long time ago. It's likely where Lazzaro's bunch is headed. Only water around."

"San Gezo?"

"That's it." With a grunt Prophet set the wounded Senor Bocangel on Mean and Ugly's back, atop his bedroll behind his saddle. Louisa sidled her horse up to the lineback dun, and she reached over to hold the man on the horse while Prophet climbed into the saddle. "Nice little watering hole there — the Oasis . . ."

"*Salon y danza pasillo del oasis,*" offered Sergeant Frieri. He smiled in the darkness. "The Oasis Saloon and Dance Hall."

"What's that got to do with anything?" Louisa asked. "The man needs a doctor, not a drink."

"No, but I do," Prophet said, touching his spurs to Mean's flanks, putting the horse ahead at a slow walk. "But come to think of it, there was a doctor there. Might still be."

"I doubt it." Chacin put his horse up beside Prophet. "I haven't been out there in years. That town has dried up, I am told. The mine there was owned by Americans, and they pulled out."

"The Sweet Hereafter Mine," said Prophet with a smile.

"*Si*, that's it. But if the mine dried up, I am sure everyone left. Everyone but scorpions and Mojaves, probably. Maybe a few of the original *Mejicano* inhabitants."

"San Gezo is cursed," said Frieri, riding behind Chacin. "The mountains, too, are cursed. That's why no one goes there. Not even the Mojaves. Of course, the Americans didn't mind. Americans will go anywhere that is cursed. They have no respect for such things. But as I said, the mountains and the *pueblito* of San Gezo . . ." The sergeant waved his hand toward the distant, dark horizon capped with stars. "All are cursed. We should not be going there, El Capitan."

"We're going for the money," said Chacin, rolling an unlit cigar around between his lips. "When we have the money, we'll head the hell out." He glanced at Senor Bocangel riding with his head against Prophet's back, snoring softly and intermittently groaning. "Did he say what he is doing out here?"

154

"No," Prophet lied. He didn't think it would be in Senor Bocangel's best interest to inform the Rurale captain that the man had chosen to remain silent on the matter of his business out here. "He was too weak to say much of anything except that he and his son were attacked by Mojaves just before sundown."

"You are wasting your time with him, Lou. Probably just some old prospector. If he lives out here in this cursed devil's land ruled by Relampago's wild Mojaves, he is better off dead."

12

"Damn, I never thought I'd be so happy to see another Mexican mountain range," said Kiljoy. "But I sure as shit am."

The stocky, ugly brigand rode at the head of the outlaw pack, the Montanas Muertas rising ahead of them. From this distance of a half a mile, the mountains appeared just another stark series of sawtooth peaks capping bulging, adobe-colored domes scored with deep canyons and washes and pleated with brown apron slopes. There were infrequent patches of lime green demarking mostly cactus. There didn't appear to be many trees or much grass.

The range shone bright in the midmorning sunlight. High in the washed-out sky, a large raptor hunted at the very edge of the range and above where a canyon gouged a steep slope, offering passage into the range for the four outlaws who were heading straight for the gate-like opening and the trail to San Gezo, where lay the only water that Lazzaro knew about within about fifty square miles.

"Just hope the well ain't dry," said Red Snake Corbin. "I'm dry as a damn gourd."

He was riding about fifteen feet behind Kiljoy and in front of Sugar Delphi, who was leading Antonio Lazzaro's wolf dun stallion. The outlaw leader looked miserable as he rode low in his saddle, favoring his wounded right side. He had one hand wrapped around a tequila bottle; the other pressed the bandanna against his side.

"You sure there's a well?" Kiljoy asked. "I'd sure hate to ride that far and there ain't water."

"There's water," Lazzaro raked out painfully. "The town has a well. That's about all it's got since the American miners pulled out."

"How long since you been here, Boss?" Kiljoy asked.

"Four, maybe five years. Holed up there when the American cavalry was after me and Heck Wallace when me and his gang robbed that freight outfit east of San Diego." Lazzaro shook his head and winced against the pain rippling through him. "Some say the mountains, the town . . . cursed. I ain't the superstitious type, but I believe it 'bout

San Gezo. Hard to get to . . . hard to get out of. It's a *trap!*"

He took a long pull from the bottle, most of the tequila dribbling down over his chin.

"We won't be there long, Tony," Sugar said. "Just long enough to . . ." She let her voice trail off and lifted her chin, her unseeing eyes wide as she appeared to stare off toward the north. But then she swung her head toward the south. It was then that Lazzaro heard the hoofbeats and followed Sugar's blind gaze toward horseback riders pounding toward them from a hundred yards away and closing fast.

"Ah, shit," Lazzaro said, seeing the bandannas holding black hair back from cinnamon faces, colorful shirts and lunging pintos.

"Injuns!" shouted Red Snake.

"Ah, no, Sugar!" Lazzaro fairly screamed when the woman pulled his horse into a gallop behind her dappled black. "I can't . . . I can't ride that hard . . . !"

Sugar checked her mount back down. "Fort up?"

"Yeah." Lazzaro crawled gingerly down off his horse and slid his carbine from the boot.

"We best head for that canyon, Boss!" This from Kiljoy staring hipped around in his

158

saddle, sunburned cheeks above his blond mustache brick red with exasperation.

"We're gonna fort up and hold 'em off with our long guns!" Lazzaro stepped away from his horse, levering a round into his rifle breech. He took one more step before groaning and dropping to a knee. Sugar was there beside him, wrapping a hand around him. "We gotta get you to cover, Tony! Show me where there's cover!"

Rifles popped in the south. The hoof thuds of the galloping riders grew louder and louder. Both Kiljoy and Red Snake returned fire, both men cursing their frustration. Obviously, they wanted to head for the canyon, but Lazzaro was holding them back because he himself couldn't make it without his wound opening up and bleeding him dry.

Lazzaro heaved himself to his feet with Sugar's assistance, then grabbed his horse's reins. "Come on!" Sugar, her hand hooked behind the back of Lazzaro's cartridge belt, followed the gang leader ahead and toward a shallow gash in the desert floor. The wash was surrounded by spindly brown shrubs and rocks, offering the only cover short of the canyon gap.

Still cursing and snapping off occasional shots toward the Indians, Red Snake and

Kiljoy leaped down off their pitching, nickering horses' backs and ran crouching toward the same gash. Lazzaro stepped gingerly into the cut, Sugar following close behind, her rifle in her hand. Red Snake and Kiljoy were the first to belly up to the side of the wash and return fire at the Mojaves. Lazzaro knelt down below the wash's shallow southern bank and raised his carbine.

The Indians were still hammering toward the wash, spread out in a ragged line, dust rising behind them. They were howling and shouting as they triggered carbines and loosed arrows, the slugs and arrows plowing up dirt around the wash. Lazzaro drew a bead on one rider and fired. His aim was off due to the hammering pain in his right side, and the rider merely dipped his head a little with a start as the bullet screeched past him.

The Indians slid down off their still-moving ponies and hit the ground running before forting up behind rocks and low mounds of sand or in slight depressions. Lazzaro turned to Sugar, who was returning fire with her own rifle, targeting sounds since her eyes were useless. Lazzaro had always thought it amazing how accurate she could be, though he was damn glad she hadn't been accurate the day before, when he'd had to pound some sense into the blind spitfire.

The outlaw leader looked back at his horse tied behind a sheltering mound of rock and squeezed the back of Sugar's neck. "The saddlebags," he said into her ear. "Fetch 'em!"

She looked at him, frowning.

"You heard me."

While Sugar rose and ran back to the horse, which she was able to smell as well as hear snorting around behind the rocks, Lazzaro turned and began pumping slugs toward the howling Indians.

"Tony!"

Lazzaro turned toward the blind woman standing near his horse with the saddlebags bulging with the stolen loot slung over her right shoulder. Sugar threw an arm out toward the southeast. Lazzaro shunted his gaze in that direction and saw two separate dust clouds — one angling toward Lazzaro from the southeast, the other moving like a vast swarm of bees from straight east.

He gritted his silver teeth and pumped another round into his Winchester's breech. "Like I said, the place is cursed, all right. And so is anyone who comes near it!"

A half hour before, Prophet turned to Senor Bocangel, who was now riding with Louisa, the man's hands wrapped around her waist. He had Prophet's bottle in one hand, and he'd been taking conservative sips from it since he'd regained consciousness just before dawn, when they'd all stopped to rest their horses.

The mountains they were heading for grew large before them, but Prophet figured they were still nearly an hour away. He knew they were headed in the right direction, however, as he'd picked up Lazzaro's gang's sign at the first blush of dawn. He was glad, because this was a hell of a place to find oneself on a wild-goose chase. No one journeyed to the forbidden island range of the Montanas Muertas without a damn good reason.

"Senor Bocangel," the bounty hunter said, "you're welcome back aboard my hoss any ole time."

Bocangel turned his drunk-bleary eyes on Prophet, and slurred, "If it is just the same to you, Senor Lou, I will remain for a bit longer with the senorita." He grinned lustily.

Louisa kept her implacable face pointed straight ahead.

"Have it your way, senor," Prophet said with a sigh. The pinto was probably strong enough to ride double for another half hour at least. Besides, Louisa weighed only about half as much as Prophet did, about the same as the wounded Mexican, and her pinto didn't seem to be straining.

"Lou, take a look!" This from Captain Chacin riding off to Prophet's left, pointing off into the desert.

Prophet kept his horse moving as he followed the Rurale's finger out toward a large organ pipe cactus standing alone amidst the tan-and-cream desert that reflected the sun's relentless heat. The lower trunk of the cactus had an odd shape. Prophet glanced at Louisa, then reined Mean and Ugly off to the left. "Best tell your men to stay here," Prophet told the captain. "No point in all of us riding into a trap."

"Who the hell you think is running this show, Lou?" Chacin glared at the bounty hunter, then turned to shout over his shoulder at the four lower-ranking Rurales and said in Spanish, "Stay here in case it's a trap!"

Prophet and Chacin rode toward the cactus. Louisa followed at a distance, hold-

163

ing her rifle across her saddlebow and looking around warily. Prophet stopped Mean in front of the cactus and stared grimly down at the naked man who'd been tied with his back to the cactus's stout trunk. He had long, black hair and a beard.

Prophet couldn't see his face, because he stood with his chin tipped toward his chest. His hands were tied behind the cactus. What was keeping him upright were the cactus's stiletto-like thorns.

His body looked like freshly ground burger. Blood oozed from dozens of deep cuts on his chest, arms, and legs. Blood oozed from an especially deep gash across his belly, and dripped down to cover what was left of his crotch.

"Damn savages," said Chacin, palming his pistol and looking around.

Prophet heard a grunt and the crunch of gravel behind him. He glanced back to see Senor Bocangel walking toward him and Chacin, his rheumy, dark eyes riveted on the man tied to the cactus.

"That's far enough, Bocangel," Prophet warned, swinging down from the dun's back and stepping in front of the short, old Mexican. Chances were good that the dead man was Bocangel's son. "He's beat up pretty bad. Let me get him down and cover him up with a blanket before you look at his face."

The Mexican looked up uncertainly at Prophet. His deeply lined mouth corners were drawn down. "Joaquin?"

"Prob'ly."

Sitting her horse behind Senor Bocangel, Louisa said, "No time, Lou."

Prophet followed her gaze eastward toward the separate dust clouds hanging above swarthy-skinned riders crouched low over their mustangs' lunging heads. The patter of hoofbeats rose quickly, until Prophet could feel the vibration through his boot soles.

Prophet grabbed the old man's arm and led him brusquely toward his horse. "We gotta move, senor!"

"No, I . . ."

"No doubt about it," Prophet said as he swung up into his saddle, then extended his hand toward the Mexican.

Chacin shouted at his men and then all five Rurales tore off across the desert, heading toward the mountains rolling up like giant mounds of bread dough in the west.

"I can't leave Joaquin," said Senor Bocangel, staring in horror at his son's stripped, bloody body.

"We'll come back for him later. Now grab

my hand or I'm gonna leave you here!"

Louisa triggered a couple of shots toward the oncoming riders as Bocangel reluctantly gave Prophet his hand and allowed himself to be swung up behind the cantle. The bounty hunter and Louisa gave their mounts the spurs, and they lunged off toward the rising dust of the Rurales, slugs ripping up rocks and sand a few feet behind them.

At the same time that Prophet began to hear guns popping angrily straight ahead, he saw that Chacin and the other four Rurales had checked their mounts down and were milling and looking confused, shuttling anxious glances between the Indians galloping toward them from the east, and the shooting in the west.

Prophet checked Mean down and stared toward the west. Ahead lay a ravine from which smoke puffed toward the Indians hunkered down in the rocks about fifty yards to the south. The ravine angled in from the north before swinging west. The men in the ravine appeared to occupy the far west end of it, not far from where the mountains rose up from the desert.

Prophet glanced behind him, hearing several slugs screaming over and around him while others blasted dirt and rocks near Mean's prancing hooves. He had no idea who the men under attack in the ravine were, but the ravine was the only near cover. Spurring Mean again, he galloped straight through the confused Rurales, shouting, "We ain't gonna stay alive long out here!"

Louisa and the others galloped behind him. Prophet slowed Mean and Ugly just a little as the brush and rocks lining the ravine grew before him. He saw a gap in the rocks and steered Mean toward it as a slug fired from behind tore a mesquite branch ahead of him.

Mean and Ugly gave an indignant whinny as the horse put its head down and plunged like a maverick Texas steer through the brush. Another mesquite branch ripped Prophet's hat off his head as the horse plunged down the side of the bank, then hit the floor of the arroyo with a bone-jarring crash.

"Ay, sheee-it!" lamented Senor Bocangel, flopping helpless against Prophet's back.

As the others came through the brush and rocks behind him, Prophet stared down the wash that appeared to narrow farther west and become obscured by jumbled boulders. He could see the thrashing tails of a couple of horses but no men though he could hear them shouting and triggering rifles.

Prophet swung his right boot over the

saddle horn, then reached up to help Bocangel down with one hand, his other hand wrapped around his Winchester's neck. "You all right, senor?"

Bocangel looked shocked and disoriented from both the Indians and the sight of his dead son. He sort of sagged back against Mean's hindquarters. Hearing the yowls and hoof thuds of the Mojaves growing louder in the east, Prophet ran past Louisa and between two Rurale mounts and shouldered up to the wash's eastern bank. The dust that he and the others in his party had lifted was still sifting.

He racked a fresh shell into his Winchester's breech and looked east between two rocks lining the bank. Seven or eight Mojaves were galloping toward him hell-for-leather, hair flying in the wind. One straight out before him loosed an arrow. It shot toward him, dropped in a perfect arc, and banged off a rock to his right, spraying shards.

13

Prophet drew a bead on the Indian's chest, fired, and watched with satisfaction as the redskin rolled off his lunging pinto's left hip just as the horse started turning to Prophet's right. The Indian landed on his head and shoulders and rolled wildly toward the ravine before piling up in a great puff of flying rocks and dirt.

Prophet ejected the spent shell, fired again but watched his slug merely blow up dust on the heels of another Indian diving for cover. Before he could get another cartridge racked, the Indian rose up behind his covering rock and sent an arrow flying toward Prophet, the missile whistling as it careened toward him, the gray flint point growing larger and larger, and bit a hunk out of the top of his shoulder before clattering onto the floor of the wash behind him.

He gritted his teeth and fired at the Indian who'd shot the arrow, but the Mojave had dropped down out of sight, reappearing a second later, running forward, then diving behind another rock about six feet nearer the ravine and loosing another arrow before Prophet could get a bead on him.

"Mierda!" one of the Rurales yelled from where the young Mexican had been firing his Springfield carbine to Prophet's right.

Prophet didn't take the time to see how badly the Rurale was wounded. It appeared that all the Indians who'd been chasing his party were all down behind cover and scrambling toward the ravine, shooting their rifles and flinging arrows at him and Louisa and the others returning fire over the arroyo bank.

He cursed as he pumped and fired, pumped and fired, watching most of his precious slugs merely hammering rocks, though one managed to drill one of the fleet Mojaves through an ankle. He intended to finish the wounded Mojave, but his hammer pinged on an empty chamber. As the Mojave lurched onto his knees, howling, he jerked back suddenly, hair falling down over his face as he grabbed his belly.

To Prophet's left, Louisa racked another shell into her Winchester's breech, and said, "Remind me to take you out target-shooting sometime, Lou. You missed an easy shot."

"I've forgot more about shootin' than you'll ever learn if you live to a hundred," Prophet said, thumbing fresh shells into his Winchester and yelling above the din of clattering rifles and ricocheting bullets as well as the dying cries of the young Rurale.

Louisa pressed her cheek against her Winchester's stock and hammered out three quick shots until her own weapon clicked. She spat out an unladylike curse and pulled her head down beneath the bank just as two arrows struck tip down in the clay dirt and sand with near-simultaneous snicks.

"What you've told me about Mojaves is true, at least," she said, quickly reloading and wincing as a bullet clipped a branch of a mesquite angling over her head. "They don't die easily!"

"And they run like the devil!" Prophet said, racking a shell into the Winchester's chamber. "And they're movin' up on us fast!"

He was about to straighten to trigger more lead toward the east when two bullets hammered the side of the bank to his right. "Shit!"

He turned, flushed and frowning, getting good and scared now as he only did when the fat was in the fire. Both bullets had come from the south. He ran to the wash's lower southern bank and saw three Indians scrambling around the rocks and saguaros about fifty yards beyond, angling toward him from the west. They'd been swapping lead with whomever they had pinned down on the wash's west end.

Prophet ran over to where Chacin was shooting at the southern Mojaves and triggered two quick shots. Two Indians leaped out from behind a low knoll and ran toward the ravine about twenty yards to Prophet and Chacin's right. They might have been trying to get around him.

"I'm gonna fix their wagons!" the bounty hunter yelled, then, racking another round, ran down the wash toward the west.

He rounded a slight bottleneck bend and stopped suddenly. A long-haired Mexican in a long, brown duster and gray sombrero was down on one knee, firing over the bank's southern lip. He had his lips stretched back from silver teeth, and he was hunched as though in great pain.

The man's identity had no sooner registered on Prophet, who hadn't had the time to really think about whom he was sharing the wash with, than Antonio Lazzaro jerked his rangy face toward him. The Mexican's eyes flashed in recognition. He'd started to swing his rifle around but stopped when an arrow cut through the air between him and Prophet. A half second later a stocky man behind Lazzaro, shooting toward the south, suddenly lurched back from the bank, stumbling and dropping his rifle to grab his lower face with both hands.

"God*damn!*" the stocky man shouted hollowly through his hands and bloody mouth. As he crouched down beneath the bank, another bullet blew his broad-brimmed, low-crowned Mexican sombrero off his head.

"Roy!" yelled the lanky man to his right. It wasn't hard to recognize the lanky gent with the tattooed forearms as Red Snake Corbin. Most of Lazzaro's men, including Lazzaro himself, graced wanted circulars from San Diego to New Orleans.

Prophet squeezed his Winchester in his hands, aiming the barrel at Lazzaro's belly. Lazzaro stared back at him, brown eyes wide and anxious. Sweat streaked the desperado's bristled cheeks and his upper lip capped with a long, thin mustache barely discernible with the rest of his beard growing in around it.

"Finish it here?" Prophet said.

Lazzaro curled one side of his upper lip, showing several silver teeth, and canted his head toward the south. "You sayin' we should fight together before we start killin' each other?"

"I reckon that's what I'm sayin'."

"How do I know you won't shoot me in the back?"

"You don't," Prophet said, curling his own mouth. "But I don't think we have time to gas over it — do you, Tony?"

Lazzaro raised his Winchester and fired toward the south. Prophet ran to the bank to Lazzaro's left and started flinging his own lead. He glanced down at Roy Kiljoy, who smiled at him despite the hole that had been drilled through both his cheeks and half of a bloody tooth clinging to his goat-bearded chin. Then the squat, blond-mustached, impossibly ugly brigand rose and began firing at the Indians closing on the arroyo's southern side.

Despite the holes in his face and the Mojave dentistry, he seemed to be having the time of his life.

"Hi, Roy!" Prophet yelled as he drilled a Mojave through the red sash around the Mojave's lean waist, crumpling the man.

"Hi, Lou! How ya doin'?"

"Fair to middlin'!"

Kiljoy spat a wad of blood to one side, winced at an arrow dug into the bank's lip about one foot in front of his ugly face, and triggered a shot, his Winchester roaring and leaping in his gloved hands. "That's kinda how it goes in Mojave country!"

Prophet felt chicken flesh spreading across his back as he tried to concentrate on his red-skinned enemies while trying to relegate the fact that he was sharing the arroyo with a passel of equally deadly white men to the back of his mind. It wasn't easy, but he managed to kill two Mojaves making a break for the arroyo and wounded another in the wrist. He pumped and fired, pumped and fired, aware that every shot he was taking meant one less shell he'd have for his return trip across the desert.

And he didn't seem to be making much of a dent in the population of Mojave attackers. They seemed to slither right up out of the ground as though from an endless source, hurling bullets at the arroyo.

After a time, he heard a skirmish behind him and wheeled to see Chacin down on one knee, his rifle at his feet. Lazzaro had an arm twisted around the Rurale captain's neck, jerking the captain's chin up while holding a bowie knife to the man's sunburned throat.

"Lou, you wanna explain to this Mescin our agreement?" Lazzaro said, showing his silver teeth.

Chacin rolled his anxious gaze toward Prophet, frowning.

"We decided to buddy up, Captain." Prophet ducked as an arrow careened over him and embedded itself in the side of the opposite bank. "At least till we can get shed of these 'Paches!"

"*Si, si!*" said Chacin, lowering his desperate eyes to the glistening steel blade caressing his neck.

"We got an understanding, then, Cap?" asked Lazzaro, jerking Chacin's neck up harder, causing the Rurale's face to flush the red of a Sonora sunset.

"*Le dije que entiendo, usted cerdo asqueros!*" Chacin yelled, spittle flecking his lips. *I told you I understand, you filthy pig!*

Lazzaro released the man, laughing. Then he made a face and groaned as he clutched his side and dropped to one knee. "Lou, I will make a deal with you," he shouted above the din. "If you cover me and my men while we make a break for that canyon, my men and I will cover you and yours!"

Prophet was sitting on the ground with his back to the bank of the wash, his rifle resting across his thighs while he punched fresh shells through the loading gate. "Took the thought right out of my head," he said, tossing the wounded desperado a wry look.

176

"But only if some of my men ride with you, one or two of yours ride with me."

He looked around, just now seeing that one of Lazzaro's "men" was in fact Sugar Delphi, crouched down at the base of the bank on the other side of Red Snake Corbin. She was staring straight off across the arroyo, a smoking rifle across her lap. He gave a silent chuff.

What in the hell was a blind woman doing out here? That rifle looked as though it had been fired. Sugar had a bullet burn across her left cheek — a very thin red line from which two red beads dribbled down toward her straight jawline.

"Yeah, I get your drift," Lazzaro said, nodding his weary head. "That way we can keep each other honest. All right. Okay. Red Snake will ride with your gang. Chacin will ride with me."

"Good enough!" Prophet said, standing and snapping off another shot, seeing that the Indians seemed to be staying hunkered down about forty yards away. He glanced over his shoulder at Chacin, who was hunkered down behind a boulder, looking vaguely suspicious and troubled while reloading his Spencer repeater. "If any of 'em start bearing down on us, Captain, blow 'em to hell!"

Chacin, scowling at Lazzaro, merely shook his head in disgust.

The outlaws gathered their horses and rode off while Prophet's group covered them from a southern lip of the arroyo.

"Nice snake pit we fell into!" Louisa shouted above the din of her own Winchester and Prophet's and those of the other Rurales.

All except Chacin and the young corporal who'd taken the arrow, that was. The corporal had died where he lay after considerable thrashing. One of the others had been wounded in the arm, and Frieri's left earlobe had been blown off. Bocangel sat huddled into himself against the wash's eastern bank, knees raised to his chest. Otherwise, the group was intact and relatively healthy.

"Should have known Lazzaro's bunch'd be the only others fool enough to get caught out here with Mojaves on the jump." Prophet turned to see Chacin, Lazzaro, the blind woman, and Roy Kiljoy galloping at an angle from the mouth of the wash toward the canyon a quarter mile beyond. The canyon stood like a stockade fort with its gates thrown wide.

Sergeant Frieri had gathered the mounts

and stood holding their reins well back from the wash's lip, in the bottleneck where he and the horses were relatively sheltered from the flying lead and arrows.

"If this keeps up," Prophet said, "I'm gonna be . . ."

He let his voice trail off as he stared out across the desert, at a lone rider sitting a black-and-white pinto pony just out of rifle range. He couldn't make out much of the Mojave except the proud way he sat his saddle, the horse turned sideways, the man's head facing the arroyo. Like a general watching a battle play out.

Prophet couldn't see the green eyes or the lightning tattoo, but he knew he was staring at El Lightning, just the same. There was a haunting, menacing, commanding quality in that dusky figure in red calico sitting so erect atop the rangy mustang. The choker of porcupine quills was a white line across his throat. Something told Prophet he'd be seeing the man again from a lot closer up.

"What's that, Lou?"

Prophet drew his gaze back from El Lightning. "I was sayin' I'm low on ammo. I got a feelin' the Rurales are, too." He glanced at Frieri standing behind him, the man's shoulder red from blood that had dripped down from his ragged ear. Only about a quarter of the loops on the sergeant's two bandoliers crossed on his chest were filled with brass.

Louisa's Winchester roared. South of the wash, an Indian gave a keening cry as he fell back from his covering rock, clamping both his hands over his blown-out right eye.

"That there is my last forty-four round," Louisa said, crouching behind the bank with her smoking rifle. "It's just my forty-fives" — she patted her left pistol holstered for the cross draw on her lean waist — "till our next visit to a gun shop."

When Lazzaro's bunch had galloped on into the canyon and took up positions around the mouth, throwing lead at the Indians beyond the draw, Prophet's bunch mounted up and wasted no time galloping their wild-eyed horses out of the draw toward the canyon.

Prophet hauled Senor Bocangel up behind him, and the old man sat there, silently atop the bounty hunter's saddlebags, still in shock over his dead son. The canyon's mouth gaped, peppered with powder smoke from the outlaws' and Chacin's blasting rifles.

Again that cold chicken flesh rose across Prophet's sweating back. It was entirely likely that Lazzaro would blow Chacin's guts out and then order his men to turn their pistols on Prophet's bunch. Out here in the open, they'd have little chance.

Prophet sucked a sharp breath as the Indians' bullets and arrows made weird gasping sounds in the air around him and glanced off rocks with eerie wails. The pops and cracks ahead of him grew louder and louder above the thumps of Mean's and the other horses' thudding hooves.

Prophet looked at Lazzaro shooting from one knee on the canyon mouth's left side. The wounded outlaw leader looked pale and yellow, as though he were suffering from jaundice. His cheeks were shrunken inward against his jaws. He was firing toward the Indians, but now Prophet palmed his Colt and clicked the hammer back as Mean drew to within twenty yards of the canyon mouth, and aimed the pistol straight out in front of him.

Red Snake and Kiljoy were firing from the canyon's right side, Red Snake high, Kiljoy low. The squat ugly outlaw's lower face was a mask of dried blood but he grinned at Prophet as he shouted, "Damn, you make a big target, Lou."

He aimed his rifle at Prophet and yelled down the barrel, "One bullet, and a whole lotta outlaws'd be buyin' me drinks!"

As Mean lunged through the canyon's gaping jaws, Prophet slid the cocked .45 across his belly, holding it on Kiljoy still grinning down his rifle barrel. Just then a bullet smashed into the rocks near the ugly outlaw's bloody face, and he jerked his head and rifle down, cursing.

It was Prophet's turn to smile as he and the others swept into the canyon. "That's what you get for waggin' that rifle around like your pecker, you plug-ugly bastard!"

14

"I was right about you, after all," Sugar said as she rode along beside Louisa, in the middle of the pack of Rurales, outlaws, and bounty hunters making its way up the canyon. "I should have killed you instead of drugged you. Cut your throat while you slept."

"Why didn't you?"

Sugar stared straight ahead but now, as before, when Louisa had infiltrated the gang and ridden as one of them for nearly two weeks, she felt as though the woman were staring straight into her soul. Sugar lifted her hat and ran a hand through her thick red hair, jostling the several beaded braids. "Not quite sure. I guess I was sentimental, thought maybe I saw something of myself in you. Felt as though we were sisters, or something crazy like that."

"We're probably more alike than I'd like to believe," Louisa said, hearing Lazzaro groan atop his horse that Sugar was trailing by its bridle reins. The outlaw leader was hunkered low and swilling whiskey with one hand while keeping a hand over the wound that had opened up during the Indian attack and was bleeding down over his double cartridge belts, thigh, and stirrup fender. "But you're the one with a price on her head. And I'm gonna collect on it."

Sugar turned toward her and gazed at Louisa's forehead, arching a thin, red brow. "You think so?"

"Yep."

"It's not too late, you know."

"What's not too late?"

Sugar lifted her chin slightly as though listening, gauging how close the others were riding around her. Prophet and Chacin rode point, with Senor Bocangel riding double with Prophet, because the old Mexican was in no condition to ride alone. Then there was Kiljoy and Red Snake riding about ten yards behind them. The three Rurales, including Frieri with his bloody ear, walked their horses about fifteen yards ahead of Louisa and Sugar, while Lazzaro brought up the rear, grunting and groaning and taking occasional, loud pulls from his tequila bottle.

As though deeming her and Louisa's

conversation private and keeping her voice down, Sugar quirked the corners of her wide, bold but feminine mouth. "You, me, Tony . . . a nice vacation along the shore of the Sea of Cortez before taking a boat down to South America. You ever been there?" Sugar shook her head. "Tony tells me it's Heaven."

Louisa chuffed. "How would he know anything about Heaven?" She glanced again at Lazzaro then frowned at Sugar. "Where's the loot?"

"Safe."

"You buried it back in the wash, didn't you?"

Sugar smiled and nodded. "Sure. With Tony's eyes. Since he's the only one who saw exactly *where* it's buried, we'd all best hope he doesn't expire."

Louisa glanced at Lazzaro riding hunched and bleeding in his saddle and sighed.

Prophet, riding at the head of the pack with Chacin, glanced over his shoulder, inspecting each of the men behind him. They'd agreed before riding up from the canyon mouth that no one would touch a gun unless the Indians were spotted on their back trail. So far, so good on both counts, he saw now as he lifted his gaze over Lazzaro's head and along the meandering course of the canyon.

A hot, dry wind had come up, shuffling dust and blowing the horse's tails, but through the grit he could see no sign of the Indians. They'd likely follow at a distance, with the intention of waiting for reinforcements then attacking later. They obviously wanted to rid the area of all white men, and Prophet doubted they had anything better to do. This was their land, so they certainly had nowhere else to go.

They rode up the canyon, which widened as the walls fell away, and Prophet found himself on a broad, flat, rocky bench, the wind swirling the dust and caking his eyes with sharp grit. He tugged his hat down lower on his head and turned his attention to his own unlikely group.

The way he saw it, there were three factions — him and Louisa, Chacin and the other Rurales, and the desperadoes. Of course, there was Senor Bocangel, who was riding behind him in shocked, pensive silence, but the old Mexican had no dog in this fight. Prophet and Chacin were after the desperadoes and the stolen loot, which shouldn't be too hard to confiscate once they'd gotten clear of the Indians and could arrest or kill Lazzaro and the others, includ-

ing Sugar Delphi, without getting themselves shot to hell.

Once Prophet and Louisa and the Rurales
had the money, however, there would still
be one more battle. Prophet had no intention of turning over even part of the loot to
Chacin, whose intentions concerning the
money were far less than noble. The money
had been stolen from the Bank of Nogales,
and that's where he aimed to take it in
return for a hefty reward on both the money
and on the bandits who'd stolen it.

Not that the stolen money didn't have its
allure to the big, Confederate bounty hunter
whose sole aim in life was to have as many
tail-stomping good times as he could find.
But he'd long ago promised himself that
he'd go about said stomping on the right
side of the straight and narrow. Never let it
be said that the son of Ma and Pa Prophet
of Ringgold, Georgia, had raised a boy who
strayed.

The wind blew a gust of sandpaper-like
grit against Prophet's face, and he lowered
his head and narrowed his eyes against it.
He turned a little to one side. When he
opened his eyes, he saw that Chacin had his
own head lowered. The captain's eyes met
Prophet's and, as though he were reading
the bounty hunter's mind, he gave a grimly

187

devilish half smile.

Prophet returned the look in kind, then blinked the grit from his lashes and peered straight ahead over Mean's indignantly twitching ears. Prophet blinked again and just as he began to hear the squawks of what sounded like a rusty chain he saw several crude corrals and buildings rise up out of the desert. The wood and weathered adobe bricks were the same color as the tan rocks, and they appeared to be a natural part of this stark, barren land.

But they were not, Prophet saw as Mean continued to clomp along, kicking stones, a couple of dilapidated stock pens appearing on both sides of the trail. The buildings were part of a town that stretched across the bench at an angle from Prophet's left to right. Higher up on the bench stretched a mantle of solid rock, like a massive eyebrow. It paralleled the town's scattered, falling-down buildings before breaking off abruptly on the town's far side.

Prophet and the others were following a worn wagon trail into the town, the trail widening and becoming the town's main street, which was a good fifty or even sixty yards wide. The buildings and pens on both sides were truly dilapidated, with windows gaping and shutters hanging and boards and bricks missing from the false façades. Porches hung askew.

Behind the buildings of the business district, the village's original Mexican adobes hunched in the weeds and rocks, looking like large stones in a long-abandoned graveyard. The wind whistled between them and the stone ovens and through the shacks' gaping windows.

The squawking, Prophet realized now, was from a shingle flopping in the wind beneath a gallery running the length of a broad, two-story building about halfway down on the left side of the street. Large, green, sun-faded letters identified the place as G.W. TODD GENERAL MERCHANDISE DRY GOODS. There was no door on the other side of the gallery, which was missing much of its floor. Obviously Todd's was as defunct as the rest of the town.

Only it wasn't completely defunct, or at least not completely abandoned, Prophet saw a minute later when he and the others reined up before a large, two-story adobe brick building that also boasted a gallery. A sign hanging down beneath the gallery's front eave announced THE OASIS SALOON AND DANCE HALL.

Prophet gave a grim smile. The place didn't look like much of an oasis these days.

But he remembered the place from a previous visit, when the town was hopping with ore wagons and drunken miners. Then, a man could find an adequate if overpriced shot of rye in the Oasis. He wondered if he still could.

The town's well stood in the middle of the street and a little to one side of the saloon — its sides built up with mortared stones and covered with a shake-shingled roof. It had a winch and a bucket. Prophet glanced over the coping and into the gaping, black hole to see the dark silvery sheen of water, and relief washed over him.

On the saloon's gallery someone was sweeping the dust and tumbleweeds that the wind continued to blow around on it, causing the two wicker rockers on the gallery to rock wildly, as though agitated ghosts were sitting in them.

The sweeper was a woman with a slender, comely shape. She turned to the newcomers now, holding the broom in front of her and sweeping her thick, curly black hair away from her eyes as she studied the gang warily.

She was a black woman in her mid- to late twenties. She wore what appeared a once fine silk blouse, the sleeves rolled up her arms, the tails sticking out over the pleated, gray skirt that blew about her long, slender legs. The silk blouse looked worn, tattered and frayed at the elbows and collar.

"Ma'am, can you direct us to a sawbones?" Prophet called above the howling wind and the banging of a nearby shutter. "We got a couple of wounded men in our party."

The black woman, whose face was strong and fine, with lustrous black eyes, shook her head slowly. Her expression was deeply vexed. "No," she said, her voice barely audible above the wind. "You can't be here. No strangers welcome in San Gezo!"

"Goddamnit, woman!" shouted Roy Kiljoy, his voice sounding weird because of the hole in both cheeks and because of the moaning wind. "Can't you see I'm leakin' blood like a damn sieve! I need these holes patched!"

Lazzaro grabbed his reins away from Sugar Delphi and rode up to the bottom of the gallery, slipping the long-barreled Smith & Wesson from its holster and thumbing the hammer back. "You ain't got no choice, Negra!" he fairly howled, scrunched low in his saddle. "We're here and we're gonna stay here till —"

He'd put his horse two steps up the gallery when he stopped suddenly and glanced over his right shoulder. Prophet had heard what Lazzaro must have heard — a ratcheting squawk like that of a rusty hinge.

Prophet glanced over his own shoulder and let his lower jaw hang when he saw one of the two doors in the loft of the barn on the other side of the street open. The wind caught the door and slammed it against the barn's front wall, revealing the wicked, brass barrel of a Gatling gun. A round, wizened face appeared above and behind the gun's six bristling maws, beneath the brim of a floppy hat.

Prophet slapped his hand to his Colt's holster but held it there when the canister dipped slightly and began to turn, spouting smoke and flames and belching wickedly above the wind. The .45-caliber rounds plunked into the dust of the street between Prophet's gang and the barn. It was a short spate of bullets, and then the canister rose, bearing down on Prophet and the others, all tightening their hands on the reins of the prancing horses. Lazzaro's horse lurched on up the gallery steps and curveted, rearing and nearly unseating its wounded rider.

Another short blast of Gatling fire tore up splinters from the gallery's steps beneath Lazzaro and his lurching mount.

"We don't cotton to strangers here in San

Gezo!" shouted the old man tending the Gatling gun. Prophet could see a pair of blue eyes blazing beneath the brim of the floppy hat. "Ride on out o' here now, and *maybe* I won't blast you outta your saddles!"

"You crazy old coot!" shouted Red Snake Corbin.

Prophet swung Mean toward the barn and rammed his spurred heels against the horse's flanks. *"Hyahh!"*

The horse crossed the street in three strides, Prophet hearing the old man yell in the loft above him. There was another short burst of Gatling fire, the slugs tearing into the dust several yards off Mean's rear hooves. Then horses and rider were in the purple shade beside the barn, and out of view from the loft.

Prophet leaped off Mean's back and, swinging his double-barrel ten-gauge around to his chest, wrapped his right hand around the neck of the wicked gun, and hooked his index finger through the trigger guard, gently caressing both eyelash triggers. He ran to the back of the barn, edged a careful look around the corner, then hurried to the back door.

He stepped back as the small door scraped open. A rifle barrel angled up from behind the door as the unseen rifleman stepped out of the barn.

Prophet lurched forward, ramming his right shoulder against the door. He heard an indignant yowl as the rifle barked, and he felt the body on the other side of the door yield to his shove. He pulled the door back against the barn wall and saw the old codger who'd been manning the Gatling gun writhing on the ground in front of the opening. The rifle lay several feet away. The oldster, who wore a coarse silver mustache and goatee, was on his right shoulder and hip, groaning and squeezing his eyes closed.

"Damn you to hell, you big, ugly lummox!" he shouted, lifting his head from the dirt and turning those fiery blue eyes on the bounty hunter. "This is our town — not yours! Skedaddle and take your pack of curly wolves with ya!"

"How do you know we're curly wolves?" Prophet picked up the rifle and set the stock against his shell belt, scowling down at the crotchety gent.

" 'Cause you're the only ones that ever come to San Gezo these days." The old man grunted and spat a curse as he climbed to his knees. He wore a wool shirt and duck trousers. Straw and dirt clung to his shirtsleeves and back, and a snakeskin suspender hung down to his bony right hip.

"You or others just like you. And we got no time for Rurales, neither!"

He spat again then winced as he tried to push off a knee. Prophet grabbed his arm to help him up, but the old man jerked his hand free of the bounty hunter's grasp. "Unhand me, you devil!"

"Dad! Dad! Are you all right, Dad?"

Prophet turned to see the black woman running around the rear corner of the barn. Louisa was a few steps behind her, cradling her Winchester carbine in her arm and looking incredulous. The woman gave Prophet a dirty look as she pushed past him and dropped to a knee beside the oldster. "Dad, are you hurt?"

"Certainly wouldn't want the old goat to be hurt," Prophet offered wryly, still indignant over the Gatling gun. The only place he liked such a weapon was in front of him. Never behind.

"I'm all right, Ivy," the old man said. "No thanks to him!"

"It was Dad's shift to mind the gun," the black woman, Ivy, said, looking up at Prophet. "One of us keeps it manned at all times."

"Mojaves?" Louisa said.

"Mojaves and banditos like yourselfs!" growled the old goat, letting the black woman help him to his feet and spitting grit from his lips.

"Didn't know there'd still be anyone here," Prophet said. "Figured on some original Mescins. You two're Americans, I take it. . . ."

Ivy said, "You take it right. Most of the Mexicans left years ago. The Mojaves have always been bad in these parts, and I wouldn't doubt it if you've led a passel of them back to San Gezo." To the oldster, she said, "Come on over to the saloon, Dad. I'll get you cleaned up and send Angel out to tend the Gatling gun."

The black woman started to lead the old man toward the corner of the barn. He stopped and gave his rifle a tug, but Prophet held fast.

"Uh-uh," Prophet said.

"What're you gonna do?" Ivy said. "Kill us all?"

"We ain't gonna kill nobody," Louisa said. "We just want some shelter from the Mojave storm out yonder." She glanced uncertainly at Prophet. "And . . . to get our bearings." Prophet knew she was trying to figure out, as he was, how they were going to bring down Lazzaro and confiscate the loot while keeping it away from Chacin. And not get themselves caught in a whipsaw.

"You likely just brought that storm to our doorstep!" rasped the old man as he let Ivy lead him around the barn corner.

Prophet and Louisa followed the pair into the main street, where the others in their mismatched gang had dismounted. They were now yelling at two men bearing down on them with a rifle and a shotgun from out front of a dilapidated gun shop. One was young and tall, the other old and thick-waisted and wearing blue coveralls and thick-soled boots.

"You fellas don't drop them guns right here and now," Red Snake Corbin was yelling at them, standing about ten yards in front of them and holding his own rifle straight out from his right hip, "you're gonna look mighty funny with third eyes drilled through your noggins!"

"Like we done said," shouted Kiljoy, "we're just lookin' for a damn *sawbones!*" He wheeled suddenly and grabbed the shoulder of Sergeant Frieri, who'd been standing directly behind him, a Schofield pistol in his hand. "You keep that goddamn pistol out of my back, you greaser bastard!"

Ivy led the old man she'd called "Dad" through the crowd. At the base of the saloon's broad veranda steps, she yelled at the two townsmen wielding the rifle and the shotgun, "Angel, LeBeouf, put your guns away. LeBeouf, fetch the doc. Angel, you get up and tend the Gatling gun and keep your eyes skinned for Injuns!"

The thick man reluctantly lowered his shotgun and began backing down the street. The younger one, who had short dark hair on his hatless head, long muttonchop whiskers, and a soup-strainer mustache mantling his pendulous lower lip, kept his rifle aimed on the gang while angling cautiously across the street toward the barn. He was tall and bony and sunburned, and he walked with a slight hitch in his step. His dark eyes owned the menacing, probing dullness of a stalking grizzly.

As Ivy led Dad up the saloon's veranda, Prophet looked around at the street. Chacin was conferring with his own men while Lazzaro was talking to Kiljoy, Red Snake, and Sugar — both factions huddled in groups on either side of the well amongst the milling horses. Chacin's men were filling their canteens from a bucket sitting beside the well coping.

Prophet continued to look around. Senor Bocangel was nowhere in sight.

At least there were no Mojaves in sight, either. Not yet. But Prophet didn't doubt he'd see El Lightning and his passel of angry Mojaves again real soon. Ivy had been right when she'd accused him of leading the Mojaves to her doorstep.

But what the hell else could he and the others have done?

He appraised the horses of Lazzaro's bunch, frowning.

Louisa sidled up to him as she squinted against the wind blowing grit and tumbleweeds against the buildings on the street's north side. She stared west along their back trail.

"If you're looking for the loot, Lou — forget it."

Prophet looked at her and kicked a tumbleweed that had brushed up against his shin. "Where the hell is it?"

"Only Lazzaro knows."

Prophet looked at the outlaw, who had just turned to the bounty hunter, curling a painful little grin and showing several of his silver teeth.

"Now what?" Louisa said tensely.

"Reckon I'll fill my canteen and tend this ole hay burner," Prophet said, leading Mean toward the livery barn. "Then I'm going to get me a tall drink and kick my heels up."

15

Captain Chacin walked his big Arab into the livery barn, dropped the horse's reins, and went back and closed the heavy door behind him. The windows provided a murky, gray light. The wind swept grit against the building with blasting ticking sounds, making the unsturdy walls creak.

Prophet was unsaddling his horse beside Louisa. Sergeant Frieri and two other Rurales were in the barn, also tending their mounts. Of the outlaws, there were only Red Snake Corbin and Kiljoy. Sugar had helped Lazzaro into the saloon to which La-Beouf had summoned the San Gezo medico.

Prophet knew something was coming, because Chacin was grinning under his ridiculously upswept albeit dust-rimed mustache. Sure enough, as Prophet set his saddle on a rotting stall partition, the captain slid his Colt Navy from his black leather holster, clicked the hammer back, and rammed the barrel into the small of Red Snake's back.

"You have come far enough, you moaning sows!" Chacin growled.

As if on cue, though a bit awkwardly, the three other Rurales grabbed their rifles and brought them to bear, some swinging them toward Prophet and Louisa, not sure just exactly who Chacin intended to bring down. Frieri grinned with menace at the blond bounty hunter.

Red Snake had just pulled his saddle and blanket off his horse's back, and now, with Chacin's pistol kissing his spine, he stiffened, then slowly turned toward Kiljoy. The bull-like desperado had already unsaddled his own mount and was slumped against a covered feed bin, weak with the pain and misery of his two perforated cheeks.

"Both of you drop your pistol belts, or I will blow you to El Diablo!" Chacin said, louder.

"Now, you just hold on," Red Snake said, still holding the saddle and keeping his back to the captain. "You still need us, Chacin. In case you forgot, there's still a whole herd of loco 'Paches down on them flats, and I wouldn't doubt it a bit if they've followed us up here to San Gezo. Prob'ly prowlin' around outside at this very moment!"

Kiljoy chuckled, then made a pained expression, gently touching two gloved fingers to the puckered, bloody hole in his right cheek. "Ooh, that hurts," he said. He chuckled again. "Put that gun down, Chacin, you crazy old coot."

Frieri and the two other Rurales were shifting their rifles around nervously, wary of getting caught in a crossfire. A young private with a pronounced overbite stepped to his right and tripped over a pitchfork.

Chacin showed his teeth beneath his mustache and narrowed his eyes under the brim of his straw sombrero. "Who are you calling crazy, you common coyote?"

Kiljoy laughed harder.

"Hold on, Captain," Prophet said wearily. "You send these two back to the hell they danced out of, and Lazzaro's gonna get his shorts in a twist."

"I do not care if Lazzaro gets his shorts in a twist."

"Yeah, but then, you see," Louisa said, "he won't tell us where the loot is. And since that's why we're all here, I suggest you holster that hogleg."

Chacin looked at Prophet, brows furled in question.

"They buried the money out on the desert

somewhere," the bounty hunter informed him.

"Not they," Kiljoy said. "Lazzaro did himself. Oh, I reckon Sugar helped, but she couldn't lead you back to it, o' course. And me an' Red Snake had nothin' to do with it. No, no, you best holster that hogleg, Chacin. Anything happens to us, you'll piss-burn Tony good. And, if Tony was to die from that belly wound of his . . ."

Chacin shuttled his gaze back and forth between Kiljoy and Prophet and Louisa, all three of whom watched the captain expectantly. Prophet knew he was wondering if Prophet and Lazzaro's men had a double cross on, because that's what Prophet would have suspected himself had the tables been turned.

"Like Roy said," Prophet said, "if you take these two down, Lazzaro'll never tell us where the loot is."

"He won't, anyway," said Frieri, standing near Prophet with his ragged, bloody ear lobe, holding a Spencer carbine straight out from his right hip. "You're a fool, Senor Prophet."

"No call to start firin' off barbs, you scum-suckin' dog. How's that ear feel? How 'bout if I come over there and lay my fist against it?"

"Boys, boys . . ." Louisa admonished the men, rolling her eyes and grabbing a rusty coffee tin off a nail in a support post and heading for the feed bin.

Prophet switched his glower to Chacin. "Holster it, Jorge. Them two lobos may not be able to lead us to the loot, but we're gonna need all the guns we got against the Mojaves. Not to mention the folks in this town don't seem to be takin' much of a shine to us, either."

Chacin's face reddened. He hardened his jaws, gritted his teeth, and stepped forward, bringing the barrel of his pistol down hard against the back of Red Snake's head. "*Fools!* Why would you leave the loot in the desert with twenty or thirty Mojaves running crazy out there?"

Red Snake screamed as he dropped the saddle and fell on top of it, lowering his head and hooking his arm over it, shielding it from another possible blow. He scowled over his left shoulder at the infuriated Rurale. "You crazy greaser son of a bitch! Roy done told you we didn't have nothin' to do with it. It was Tony and Sugar that buried it! You think we like it? Shit, we robbed that loot same as they did, and we deserve our cut of it, but how we gonna get it if Tony dies?"

"Which he most likely will," Kiljoy said, as red-faced as Chacin now.

Prophet looked at Frieri, who was only an inch or so taller than Kiljoy and just as ugly, his shoulder covered in blood from his shredded earlobe. He stared with silver-eyed menace at Prophet, who lunged forward quickly, swept the barrel of the little sergeant's rifle aside.

The Spencer roared, the slug drilling into the ceiling over Prophet's head. Prophet grabbed the barrel with his right hand, jerked it toward him and out of Frieri's hand. The sergeant lurched forward with a startled yelp, and his flat, round face met Prophet's balled fist with a resounding smack.

The sergeant's head jerked back as though he'd run into a stone wall. His nose exploded like a blood-filled bladder flask. He screamed and stumbled back against Kiljoy's horse, which sidestepped, sending the howling Frieri to the barn's straw-strewn earthen floor.

Another gun roared — a deafening thunderclap in the close quarters. Chacin shrieked and grabbed the wrist of his right hand, the hand now missing the gun that had been in it a moment before. The hand shook as the captain stared down at it in disbelief, his smoking revolver on the floor near his boots.

Louisa's own Peacemaker was smoking in her right fist as she turned it toward the other two Rurales, who wanted nothing to do with the notorious, man-hunting gringa. They lurched fearfully backward and lowered their rifles. They probably knew that even if Chacin was to get the stolen Nogales loot, their cuts would be too small to die for.

"*Puta* bitch!" Chacin rasped, clenching his bloody hand — it looked as though Louisa's bullet had carved a notch through the little-finger side of his hand after ripping the gun out of it.

Louisa clicked the Colt's hammer back and swung it back toward the indignant captain. "Thought we agreed we weren't going to keep slinging shit around, Captain."

"Wouldn't be the first time he double-crossed me," Prophet said.

The barn fell silent. All the players looked around at each other, faces hard and scowling. Then, suddenly, Kiljoy gave a snort and started laughing. He leaned back against a stall, threw his head back sharply, and loosed loud guffaws at the ceiling. Chacin was next to start laughing, and then Prophet started in, as did Red Snake, still rubbing his head.

The two low-ranking Rurales began laughing uneasily and a little uncomprehendingly, as they didn't understand English. The barn fairly erupted with laughter, frightening the horses that were already prancing and snorting from the previous violence. Even Louisa, who was normally sober-faced, loosed a few red-faced snorts before brushing a sheepish fist across her face. The only one not laughing was Frieri, who, sitting on his butt, was holding both hands over his profusely bleeding nose. He looked a little dubious, as though feeling that he himself were the butt of the joke.

It was a hell of a pickle. Such a pickle, in fact, that there was really nothing a man could do but laugh.

"What do you say?" Chacin said when the laughter had died somewhat, holding his bloody hand to his belly, "that we all go on back to the saloon and have a drink and pull our horns in for now. Isn't that the expression, Lou? Obviously, we need each other's help, huh?"

"Took the words right out of my head," Prophet said, chuckling and gingerly helping the stone-faced Frieri to his feet. "Sorry about that, Sergeant. Sometimes my drawers get tight, and it gravels me." He brushed the dust from Frieri's bloody, gray uniform tunic. "I hope we can still be friends."

The saloon was a veritable medical tent. A more sedate and less gruesome version of what Prophet had seen during the war, but a hospital tent, just the same.

Lazzaro was laid out on a table near the bar that ran along the building's right side. The doctor — a tall, leathery, severe-looking man with a cap of coarse, silver hair sitting close against his skull — had cut the outlaw's shirt off. While Sugar and Red Snake held Lazzaro down, the doctor, whom Prophet had heard addressed as Shackleford, poked a forceps through the wound that looked like a massive slathering of cherry jelly on the man's lower right side.

Lazzaro was biting down on a well-chewed length of razor strop, which the doctor had produced from his black medical kit for just that reason, and was wagging his head from side to side. Purple veins bulged in his forehead, and ropelike cords stuck out in his neck.

"Hold him, now!" the sawbones said in his deep baritone that boomed like thunder around the cavernous room. "Hold him, now! Hold him or I'm liable to pull out somethin' that needs to stay!"

The tall man, who Prophet thought looked more like a preacher than a doctor, loosed a thunderous laugh at his own joke. He had a rolling-voweled, almost songlike southern accent that Prophet, being a southerner himself, identified as Alabama.

The Rurales were grouped in the back of the dimly lit room, tossing dubious glances at the outlaws as well as at Prophet and Louisa, who sat near the front. Prophet had his back to the side wall off the end of the bar. From this vantage he could keep an eye on the room as well as on the street. Louisa had her back to the room. She didn't seem to care, knowing that if trouble broke out, Prophet wouldn't keep it a secret.

She was turning a shot glass of rye whiskey between her thumb and index finger, staring at the amber liquid. She'd been oddly quiet the whole trip, Prophet was thinking. Something had happened during her time with Lazzaro's bunch that she didn't want to talk about.

Since she didn't want to talk about it, Prophet didn't try, knowing that a herd of wild horses couldn't drag out of Louisa what she didn't want to share. He sensed it had something to do with Sugar, as he'd seen the two riding together up the canyon, but he had no idea what.

Maybe she sensed some good in the blind woman. Or, on the other hand, maybe she sensed more evil than she'd at first thought. From what Louisa had told him, in these parts, Sugar Delphi had a wicked reputation for coldblooded murder, despite her blindness.

She'd ridden with Lazzaro for nigh on four years, and her pretty face that owned a strange, foxy quality, likely due to the fact she couldn't see, adorned as many wanted circulars along the border as did Lazzaro's. Prophet hadn't been through here in a while, which was likely why he hadn't heard about her. Louisa obviously had. Sugar couldn't be a very good shot, but at relatively close range she could smell or hear folks, and that's all she needed to get a bead on them. She'd told Louisa that she could see shadows — not with her eyes but with her mind.

A strange sixth sense, she called it.

Prophet only knew that, from what he'd heard and the number of murders she was said to have committed, Miss Sugar Delphi needed to stretch hemp.

First, the loot. And how were he and Louisa going to cross that long, flat stretch of open desert again without getting slow-roasted over a hot Mojave fire?

The black woman, Ivy Miller, who apparently ran the Oasis, was sitting at a table directly in front of the saloon's double doors, which were closed against the wind. She sat with the liveryman, Dad Conway, who was nursing a beer and glowering at the newcomers, and a plump redhead with one purple and one black feather in her hair. Obviously a whore, the redhead was one of those pale, heavy, rounded women whose age it was hard to figure, but Prophet guessed she was somewhere on the back side of thirty.

She must have thought that Prophet's quick appraisal was an invitation, because she'd been giving him smoldering looks since he'd entered the saloon with Louisa. Now, not wanting to encourage her, he tried to keep his eyes off her. While he certainly had nothing against whores — in fact, he preferred whores to almost all other women aside from Louisa — she held no charm for him. Despite the lust in her eyes and her forever quirked, red lips, she looked like a harpy who would give a man little pleasure and no rest.

Miss Ivy, nursing her own whiskey shot, sat sideways to her table, one ankle hiked on her other knee beneath her tattered, gray dress. She sat staring at her drink, the skin above her brows deeply furrowed, as though she were perplexed. Probably over Prophet's and the others' presence. He couldn't blame her. He supposed he and Louisa looked as raggedy-heeled as Chacin, Lazzaro, and the others, but at the moment the situation couldn't be helped.

It wasn't about to get any better, either, Prophet saw as he stared out the window before him. A man wearing a town marshal's badge was walking toward the saloon, the tails of his black frock coat blowing in the wind. He paused to shake his leg free of a pesky tumbleweed, then continued toward the veranda.

He wore three pistols and was holding a long-barreled shotgun on his shoulder. On his mustached, ferret-like face was a grimace that meant he wasn't just looking for a drink.

As the marshal started up the veranda steps, a door opened at the back of the saloon, and three more quiet, steely-eyed townsmen came in, armed for bear.

16

Prophet made no sudden movements as he studied the three men at the back of the saloon. They wore pistols and shell belts, and they'd armed themselves with rifles. One he recognized as the townsman called LeBeouf — a burly gent with a wandering eye. The three stood near a door in the middle of the rear wall and to the left of a stairs that angled toward the second story.

Louisa had followed Prophet's gaze to the three, craning her neck to look behind her. The only other person in the saloon to have noticed the newcomers was, oddly, Sugar Delphi, who had turned slightly away from holding Lazzaro down to cock an ear at the room's rear.

"Got it!" the doctor roared, pulling his bloody forceps out of the hole in Lazzaro's side.

Lazzaro screamed, bucking up off the table, then promptly passed out, the leather swatch falling out of his mouth.

"I didn't think that stupid gringo was ever going to shut up!" exclaimed Sergeant Frieri, sitting with Chacin and the other Rurales around a single tequila bottle.

Red Snake turned his head sharply toward the Rurale and opened his mouth but before he could retort, one of the saloon's two front doors opened, rattling the rusty bell. The town marshal walked in on a gust of wind-blown grit, scrubbed his boots on the hemp rug, and closed the door behind him.

Prophet kept one eye on the three men at the back of the room and one on the newcomer — a medium-tall, small-boned, potbellied man with curly, dark brown hair puffing out around his tan Stetson. His black frock coat was dusty, and his string tie had been blown back over his shoulder.

He had dark brown eyes, and they both seemed to twitch as he studied the room, grimacing, shoulders slightly slumped, all in all appearing vexed or negotiating a chronic, generalized pain. Prophet judged him to be in his late thirties, early forties.

"Well, well, well," the marshal said in a high-pitched, gravelly voice, and none too happily. "Ain't this a party?"

"Come on over and take a load off, Marshal," Prophet said, raising his shot glass

214

and grinning. "I'll buy you a drink."

"Who the hell are you?"

"Lou Prophet. You are . . . ?"

The lawman swept the room with his twitching, disapproving gaze — his eyes seemed to be blinking out of sync with each other — and raised his gravelly voice. "Bill Hawkins is my name. Town marshal of San Gezo. And I reckon you fellas ain't got the word, but here it is: strangers are not allowed in San Gezo. Especially obvious outlaws." He extended his left arm and pointed his index finger at Chacin, narrowing one of his forever-twitching eyes and shouting, "And that goes for you, too, Captain. Anyone can wear the uniform of a Mexican Rurale. Besides, all of us here are citizens of the United States of America, and we do not recognize the government of Mexico."

"You don't think so, uh?" Chacin's face reddened and he curled his upper lip as he twisted the right upswept end of his mustache. The other Rurales stiffened as they glowered back at Marshal Hawkins.

Hawkins looked meaningfully at the three men at the back of the room, who slowly spread out to form a semicircle at the room's rear, hefting their rifles. Two were relatively young but hard-eyed, and they

215

wore their guns and wielded their rifles as though they knew how to use them. La-Beouf scowled at the Rurale captain as though filled with an old hatred. Appearing in his early fifties, his pale skin was pink behind his cinnamon beard. Several warts bristled on his double chins and on his small, blunt nose. He cocked his Winchester loudly and worked the gob of chew in his mouth.

The marshal set the butt of his shotgun on his shell belt, aiming the double barrels at the ceiling. "Those three men you might have noticed at the back of the room feel right at home here in Mojaveria. They're well armed and well schooled in the implementation of said firearms. They are shop owners here in San Gezo and my sworn deputies.

"They've been ordered to defend themselves and the good citizens of this town at all costs, for we are the last inhabitants of San Gezo, and we will not be pushed around by Indians or border bandits." He slid his owly gaze to Captain Chacin. "Or anyone wearing a gray monkey suit and callin' themselves a Rurale."

Chacin glowered back at the man, grinding his jaws.

Hawkins looked at the table before him.

"Miss Ivy, Miss Tulsa, Dad . . . you all walk back behind the bar and get ready to lower your heads if the situation gets ugly, which it very possibly might. Doc, you, too."

The two women quickly climbed to their feet. Huffing and puffing and looking deeply dismayed, the hefty, redheaded whore shuffled toward the bar. The black woman took Dad's arm and moved less quickly, leading the old man, who continued to glare at Prophet, around behind the bar. The whore popped the cork on a bottle and, her pudgy, pale hand shaking, splashed whiskey into a tumbler.

Prophet sighed and slacked back in his chair, hooking his thumbs behind his cartridge belt. "Look, Hawkins, you can talk loud as you want since you're holdin' that barn burner an' all. But know you can't legally kick us out of your town. We ain't broken any of your laws, and your town is in Mexico, of which I doubt you ain't even a citizen. Now, why don't you come on over here and let me buy you a drink, you ole hornswoggler, before this gets a whole lot nastier than it should."

The marshal looked at Prophet, one eye wide, the other twitching wildly. He appeared to be puffing up and on the verge of exploding.

217

Prophet saw something out the corner of his left eye. At the same time, Ivy, standing behind the bar, gasped, "Oh, my god!"

Prophet turned his head to see the tall, dark hombre who'd been manning the Gatling gun fall out of the open loft door on the other side of the street. He turned one somersault and hit the ground in front of the barn with a thud. He bounced slightly and lay still on his belly, dust puffing around him.

An arrow protruded from his back. Prophet lifted his shocked gaze to the open loft door to see the maw of the Gatling gun swinging around slightly and becoming level with the saloon. A dark face beneath a red bandanna smiled wickedly, green eyes flashing in the afternoon light as El Lightning's fist began turning the gun's wood-handled crank.

Prophet shouted, "Everyone down!"

He threw himself back in his chair, and he and the chair hit the floor with a resounding boom that was almost instantly drowned by the savage hiccups of the blazing Gatling gun and the screams of everyone else in the room.

Bam-bam-bam-bam-bam-bam-bam-bam-bam!

The moaning wind only partly covered

the gun's savage cacophony. It did not at all cover the screeching of breaking glass as the bullets hammered the front of the saloon and blasted out the window to send the bullets screaming through the saloon and into tables and chairs and support posts and the bar and the back-bar mirror and shelved bottles and glasses. The bullets shredded the dull red carpet on the stairs at the room's right rear and blasted the newel from its post.

Prophet had turned onto his right shoulder and cast a quick look around the room to see everyone on the floor amidst the flying splinters. When the Gatling gun died, its cartridge belt apparently having run out of bullets, Prophet grabbed his rifle off the table, where he'd left it. He pumped a shell into the chamber, rose to his knees, swiping his hat from his head, and edged a look up above the sill of the front window nearest him.

He could no longer see El Lightning in the barn loft. Only the Gatling gun sat there, its smoking canister tilted upward. Howls and the thuds of galloping horses rose, and Prophet saw Mojaves galloping toward the saloon from both sides of the street while several others appeared in the breaks on either side of the livery barn. One bolted out from the barn's right side and dove behind a stock trough, a carbine in his hands.

Prophet rested his Winchester's barrel on the sill of the blown-out window and triggered two shots at the stock trough, blasting the carbine out of the Indian's hand with the first shot and drilling the Mojave's neck with the second. Both his spent cartridges rattled onto the wooden floor behind him as he pumped a fresh shell into the rifle's breech.

Two shots for one Injun, he thought with an inward grimace, knowing he had to make every shot count.

Around him, the other men and women were shouting and shifting themselves into position to cut loose on the Indians now triggering rifles and arrows from horseback as they galloped in both directions past the saloon. The Mojaves were howling angrily but moving too quickly for an accurate shot. As two arrows whistled past his head and a bullet drilled the sill, spitting prickly slivers against his face, Prophet lowered his head and put his shoulder to the wall beneath the window.

He ran a sleeve across his face and cast a quick glance behind him. Lazzaro was on the floor, and Sugar was crouched over him, her sightless eyes showing gray in the light from the saloon's front windows. Louisa was on one knee, triggering both her pistols through the front door that had been blown open by the Gatling's blast.

Marshal Bill Hawkins was down on his shoulder behind Louisa, holding one arm while sliding himself toward the front window on the far side of the door, holding his big Greener in one gloved hand. His hat was off and his dark curly hair glistened with broken window glass.

Chacin and the other Rurales and Red Snake and Kiljoy were firing pistols and rifles through the larger front window on the right side of the door. One of the three townsmen who'd entered through the rear door was down and unmoving in a pool of blood while the others, including red-bearded LeBeouf, were hunkered behind overturned tables, looking fearfully toward the front of the room.

Prophet broke open his barn blaster, made sure he had a wad in each barrel, then, growling through gritted teeth, said, "I'm getting awful tired of these damn redskins!"

He triggered the left barrel through the window, blowing one Mojave off his horse and causing another behind him to yelp and grab his face. While the first Mojave was still airborne and howling, Prophet triggered the coach gun's second barrel.

A Mojave had worked his way over to the saloon and was just bounding up the veranda steps when Prophet's blast shredded the Indian's calico blouse, peppered his neck and face, and threw him back down the steps and into the street with a clipped cry.

There was a window in the side wall off the end of the bar, behind Prophet. While the others continued to throw bullets at the Indians, Prophet reloaded the double-barrel gut shredder and hurled himself through the window. He landed in the alley between the saloon and another adobe-brick building, with a great "Uhfff!" of air ejected from his lungs.

He rolled over, wincing at the glass pricking under him, and triggered his shotgun at the first Indian he saw, blowing the howling brave off his horse. Heaving himself to his feet, Prophet ran up to the mouth of the alley and blew another Mojave off his horse, as well.

He started to crouch behind a rain barrel to reload but then he heard only a few rifles popping from the front of the saloon to his right. Looking around, he saw the Indians galloping off in both directions along the street before him, leaving a half-dozen dead in their wake.

"Hold your fire!" Prophet shouted, squinting against the windblown dust. Beyond him, the broad main street was a dirty, washed-out yellow amidst the curtains of blowing grit and tumbleweeds.

He whipped around, thinking he'd seen something moving at the other end of the alley. Quickly breeching the shotgun, plucking out the spent loads and thumbing fresh ones in the barrels, he ran down the alley, then sidled up to the rear of the saloon. Thumbing the barn blaster's rabbit-eared hammers back, he moved slowly around the corner. Two Indians were standing in front of the back door, one nocking an arrow, the other shoving cartridges into the loading tube of his Spencer carbine.

They saw Prophet at the same time and gave a startled yowl. Prophet raised the coach gun, turned sideways, and — *Boom! Boom!* — blew both braves up off their feet and sent them flying down the alley in clouds of blood that the wind blew against the saloon's rear wall.

The rear door creaked open. Prophet swung toward it, dropping his empty shotgun and bringing up his Colt. Louisa stepped into the open doorway, both her silver-chased Peacemakers in her fists. She raised both barrels and depressed the hammers as Prophet lowered his own weapon.

She poked her head out to inspect the two dead Indians. Then she looked at Prophet. She pursed her lips and arched a brow. "I hear your Devil friend laughing at us, Lou."

"Ah, hell," the bounty hunter said. "We been in tighter places before this." He picked up his shotgun, breeched it. Uncertainly, he added, "Or . . . just as tight, anyway."

17

Later that night, around midnight, Prophet
set his rifle and shotgun on a table and
glanced at Ivy Miller scrubbing off the
counter behind the saloon's main bar, where
she'd prepared a hardy stew. "Mind if I have
a cup o' that mud, Miss Miller?"

He and she were the only two in the
saloon's main hall. The others, including
Louisa, were upstairs or out on the veranda
or scattered around the village, watching for
the Indians whom they were certain would
attack again, though their number had been
depleted by eight, their guns and ammunition confiscated. Prophet, with an extra
bandolier filled with .44 shells for his rifle
and .45 shells for his Colt slung over his
neck, had been stationed atop the saloon's
roof until Chacin and Frieri had relieved
him a few minutes ago.

"Of course, Mr. Prophet." The black
woman tossed her sponge into the sink

beside the stove and used a swatch to lift the big, blue pot from a burner and fill two white stone mugs at the bar. "How could I refuse a man who trailed a passel of blood-hungry 'Paches into our fair town?"

Prophet sat back in a chair, doffed his hat, and ran a hand through his hair. "I do apologize, ma'am."

"Oh, stow it. I reckon there wasn't much else you could do, could you?" She came around from behind the bar and set one of the steaming mugs on the table before him. "Except stay out on the desert where they'd deplete you of ammunition, food, and water."

Prophet lifted the mug, blew on it, and sipped. "Much obliged."

"You can call me Ivy. You're the only one, though. The others may call me Miss Miller if they call me anything at all."

"You don't like my friends?"

She pulled out a chair across the table from him and slumped into it, giving him a pointed look across her steaming coffee mug. She had a very slight scar, like that from a knifepoint, on her otherwise smooth, chocolate-colored right cheek. "Are they really your friends?"

"Just that blond bundle of blue-eyed dynamite — Miss Bonnyventure." Prophet canted his head to one side and gave the saloon owner a wry look. "How'd you know?"

"I been around the frontier once or twice, mister. In my business, you get to be a good judge of character. Don't get me wrong — your character is far from what I'd call *good*." Her clear, dark brown eyes dropped to his chest before flicking back to his face, her cheeks darkening beneath the natural coco of her skin. "I bet you can really stomp when you get the urge. But you shine in comparison to them you rode in with." The look grew more pointed. "Right?"

Prophet chuckled, not sure what to make of the gal though he had a feeling she could do some stomping of her own. "Speaking of them I rode in with, you ain't seen the bandy-legged ole Mescin, have you? Senor —"

"Bocangel?" the woman finished for him. She'd arched both her brows and put some extra starch in her voice.

"You know him?"

"Of course. He's been holed up here himself, the old desert rat." She sat sideways to the table, an ankle hiked on a knee beneath her dress. An unladylike pose, but on her it seemed natural and not unalluring. The first three buttons of her silk blouse

227

were open, revealing her deep, dark cleavage between the two full mounds of her breasts.

She looked up at him, caught the direction of his gaze, and smiled with one side of her mouth. Prophet sipped his coffee, then said over the mug he held to his lips to cover his chagrin, "What do you suppose happened to him? He got caught out on the desert, had a Mojave arrow in his arm."

"I reckon that's his business, ain't it?"

Prophet frowned at her curiously. Obviously, she wasn't on friendly terms with Senor Bocangel.

"His boy's dead," he said, as though that might temper her view of the man.

She had no reaction to that. After a short, taut silence, she glanced at the ceiling and said, "You and that blond barrel of dynamite . . . ?"

"We're partners."

"In what?"

"Bounty hunting."

"And just what kind of bounty hunting are you doing here in San Gez . . . ?"

Ivy let her voice trail off when boots pounded the veranda outside the closed front doors. The adobe building's blown-out windows were shuttered against another Indian attack. Prophet picked up his barn blaster and thumbed one of the hammers back but lowered the gun when the door opened and Marshal Bill Hawkins walked in. He had his left arm in a sling, and a bandage showed through the ragged hole in the sleeve of his frock coat bored by the Gatling gun.

Hawkins had been on patrol around the town. The nervous, angry-eyed little man was dust-rimed, as the wind was still blowing half the sand of the Sonoran Desert around in swirling clouds. He closed the door, paused before it, and spat grit from his lips, brushed it from his mustache, and beat his hat against his legs clad in brown wool, the knees silvered from wear.

"Coffee, Bill?" Ivy asked him.

"Yeah. Good and black." As Ivy got up and walked back behind the bar, Hawkins glanced at her round backside, then walked toward Prophet, his nervous, perpetually frustrated eyes twitching. "Prophet, you and your boys . . . and gals . . . got this town in a peck of trouble. Not to mention its good citizens, of which I am one, in serious danger."

He pulled out a chair, set his Winchester on the table near Prophet's own mini-arsenal, and sat in the chair with a grunt. He ran a weary hand through his curly hair poking up all over his head and glowered across the table at Prophet. "I didn't ask this of Chacin or them others, because I knew I'd get run around the well house. I'm askin' you 'cause you seem the only one a man could half-ways trust."

Ivy set a mug of coffee down in front of the marshal. He glanced at her. "Thanks, Ivy."

"Don't mention it, Bill. And don't let me interrupt." She smoothed her skirt down against her rump and the backs of her well-turned thighs — at least, Prophet guessed they were well turned in the vague way he'd thought about and appraised her, as men were wont to do — and sat down in her chair.

Prophet shuttled his gaze from the woman to Marshal Hawkins. "I reckon you deserve to get the whole wheelbarrow-full." He sipped his coffee, tilted the mug, and rolled the bottom edge of it around on the table. "My partner Miss Bonnyventure and me been trailin' Lazzaro's bunch. They hit a bank in Nogales, got away with sixteen thousand dollars in Mexican coin and paper. There's a reward for the money and for the heads of each of Lazzaro's bunch."

Hawkins said, "The blind woman . . . ?"

"She's part of 'em. And while she may be

blind, don't give her your back."

"Somehow, I knew that."

"Go on, Mr. Prophet," Ivy urged, wanting to hear it all.

"Call me Lou." Prophet gave her a little cockeyed half smile, enjoying the distraction of sort of halfway flirting with the pretty, sexy woman despite the gravity of their situation. She merely pursed her lips and looked down at her coffee before lifting the mug to her mouth.

The marshal glanced incredulously from Prophet to Ivy then back to Prophet. "Please, do go on, bounty man," he said with a sarcastic edge.

Prophet laid it all out for him and Miss Ivy — the loot, the Rurales, the Mojaves, and his stumbling across Bocangel in the dark desert, then finding the man's son crucified on a cactus earlier that day.

"So take the loot and git," Hawkins growled.

"I'd love to oblige you." Prophet sipped his coffee. "But Lazzaro and Miss Delphi hid the loot in the desert. Somehow, we're going to have to get the son of a bitch to tell us or show us where it is."

"Pistol-whip him till his teeth fall out. That oughta do it. Hell, I'll do it for you if you're squeamish."

231

"Wouldn't work on Lazzaro. Besides, in his condition, he'd likely die. Where would that leave us?"

"Hell, he's probably gonna die, anyway. Doc Shackleford says he's back and forth — mostly back. Lost too much blood." The marshal sat back in his chair. "Maybe Miss Delphi can feel her way back to it. They say them sightless folks have another sense."

"They say it about Sugar, but her extra sense is mostly reserved for killing, not leading men back to money she's helped steal." Prophet picked up his rifle and set the butt on his thigh, opening the breech. "Them Injuns been causin' a lot of trouble around here, have they?"

He caught Ivy casting the marshal a furtive glance.

Hawkins wrinkled his brows and said, "Not till you folks led 'em here. I doubt they had any idea San Gezo even had any folks left in it. Most everybody left with the mining company. There's the well out there but the Injuns know of other tanks in these mountains that white men don't.

"There's another well out on the other end of the range, and most of the long-lost desert rats and curly wolves use that one. This town, you see, is cursed. Or so the Mexicans believe. Bad luck is as common here as the wind. We keep our heads kinda low here, so's not to piss-burn the red men and attract attention. Kinda helps, havin' the place cursed, you see."

"What're you folks doin' here?" Prophet said, sliding his curious gaze from the marshal to Ivy and back again. "Got nowhere else to go, do you? Don't get along well with others?"

"That's about the size of it," Ivy said. "The world has gone to hell in a handbasket. You can have it." She lifted her cup and threw the last of her coffee back. "Well, then, I reckon I'll try to catch some shuteye. There's a little stew and a few biscuits left." She canted her head toward the bar. "On the warming rack."

"I'm full, Ivy — thanks," the marshal said, casting another glance at the woman's enticingly round backside.

She walked halfway across the room, then stopped and cast an inscrutable look over her right shoulder, her eyes quickly meeting Prophet's before flicking away. "I'm in room eighteen, top story . . . anyone needs anything."

Then she headed on up the stairs.

Hawkins scowled at Prophet and said angrily, "That's funny. I been here as long as you, Ivy, and I never until now knew which room you bedded down in up there."

Ivy said nothing. She merely turned at the second-story landing and continued on up the stairs. Hawkins snorted without mirth.

Prophet looked again at the rifle sticking up from his thigh, opened and closed his hand around the neck of the stock.

Hawkins gave a wolfish grin and raised his dark brown eyes to the hammered tin ceiling. "You steer clear of Miss Ivy, hear?"

"Maybe you never knew what room she holes up in, because she don't want you to know, Bill." Prophet glanced sidelong at the riled marshal. "Ever think of that?"

Hawkins jerked his chin down with menace. "Just steer clear, bounty man. Wouldn't wanna catch a stray bullet here in San Gezo — now, would ya?"

Prophet's pale blue eyes sparked with mockery. "That'd be a black eye on your fair city, wouldn't it?"

Hawkins finished his coffee, stood, and plucked his Winchester off the table. "I'm goin' to bed."

"Don't let the bedbugs bite," Prophet said as the man climbed the stairs. Everyone in San Gezo had taken a room in the saloon, it appeared. All except for Senor Bocangel.

Prophet kicked back in his chair for a time, pondering the situation. Finally, he thought about Hawkins and Ivy and the others here in San Gezo.

Damn curious they remained here, few as there were. With Bocangel, they numbered less than ten. Prophet could understand folks wanting to keep to themselves. He harbored much the same sentiment. You didn't have to be around other humans long to get tired of their bullshit. And all men . . . and women, for that matter . . . owned a good dose of bullshit. He had enough of his own to make him want to hack his own head off with a rusty saw. Prophet preferred the company of his horse, mean and ugly as he was. . . .

The bounty hunter heaved himself to his weary feet, grumbling at the marshal's admonishment about Miss Ivy, and picked up his guns. He muttered an indignant curse and tramped up the stairs, making no effort to cushion his footsteps. He went on up to the third floor and rapped on the door bearing the tarnished-brass number 18.

18

"Lou?"

Louisa lifted her head from her pillow, looking around, wondering where she was and where Prophet was. It took nearly half a minute for Chacin, Lazzaro, Sugar, the Indians to come back to her. When they did, she turned to see that the side of the double bed in Miss Ivy's saloon that she'd reserved for Prophet hadn't been slept in. The covers hadn't been pulled back.

The oil lamp on the room's dresser sputtered in drafts scurrying in around the closed wooden shutters over the sole window. The room was small, its wooden walls papered in red with phony gold palm leaves that had long since faded to pink and peeled off in strips. The air was foul with mouse droppings. A chair with scrolled arms and back upholstered in green brocade sat in a corner. It had once been elegant, but now its seat was nearly worn through, and a chunk was missing from one of the arms. The back was stained with what appeared blood.

A remnant from San Gezo's last heyday.

A washstand stood in front of the window. Awake now and feeling restless and wondering what time it was and what was going on outside — where the hell was Prophet? — Louisa threw the covers back and moved naked to the stand. She used the sliver of soap there and the sponge to give herself a quick sponge bath, then dried herself with a scrap of towel, picked her clothes up off the chair beside the bed, and dressed.

She pulled her tarnished timepiece out of the pocket of her calico shirt and clicked open the lid in which rested a wedding picture of her mother and father. When the picture had been taken, they'd been younger than Louisa was now, her father boyishly handsome with his slicked-back hair parted in the middle, her mother too severe-looking for the happiness she must have been feeling. Married to the man she loved. About to buy a farm, start a family.

She wore her thick blond hair elegantly back and parted and gathered in a fist-sized bun at the crown of her head. The thickness of her hair accented the fine, smooth Nordic planes of her face.

Dead. Louisa's parents and her brother and sisters. All dead.

Louisa caressed the slightly water-stained photo with her thumb, and not allowing the remembered screams to enter her head as they did so often and with such persistence that she thought she'd surely go mad, she read the time.

Three o'clock.

The large building sounded eerily quiet in the wake of the wind. There was a freshness in the air that told her it must be raining.

She returned the piece to her pocket. She adjusted her cartridge belt and pistols on her hips, made sure each gun was fully loaded, rolled each cylinder across her forearm, comforted by the smooth, certain sound of the clicks, and left the room.

As she walked along the second-story hall, she heard snores from behind several scarred doors. Descending the stairs, she saw two Rurales filing through the saloon's open front door, muttering to each other wearily as they headed for the bar. The room was lit with three or four lamps bracketed to posts or hanging from the ceiling, and in the flickering, buttery light she recognized Sergeant Frieri and one of the Rurale corporals whose name she'd never learned and had no interest in learning.

"Senorita, what a pleasure," Frieri said, standing at the bar while the corporal stood behind it, filling two tin cups with coffee from the large, blue pot that had been warming on the range.

"The pleasure's all mine, Sergeant," Louisa responded, in no mood for the man. "What's happening out there?"

The sergeant leaned an elbow atop the bar. He was just barely tall enough to do so. He smiled at Louisa, showing the gap where his front teeth had been, and several crooked teeth in his lower jaw rimed with crusted coffee and tobacco. "It's raining very softly. Perhaps we could take a walk together. The air is fresh."

"You need your balls busted again?"

The sergeant closed his mouth, his long, reptilian eyes darkening. The corporal chuckled but stopped when Frieri fired a glance at him.

"Pour me one of those," she ordered the corporal.

A little nervously, the man did as she'd ordered, and then, silently, he and Frieri took their coffee and filed on out to the veranda, where Louisa could hear them muttering as they sat in wicker chairs. They'd left one of the two doors open, and she could hear the welcome, soft patter of

239

the cool rain that smelled like fresh chili peppers and almond extract. Somehow, the sound took the edge off the night though she knew that the Mojaves wouldn't be waylaid by a little rain. Their superstitions might keep them from attacking until daylight, but rain wouldn't stop them.

Louisa carried her mug over to the table that she and Prophet had been sitting at earlier. Where was he? There were three empty stone mugs on the table. The one on the left side, nearest the sidewall, was turned to the left. Prophet always drank with his left hand, leaving the right one free for his gun.

No telling whose the other two were. One might possibly have been Miss Ivy's. Louisa had a keen sense about the attractions between men and women — especially between Prophet and other women. And she'd seen right off — she couldn't have said how exactly — that there had been an attraction between Prophet and the pretty, cocoa-skinned saloon owner.

"Getting you a tussle, eh, Lou?"

Louisa sat down in his chair, curling one leg beneath her. She looked up when she heard someone descending the stairs. Sugar's red braids and thick red locks bounced around her shoulders. She came down slowly, running her left hand lightly along the rail.

She stopped at the bottom, stood there for a time, her head forward. "Louisa?"

Louisa sipped her coffee. "How'd you know?"

"Your own particular smell," the blind woman said. "And the smell of coffee. No better pairing in this world."

"You want me to pour you a cup?"

"That'd be nice." The blind woman came forward slowly, tentatively. "Any chairs in my way?"

Louisa got up and walked around to fetch the coffee. "Not if you stay close to the bar."

Sugar walked along the bar, brushing an arm along it before pulled out a chair from the table at which Louisa had been sitting and slacked into it. Louisa set the fresh cup of coffee down before Sugar, then sat in her own chair, leaning forward with her elbows on the table and lifting her own mug with both hands.

"Good and hot," Sugar said, sipping her mug of the brew. "Got chilly with the rain."

"Couldn't sleep?"

Sugar shook her head. "You?"

"Nerves are a little jangled, I reckon."

"I didn't think your nerves were ever jangled, Leona. Or . . . it's Louisa, I guess, isn't it?"

Sugar sat back in her chair. She met Louisa's gaze and it was like she was seeing her. There was a slight tightness in her features, a pensive cast to her sightless eyes that wasn't normally there.

"Lazzaro kick off?"

Sugar smiled. "You'd best be grateful he hasn't."

"That's a hard one."

Sugar leaned forward, sliding her hand across the table, closing her fingers around Louisa's left forearm and squeezing. "You and I could go far together, Leona. Do you mind if I call you Leona? It's hard to call you Louisa. To me, that's not who you are."

"I'd just as soon you didn't."

Sugar squeezed Louisa's forearm harder. "Answer my question, dear."

"I already did."

Sugar released Louisa's arm, lifted her coffee to her red lips, and took a sip. She sucked her upper lip, set her coffee down, and ran her hand down along the side of her head, fingering one of the two small, beaded braids hanging there. She canted her head slightly, and she looked like a young girl thinking out a troubling matter.

"How many men have you killed, Leona?"

Louisa hiked a shoulder. "I'd say upward

of fifty. And every one deserved it. They all had prices on their heads. Most had killed women and children, just like your bunch."

"That makes it all right, does it? The fact that you've killed men with prices on their heads — who, as *you* say, deserved it?"

Louisa shook her hair back from her face and gave Sugar a tolerant look. "Are you going to recite the Constitution to me now? Or the Bible . . . ?"

"I'm just sayin—"

"I know what you're saying. That I'm a killer same as you. While I don't deny my vengeful nature that does, indeed, border on vigilantism at times, I'm nothing like you. I kill those who've killed innocent folks, and I'm going to keep on with that until I die of old age or lead poisoning. You, sweet Sugar, are going to hang."

Sugar laughed, showing her white teeth. "Oh, come on, Leona! How are you going to take me and the boys in? Lazzaro can't ride, and in case you hadn't noticed, Chacin has made his own claim on our heads. Let's not even get started on the Mojaves."

She sipped her coffee, swallowed, and laughed again, choking a little on the hot liquid. "None of us will get out of here alive. At least, not as a group. Now, two could take off south across the mountains, head for the Sea of Cortez . . ."

"What about your beloved Tony?"

A genuinely vexing expression clouded Sugar's pretty, oval-shaped face. Tears glazed her eyes. She looked away. "Tony will be dead soon. The doc says he had to go too deep to find the bullet. Infection is likely."

She wiped a tear away from her cheek with the back of her hand, staring toward the shuttered window on her right. "I can find the money. If you lead me to the draw, I can find the money, Leona. In the dark, when no one else will track us and the Mojaves will be lying low. Then, just as I said . . ."

"Stow it."

"Think about it?"

Louisa stared at her, a troubled expression of her own furling the tawny brows over her hazel eyes. A recent memory washed over her. She looked at Sugar's red lips, her sightless, cobalt eyes, her thick red hair caressing her slender, pale neck, hanging down past her shoulders. Her hands were long and slender, tanned by the sun. She thought of Lou upstairs with Miss Ivy, and a wretched feeling bit into her. A depression like a lead weight on her soul.

He was not hers. She, not his. No one's.

Her life was a desert, and she was alone in it. Same as Sugar.

She did not like the way her thoughts were suddenly angling. It made her head feel light, her lungs tight. Suddenly, she couldn't get a breath.

"Oh, Christ," she heard herself mutter as she slid her chair back. She heaved herself out of it. As she moved around the table, she caught her boot on a leg, and stumbled, nudging the table with a noisy bark.

"I need some air," she said, moving to the door, striding through it and moving across the veranda and down the steps and into the soggy street.

Behind her, Sugar ran the tip of her index finger along the rim of her coffee mug. The pensive little-girl expression had returned to her pretty face.

Louisa strode across the street toward the livery barn. One of the Rurales was sitting between the open loft doors, smoking, dangling his legs with their high, black boots down over the barn front.

"Ay, chiquita . . ." he muttered.

Louisa ignored him. She strode down along the left side of the livery barn and past the rear paddock. There were no horses in the paddock; she and the others had stabled their mounts in the barn, where the Mojaves couldn't so easily get at them.

Behind the paddock was brush and rocks and small, ancient pueblos grown up with weeds and cactus, some nearly concealed by greasewood and mesquites. Louisa kept walking, angling through the desert. She did not know where she was going. She knew only that, despite the Mojave threat, she needed to walk and to breathe and get the cluttered, ugly thoughts out of her head.

She moved between two hovels that were low, black shapes in the darkness and stopped. She'd heard the thudding crunch of a boot in gravel somewhere ahead. Her heart leaped, and she closed her hand over the grip of the .45 on her right hip. Before she could slide the gun from its holster, she heard another, louder footstep behind her.

An arm whipped around her neck. A hand closed over her nose and mouth, jerking her back so suddenly that she released the pistol to break her fall. She hit the ground on her belly, was turned over by a brusque hand. Looking up, she saw the flat, round face of Sergeant Frieri grinning down at her, eyes bright, ambient light glistening off his rotting, wet gums.

In Spanish, he said to someone behind him, "Hold your pistol on her while I give this Americana the fucking she deserves!"

Louisa saw a gray-clad figure move up behind Frieri. At the same time, the sergeant slapped her with the back of his hand, and, giggling bizarrely, straddled her, squeezing her left breast with one hand while he began opening his fly with the other.

Frieri froze. His grin faded. He loosed a little chirp as he grimaced. He shifted his weight slightly.

"How deep you want me to shove this thing, Sergeant?"

Louisa had slipped her short but razor-edged stiletto from the sheath sewn into the inside of her short deerskin jacket. Now she poked the tip against the man's scrotum, steadily increasing the pressure.

In Spanish, he rasped, "Put your gun away, Corporal, you fool! Help the lovely senorita to her feet! She seems to have fallen!"

19

Prophet had a busier night than he'd intended. It seemed that Ivy Miller hadn't had a good ash hauling in recent months and badly needed to satisfy her natural female desires and also to waylay the anxiety that Prophet's gang had evoked when they'd led the Mojaves into her quiet little town.

Prophet had been more than happy to distract her, as she did him, from their recent travails. She woke him around four thirty for one last tussle before she dressed and headed downstairs to begin her morning saloon chores.

Prophet fell back asleep for a time, feeling he'd just been run over by a whole cavvy of Mojave war ponies. Then, hearing birds chirping outside and seeing that gray morning light was pushing between the cracks in the shutter closed over the window of Ivy's room, rose up from the rumpled bed with a groan.

He stumbled naked to the shutter, drew it open, and stared down into the broad main street. The sun was up but hidden behind low, gray clouds. The wind had resumed its harassment of this high bench, groaning under the saloon's eaves and tossing dust and tumbleweeds along the street. *Bad luck was as common as the wind in San Gezo.* A couple of Chacin's men were stationed up and down the trace, and someone — Prophet couldn't tell who from this distance — was manning the Gatling gun in the barn loft on the street's other side.

According to the group's agreement, five guards would stay on watch all night with orders to shoot twice quickly if anything looked amiss. No shots had been fired. The Indians must have stayed hunkered down out in the desert, but Prophet figured they'd attack again soon. He was a little surprised they hadn't at first light.

He drank some water from his canteen, then corked the flask and went around the nicely appointed room, gathering his clothes that Ivy had tossed every which way when she'd undressed him. She, however, hadn't been wearing a stitch when she'd answered his knock on the door, and he'd found her body to be not only lush and ripe but ready.

Prophet wrapped his shell belt around his

waist, made sure his Colt showed brass in all six chambers, then hooked his shotgun over his neck, picked up his rifle, and headed on into the hall, gently closing Ivy's door behind him.

Most of the doors up and down the hall were closed. A window on each end of the hall lent a murky, gray light and revealed the dull red carpet runner on the floor. As he strode along the hall toward the stairs, he saw that the last door on the right was open a foot.

He passed the door, glancing inside, and stopped. He backed up one step and turned to the door, frowning.

Through the one-foot gap he could see Sergeant Frieri lying on a broad, canopied bed. The ugly little Rurale looked so out of place in the frilly room with the four-poster bed, quilted bed covers, lace-edged canopy and dark blue carpet trimmed with red roses that Prophet almost loosed a chuckle.

Then his scowl deepened, and he blinked his eyes as if to clear them.

Frieri's dark head poked up above the bedcovers. His eyes were open. So, too, was the man's mouth. His lips were stretched back from his face in a grimace. Beside him, the plump redheaded whore, Tulsa St. James, lay on her side, facing the sergeant, her hands sandwiched together between her right cheek and her silk-covered pillow. The whore was snoring very softly, making her lips flutter.

Prophet nudged the door open another two feet with his rifle barrel and stepped softly inside, trying to keep his spurs from chinging. On a table beside Frieri's side of the bed were two empty bottles and two empty shot glasses. Prophet walked over to the bed and stared down at Sergeant Frieri.

The man's covers were pulled down to his upper chest, exposing the long, deep gash across his throat and from which thick, dark red blood had oozed out onto his chest, staining the quilts.

The man stared sightlessly up at Prophet, his wide eyes shining dully in the light emanating through the cracks in the window shutter on the other side of the whore. She stirred now, groaning and blinking and lifting her head slightly.

"What?" she muttered, blinking up at Prophet as she raised her head from her pillow. She'd taken her hair down and it lay in a tangled mess about her head and bare shoulders. "Well . . . hello there, big feller. I'd be happy to oblige you, but I ain't much good till noon. Run along, now, and we'll talk late—" She cut herself off when her eyes found Frieri lying beside her.

Her mouth opened and her eyes nearly popped from their sockets.

"Now, don't start caterwaulin', for chrissakes!" Prophet said, keeping his own voice down.

She clapped a hand to her mouth and bit down on it, moaning and scuttling away from the dead Rurale. She backed too far away and gave a startled shriek as she dropped over the side of the bed and hit the floor with a boom.

"Shit."

Prophet looked around the room, making sure the killer wasn't still present though judging by the thick texture of the blood, the sergeant had been killed at least a couple of hours ago. He doubted Miss St. James was capable of such a grisly act. Hearing boot thuds on the stairs and the rumble of surprised voices rising from the first two stories, Prophet walked around the far side of the bed and dropped to a knee beside the whore.

Holding a quilt over her breasts, she scuttled against the wall below the window, saying "Oh, god! Oh, god! Oh, god!" Then she raised her terror-stricken eyes to Prophet. "Why'd you have to kill him in my bed, ya fuckin' *savage?*"

"I didn't kill him," Prophet said, trying to keep his own voice calm in an effort to calm the whore. "I take it you don't know who did."

The whore just shuttled her gaze to her last customer and covered her mouth with a pudgy hand, muffling another gasp. Meanwhile, the boot thuds grew louder until Prophet turned to see Red Snake Corbin and Roy Kiljoy walk into the room.

Kiljoy had a white bandage wrapped vertically around his head and knotted beneath his chin, covering the two holes in his cheeks. Blood showed where the holes were. While the wounds had to be sore as hell, Kiljoy looked no worse for the wear. Judging by the rheuminess of his eyes, he wasn't sparing the painkiller.

"Well, well, well," Red Snake said, lowering the pistol in his hand as he and Kiljoy inspected the dead Rurale.

Kiljoy looked from the whore to Prophet and back again, his eyes questioning. More boot thuds grew louder until Captain Chacin appeared, flanked by one of his corporals.

The man looked as though he'd just gotten up, his tunic unbuttoned to show a greasy undershirt. He wasn't wearing his shell belt and holster, but he had his Colt

Navy in his hand. As he turned his head and dropped his gaze to the bed, his brows furrowed and his jaws hardened.

He turned to Prophet, slowly raising the pistol in his clenched fist. The bounty hunter straightened, stepping back away from the whore and raising his Winchester to his shoulder, loudly racking a shell into the chamber. "Think about it, Chacin."

That's all he said as he aimed down the Winchester's barrel at the Rurale captain. It appeared all he needed to say. Chacin lowered his pistol. He knew that Prophet wouldn't have cut a man's throat in cold blood. Not even one of Chacin's Rurales. Whoever had done the grisly deed would have been covered in blood, for it had sprayed all the way down to the sergeant's feet poking up from beneath the quilts.

To Prophet, Chacin said, "Mojaves?" He looked at Red Snake and Kiljoy, who could not conceal their pleasure at seeing Frieri lying with his throat laid open, his eyes etched with the horror he must have felt when he'd awakened from his tequila-induced slumber to see his blood geysering from the severed arteries in his neck. "Or one of these bastards?"

"Hell, I had better reason." Louisa had just stepped through the door to stand beside Chacin, regarding Frieri with her implacable gaze. She hiked a shoulder. "In fact, last night I almost saved the butcher from this messy job."

"Senorita, your clarity does not match your beauty."

"Frieri and one of your corporals insisted upon showing me the finer points of love-making out behind the livery barn . . . until I let the pig feel the fine point of my stiletto." Louisa crossed her arms on her chest. "Forgive me if I don't grieve."

Chacin turned his angry gaze on Prophet. "We had a deal, Lou. A deal!"

"You're preachin' to the choir, Captain." Prophet walked out from behind the bed, fingering his beard stubble pensively. He glanced at the sobbing whore, then turned to Red Snake and Kiljoy. "You two haul him outside. He don't exactly match Miss Tulsa's décor."

"Why the hell should we do it?" Red Snake balked.

Prophet raised his Winchester, aiming it out from his hip at Red Snake's belly. "Because I got the drop on you."

Grumbling, the two outlaws went over to the bed, pulled Frieri out from under the bloody, soggy covers, and dropped him on the floor. They rolled him up in a bloody quilt, then, making disgusted faces and each taking an end, carried the dead Rurale on out of the room and into the hall.

Prophet walked out after them. Chacin and Louisa flanked him, Chacin looking indignant. "This is very nasty business, Lou. Very nasty. If someone was going to kill my sergeant, they could have at least done it out in the open instead of skulking around like a damn coward!"

"I can't say as I'm going to lose any more sleep over Frieri than my purty partner will," Prophet said as they started down the stairs. "But it does make me right uneasy — this underhanded killin'. Makes me sorta wonder who's next."

"Any way a Mojave could have slipped in last night?" Louisa asked as the three turned at the second-floor landing and continued on down the stairs behind the cursing, grunting Red Snake and Kiljoy.

Ivy stood at the bottom of the stairs, both fists on her hips. A cooking spatula stuck out of her right fist while she regarded the bloody bundle with disgust in her chocolate brown eyes. "Your handiwork, Lou?"

Prophet grinned as he came down the stairs, keeping his voice intimately low as he pinched his hat brim and grinned. "Hell, you didn't leave me with that much energy."

Behind him, Louisa gave a caustic snort.

"If you boys are gonna start killin' each other, I'd ask that you did it outside," Ivy said as Red Snake and Kiljoy hauled Frieri toward the saloon's open front doors. "That's a mighty expensive death shroud. Damn near as expensive as my windows!"

Marshal Hawkins sat at a table near the front of the room with Doc Shackleford and two other townsmen — two of the three who'd snuck through the saloon's back door yesterday afternoon, just before El Lightning went to work with the Gatling gun.

One was the red-bearded George Le-Beouf. The other man, who wore his long, gray-streaked blond hair in a ponytail and was dressed in a gaudy green suit with checked trousers, was Casey Blackwell. His long, angular face was clean-shaven and pink with sunburn though beneath the burn he appeared almost sickly pale. He had watery gray eyes and a straight, four-inch, slash-like scar under the right one.

The four men sat over breakfast plates. The doctor was the only one still eating. Coffee mugs steamed on the table before them as they cast their grim gazes toward the bloody bundle that Red Snake and Kiljoy were just now hauling out the doors.

"Well, what do you say, boys?" Marshal

Hawkins said. "One down — how many left?"

The four townsmen laughed.

20

Prophet had a cup of coffee to get awake. Ivy did not talk to him. She was too busy cooking and serving breakfast.

Louisa didn't talk to him, either. She merely sat cleaning her pistols at the same table as him but without looking at him. She could be like that, especially if she knew he'd made time with another woman. Or maybe something else was bothering her entirely.

The fickle moods of his blond partner were the least of Prophet's worries. It was true he did not lament the demise of Sergeant Frieri, but the fact that the man had been murdered here in the hotel made Prophet uneasy. He had a feeling the killer was one of the townsmen. Hawkins, maybe, or one of the other men sitting with him. Each likely had other clothes they could have changed into after accomplishing their bloody task.

But why had the killer singled out Frieri to kill?

The question was sharp badger teeth nibbling at the edges of Prophet's mind. When he finished his coffee, he left Louisa to her guns and went outside, closing the door behind him on the wind that had picked up, blowing with nearly as much fury as it had the previous day. It was a hot, dusty, nerve-jangling wind. Its moaning and groaning and loud gusts could cover the approach of a galloping horde of Mojaves, so that neither he nor the others would know they were under attack until the Indians were already flinging lead or ash-shafted arrows.

If anything had cursed this town, the wind had.

He looked across the street to see a Rurale corporal sitting in the barn loft beside the Gatling gun, his knees drawn up as he smoked. He regarded Prophet dully through the screen of blown desert sand.

Looking up and down the street at the well and the mostly abandoned and dilapidated buildings, he saw no one else. There was no movement except sand and weeds and shingles blowing on their chains and lifting a bizarre squawking. A cat slinked along the front of a low-slung blacksmith shop, tail down, ears back, and disappeared through a knot-sized hole in the bottom of one of the two closed doors.

His shotgun hanging down his back and holding his Winchester on his shoulder, Prophet stepped down off the saloon veranda and tramped left along the street. There were a total of six buildings at this end of the near-abandoned town, three to Prophet's right, four to his left. He'd had only a vague idea where he was heading, but now he realized he was tramping out to take a look at the old mine.

The folks here in San Gezo were more private than most. There had to be a reason for that. They had to be protecting something valuable, and the only thing of any value here had been the mine.

Of course, the mining company had pulled out, so the chance of the mine still being worth anything was slim, but Prophet could think of no other reason — aside from mere reclusiveness — that the townsfolk could be wanting to keep any possible visitors moving along.

The street narrowed, became an old wagon trail. Along both sides of the trail, the ancient adobe or stone hovels of the original village shone in the greasewood, ironwood shrubs, and clay-colored rocks and boulders. There was a grove of dead pecan trees on the right side of the trail. Far to the left, two ridges humped up, craggy and uneven ridges forming a canyon between them.

Prophet stopped, narrowed his eyes. A shadow had flickered in an arroyo mouth just ahead.

He'd just started pulling his rifle down from his shoulder when a Mojave wearing a cap of hawk feathers, his broad, tan face striped with ochre war paint over the nose, bounded out of the arroyo mouth, drawing an arrow back from a bow. Prophet threw himself left as the arrow shot toward him, making a *zip!* as it passed six inches past his right cheek.

Prophet hit the ground and, seeing the Indian bound toward him while nocking another arrow, he bounded off his heels, throwing himself into a tangle of greasewood and flood-deposited rocks and driftwood. Something slammed into the side of his boot, whipping his leg sideways.

Prophet ignored it, rose to his knees, pumped a shell into the Winchester's chamber.

A figure dashed past him down the arroyo, just beyond a screen of catclaw and spindly willows. Prophet fired once, twice, three times. The Indian lowered his head and raised his arms and kept running as Prophet's slugs blew branches off the shrubs on the other side of the arroyo. He dashed out of sight beyond a thumb of rock to Prophet's left.

Cursing, stumbling, Prophet dashed out into the arroyo, snapping branches under his boots. He dropped to a knee and swung his rifle up the narrow, meandering ravine and held fire. The Indian was gone. Dust sifted in the wind behind him. Prophet tried to stand but his right boot got hung up on something. He looked at it. A Mojave arrow stuck out of his heel, the flint point half buried.

He reached back, pulled the arrow out of his boot, and tossed it away. "Bastard," he said through a growl. "Gonna need a new heel . . . son of a bitch."

He stood, tested the heel. Seemed sound enough though it squeaked a little. He ejected the spent cartridge from his Winchester, heard it ping off a rock as he seated a fresh one in the chamber and started walking forward. He pivoted on his hips, swinging the rifle around, expecting similarly war-painted Mojaves to bound toward him from both sides of the arroyo at any second.

None showed by the time he came to the

end of the arroyo as it curved into the canyon dug into the valley between the two ridges. None showed when he had made his way carefully up out of the arroyo and stole along the canyon bottom, crouching behind boulders and perusing the rocky ridges nearly surrounding him. Here, a wagon trail angled into the canyon from the direction of San Gezo. Prophet had never visited the Sweet Hereafter Mine, but he figured the road led to the mine. Not much else out here. This certainly wasn't ranching or farming country.

He did not walk along the trail but kept to the brush and boulders to the left of it, near the base of a steep ridge on his left. Ahead, the trail wound deeper into the canyon, turning around a hill on the left and likely jogging into the steeper canyon beyond, where the mine probably was.

Prophet knew it was crazy for him to be out here alone. There were probably twenty Mojaves lurking around in these rocks and cuts. But the Sweet Hereafter gave him a strong tug. Continuing to look around him carefully and angling between boulders and brush clumps, he kept walking.

Dust puffed from a boulder ahead and to his right, a quarter second before the screech of the ricocheting bullet filled

Prophet's ears. Instantly, he saw the shooter halfway up the ridge on his right and about sixty yards beyond him.

Prophet wasted no time triggering two quick shots from his shoulder, saw the shooter tumbling out from behind his covering boulder, dropping to his belly, and sliding several feet down the hill. The shooter had dropped his rifle, and it slid down the hill beside him.

Prophet pumped a fresh round and scowled at the shooter. Not an Indian. A white man. Prophet looked around in case other ambushers were near, then strode quickly over to the base of the hill, giving his gaze once more to the shooter who was struggling to haul himself to his knees.

He was an elderly Mexican in a green plaid shirt and faded denims with patched knees and lace-up boots. His battered Stetson had rolled to the base of the hill near Prophet's feet.

"Bocangel?"

The man groaned as he sat back on his heels, pressing both hands against his left thigh. Prophet glanced around once more, then climbed the slope at an angle, loosing stones in his wake. "Why the hell you're tryin' to perforate my hide, old man?" he asked, reaching down and scooping the oldster's Springfield carbine out of the gravel.

"I didn't know it was you, Lou!"

"Who'd you think I was?"

"One of . . ." Bocangel gasped, gritting his teeth. ". . . them . . ." He flopped back, twisting around on his side as he passed out.

"One of who?" Prophet snarled, scowling down at the man.

Bocangel lay twisted back on his side at an awkward angle. A wing of his thick, black, silver-streaked hair covered one eye. Prophet tossed the man's rifle down the slope, then stooped to grab his arms and haul him up and over his left shoulder. Grunting and cursing and looking around warily for Mojaves, he headed on down the slope and made his way back the way he'd come. Bocangel was not a heavy load, but Prophet stopped twice on his way back to the saloon to look around, making sure he wasn't being shadowed.

The wind blew a furnace-like heat, peppering his face with grit. The moisture that had fallen last night was gone without a trace. Sweat slithered down Prophet's cheeks, pasted his buckskin shirt against his back.

Prophet made it back to the main street and continued over to the saloon, where

Chacin and his two remaining Rurales and Marshal Hawkins and the townsmen Le-Beouf and Blackwell were sitting on chairs they'd hauled out of the saloon, nursing beers and holding rifles.

"Well, I'll be damned," said Casey Blackwell, his watery gray eyes even more watery now from the beer. "I was wonderin' where that old coot was hiding out."

Prophet stopped on the veranda. "Why was he hiding out?"

"Who shot him?" Hawkins jumped in before Blackwell could reply.

"I did. He shot at me first."

The burly LeBeouf chuckled. "Didn't know the old goat had it in him."

"What were you doin' out there, anyways?" Hawkins asked, both eyes twitching as they bored into Prophet.

"Figured it was a nice day for a stroll." Prophet carried Senor Bocangel into the saloon, blinking as his eyes adjusted to the near darkness.

"Don't appreciate that, Prophet!" Hawkins walked in after the bounty hunter. "You and your people are restricted to the main street of this town and no farther!"

Prophet lay Bocangel down on a table just inside the door as Ivy came around from behind the bar with a bottle and a kitchen rag. "What happened to him?"

"I shot him." Prophet looked at Doc Shackleford, who was scowling back at him from over a plate of ham and eggs at the back of the room. The doctor had a Sharps carbine and a box of shells on the table near his plate, close to hand if the Mojaves came. "More business here, Doc."

Louisa sat at the table off the end of the bar, kicked back in her chair, boots crossed on the table, arms crossed on her chest. Kiljoy and Red Snake were on the other side of the room, playing cards and drinking tequila though it wasn't much past nine o'clock. Sugar Delphi stood at the bar, a cup of coffee in front of her. She was staring out the window beyond Louisa, her sightless eyes glowing eerily in the washed-out light of the street.

"Goddamnit!" Shackleford angrily cut into a thick slice of ham. "That bean-eatin' son of a bitch can wait. Next thing you know, you're gonna bring me his son and ask me to fix his worthless hide, as well!"

Bocangel was semiconscious and groaning, wagging his head back and forth atop the table.

"Come on, Doc," Ivy said, pouring some whiskey into the cloth and pressing the cloth to the bloody wound in the old Mexican's

268

skinny left thigh. "He's liable to bleed to death. I know you pill rollers take an oath of some sort or another. Haul your ass over here."

She looked at the bloody bandage wrapped around the man's right arm and glanced at Prophet, "Once wasn't good enough?"

"Mojave did his arm for him yesterday. He disappeared as soon as we came into town." Prophet looked at Hawkins and the other two townsmen who'd walked in behind the marshal. "What the hell you folks have against this man?"

"Look here, Prophet!" Hawkins pointed an admonishing finger at Prophet, his eyes furious. "You just stay out of this town's business! As long as you're here, you will remain right here in this saloon, and keep your questions to yourself. There ain't nothing about this town that's any of your damn business, you hear?"

Ivy's cajoling had worked. Shackleford had tossed his napkin down, took a last slug of coffee, and was ambling toward Bocangel's table, growling.

"Maybe they oughta hightail it right now," the doctor suggested with a snarl at Prophet. "That killer upstairs is likely gonna cash in his chips if he ain't already. I got Miss Tulsa watchin' him, but she likely nodded off. Her nerves are shot, and she said she was kept up half the night by that sergeant who had his tonsils removed the hard way."

Despite his rage, the doctor couldn't help chuckling at his joke. He brushed a fist against his nose as he crouched over Bocangel's wounded leg. "If you'd aimed a little more to the right, Mr. Prophet, you'd likely have severed the artery and saved me from eating a cold breakfast. As it is, looks like I'm going to have to clean this hole . . . looks like the bullet went all the way through, indeed . . . and sew *the gentleman* up."

"Hey, gringo." This from Captain Chacin standing in the open doorway behind Prophet and glaring at the sawbones. "What you got against Mexicans, uh?"

"Now, hold on, there, amigo," Hawkins said, flaring his nostrils at the Rurale and closing his hands over the grips of his holstered revolver. "If you're askin' for trouble, you just keep usin' that tone."

"You are in *Mejico* — *our* country," Chacin yelled, poking his thumb against his chest. "You will show us respect or it is *you* and your gringo friends we will run out of town, and take everything here for our own!" He glanced at Ivy standing near the

270

doctor and Bocangel and curled his lip.

Then he grunted, his seedy expression replaced by a sudden shocked glower. He stumbled forward suddenly, head jerking back, lower jaw dropping. He fell forward into Prophet's arms, a Mojave arrow sticking out of his back.

21

Prophet eased the quivering Chacin to the floor, then grabbed his rifle off the table beside Bocangel. Everyone in the room had jerked to attention, grabbing their weapons. Louisa had slammed her chair down and run to the front window, her own carbine in her hands.

Prophet racked a shell, pressed a shoulder to the side of the front doorframe, looking across the street to see a skinny brave in a white bandanna just then drawing back behind a small adobe-brick building with a barber pole right of the livery barn. Prophet fired, his slug blowing adobe shards from the side of the barbershop a full half second after the Mojave had disappeared.

Prophet's spent casing clattered onto the wooden floor behind him. Chacin groaned and cursed in Spanish. Kiljoy and Red Snake were crouched before the broken-out front window right of the door, breathing hard. Marshal Hawkins was crouched between them, turning his head sharply back and forth, long-barreled pistol extended out the window.

LeBeouf and Blackwell were out on the porch, both on one knee, swinging their extended guns up and down the street and then up toward the rooftops of the buildings on the street's other side.

"Where the hell are they?" Red Snake shouted, his voice pitched with anxious rage. "Where the hell are they? I'm so mad I'm pissin' lead!"

"Don't get up on your ear," Prophet told the tattooed brigand. "That's just what they want us to do. Piss away our ammo supply."

If the Indians remained persistent, he and the others might need more caps again soon.

Prophet and the others stared out the window, casting their gazes up and down the street, at the roofed well and into every nook and cranny in which a Mojave might be lurking. After a tense half a minute, LeBeouf and Blackwell scrambled nervously through the door, brushing past Prophet, and hunkering down behind the saloon's front wall.

The doctor was down behind Bocangel's table, leaving his half-conscious patient clearly exposed. Ivy knelt behind a chair, both hands on the back, her chocolate eyes rolling nervously. She looked at Prophet. "The back door," she said tonelessly.

Prophet pushed off the front doorframe and ran down the length of the saloon and through the door at the back. The door entered into a storeroom of dusty barrels and crates and a wooden door in the floor that likely indicated a root cellar.

Prophet continued through the musty darkness relieved only by a sashed window in each side wall and paused a foot before the saloon's rear door. It was a heavy, Z-frame door fixed to its frame with a nail and hasp. Light pushed between the cracks in the door's slightly warped boards and through the one-inch gap between the door and the floor.

Prophet waited, listening. He could hear only the wind scurrying around in the lot behind the saloon and the scratching sounds of the brush blowing up against the saloon's rear wall. The vague smell of flour and cured meat and old potatoes filled his nostrils, though he saw no sign of any food stores. The smells had likely remained in this pent-up place from when San Gezo was bustling. Stronger was the ammoniac smell of the privy that stood a hundred feet behind the saloon.

Prophet nudged the nail from the hasp with his rifle. He wrapped his hand around the door's iron handle, and pulled.

He had to jerk the door out of its shrunken frame. It vibrated a little when it came loose, its heavy hinges squawking. The gap opened. Prophet, standing a foot behind the threshold, stared out at the empty lot with the two-hole privy beyond and a pile of rotting lumber and two larger piles of split mesquite and pinyon pine.

An Indian stepped out from behind the wall on Prophet's left and into the open doorway. He was so close that Prophet could smell the rancid odor of the young savage, who had a round, fat face with blue and ochre war stripes painted across his nose.

He smiled, showing two chipped front teeth as he extended a saddle-ring carbine with a leather lanyard straight out from his waist. The gun exploded into the door that Prophet had just thrust closed. The slug tore through the door, flinging splinters and passing an inch to the left of Prophet's side.

Prophet opened the door again, fired his own Winchester from his waist, hammering a round at point-blank range through the Mojave's bared belly button. The brave screamed, dropped his carbine, and grabbed his belly with both hands as he leaped bizarrely off the ground, screaming. He landed awkwardly as he twisted around and dropped to his knees with his back to Prophet.

He slowly lowered his head as if in prayer, mewling as he died. Prophet spied movement behind the privy and stepped to one side of the door. Another Mojave was running away through a gap in the eroded, brush-stippled hills beyond the outhouse. Prophet held fire as the Indian disappeared.

Quick footsteps sounded to Prophet's right. He stepped out behind the saloon but lowered his Winchester when Louisa came around the corner, her own Winchester aimed out from her right shoulder. She lowered the gun, looked around, and dropped her eyes to the Mojave whom Prophet's slug had gutted.

"Too bad for him."

"There was another one. Probably more. Not showing themselves."

As he looked around at the privy and the woodpiles and the rocky hills rising behind the privy, he knew a creeping feeling in his bowels. He felt like a kid whose imagination was haunted by ghosts. Only the ghosts out here in this semi–ghost town were real. And they were Mojaves, the very worst kind of ghost a man could be haunted by.

And these ghosts seemed to be having a grand old time haunting him and the others holed up at Miss Ivy's.

"Any more up front?" Prophet asked Louisa.

"None showing themselves."

"We'd best check the livery barn. If they get the horses . . ."

Prophet walked back through the storage room and into the saloon's main hall, Louisa on his heels. Chacin was sitting up against the front wall holding a tequila bottle, one of the Rurale corporals standing nearby with a bloody rag in his hand, chuckling nervously.

"Figured you'd gone to your reward, Cap," Prophet said, genuinely surprised to see the man alive.

Chacin held up the arrow with its bloody tip. "Only went in a couple of inches. My bandolier broke its force." He took a long pull from the tequila bottle. "Still hurts like hell, though." He shook his head. His face was beaded with sweat, his mustache bright with it.

The captain and the corporal were the only two in the place. As Prophet stepped outside, he saw Sugar standing on the veranda, cradling a carbine in her arms. The others were scattered up and down the street, peering into breaks between buildings and into the buildings themselves.

"They're close," Sugar said. "I can smell 'em." She turned to Prophet. "How many were behind the saloon, bounty hunter?"

"Two." Prophet didn't bother asking her how she knew it was him standing beside her. She likely knew his smell and the sound of his tread.

She glanced across him to where Louisa stood to his left. Louisa didn't look at her, and Sugar didn't say anything. She turned her head forward and worked her nostrils like a cat, running the tip of her tongue along the underside of her upper lip.

"That hooligan still kickin'?" Prophet asked her, meaning Lazzaro.

Sugar smiled as she stared straight ahead. "Yes." She chuckled softly.

"Best haul your ass inside," Prophet said as he stepped off the veranda and into the street, Louisa following him. "Wouldn't wanna get your pretty head shot off."

Sugar told him to do something physically impossible to himself.

As Prophet crossed to the barn, the young Rurale standing near the Gatling's maw and peering apprehensively out the loft's open double doors, Prophet said, "I see where

278

you acquired your farm talk."

Louisa said nothing as Prophet went into the barn. The hoof-churned dust was soft and noiseless under his boots, though occasionally a piece of straw crackled quietly. The barn was long and narrow with here and there a ceiling support post behung with moldy tack covered in dust and cobwebs. The double rows of stalls on either side of the narrow alley were filled.

The horses snorted and stamped and nudged the stall partitions. Mean and Ugly, his eyes ringed with white, nodded at Prophet. The horse was tired of the close quarters and wanted to be on his way.

"Soon, Mean," Prophet said, running a hand down the horse's lumpy snout with its long, irregular white blaze. "At least, I hope soon."

Louisa leaned against the stall housing her nameless pinto. She held her carbine slanted down over her right arm, her right hand around the neck, index finger curved through the trigger guard. "Let's go now."

Prophet glanced at her. "What's that?"

"Let's pull foot, Lou. I'm tired of this town."

Prophet studied her, frowning. He wanted to ask her what was eating her, but something told him he didn't need to know. He knew it wasn't the Mojaves she wanted to run from. "Can't say as I admire it all that much myself. But I ain't leavin' without the money. If not the money, then at least them outlaws tied up good and tight and strung out behind Mean and Ugly's ugly ass."

She didn't say anything but just stood there, shoulder pressed against the stall door, an oblique look on her pretty face, hazel eyes shaded by her hat brim. Finally, she pushed away to retrieve grain and water, as Prophet did himself, and said, "Where'd you go earlier?"

"I walked out to inspect the mine north of town."

"What about it?"

"I don't know." Prophet poured a small bucket full of oats into Mean's trough, the horse rudely nudging him aside to get at the breakfast. "I thought maybe it would tell me why Hawkins doesn't want us here."

"Didn't the company pull out?"

"Yup."

"But you think there might still be gold in the mine."

Prophet hiked a shoulder. "Wouldn't be the first time a mine company pulled out, leaving a rich vein behind 'em. Not that it's any of my business. Curiosity killed the cat."

Louisa filled a wooden bucket from the

water barrel near the barn's open front doors. "Yeah, you best get that gold out of your brain. Hawkins ain't gonna like you snoopin' around."

"So he told me."

"Now don't go gettin' ornery and try to spite him. Stay away from that mine." Louisa splashed water into her pinto's water trough, then grabbed the front of Prophet's grimy buckskin shirt. "I mean it, Lou. We got enough troubles with the Mojaves. Let's stick to the plan and pull foot just as soon as we can get that loot and head for the border."

"I'll dally that." Prophet took the bucket from her and used it to water Mean. When he returned the bucket to the rain barrel, he said, "I reckon our main point of business for now best be to get all them Injuns off our trail." He picked up his rifle, which he'd leaned against Mean's stall door. "And you know what that means."

"Kill 'em all?"

"Kill or be killed, Miss Bonnyventure."

"It's *Bona*vent—" Louisa stopped and took a step back, scowling at the rafters over her head.

"What is it?" Prophet asked her.

Louisa doffed her hat, showed him the fresh blood staining the brim. They both looked up once more. Blood dribbled out between two ceiling boards. It looked like molasses and it sort of webbed down from the ceiling before forming a single drop that dripped to the soft earthen floor, puffing dust.

Prophet and Louisa exchanged a meaningful glance. Then Prophet walked over to the wooden rungs running up the far wall. He climbed the rungs into the hayloft with its mounded hay and straw and steeply pitched roof. The Gatling gun sat a few feet back from the open doors, a chair from the saloon behind it.

The Rurale corporal — the oldest of Chacin's remaining men — who'd last been manning the gun lay belly down in the straw beside it. His rifle lay beside him. His head was turned onto one cheek, arms hanging straight down against his sides. His leather-billed forage cap lay on the other side of the gun. His black hair was parted in the middle, the part showing the man's pale scalp.

Flies buzzed around him.

Louisa walked up to Prophet just as the bounty hunter kicked the body over, revealing the deep, grisly gash across the corporal's neck.

"Well, lookee there," Prophet said without

mirth. "Another sloppy tonsillectomy."

Louisa sighed. "I don't recollect hearing the poor man even complaining about a sore throat."

22

"Help me here," Prophet said, crouching and snaking his arms under those of the dead Rurale.

"What're we going to do with him?"

"Haul him out in the desert. We leave him here, he'll attract coyotes or mountains lions."

Awkwardly, they carried the dead corporal over to the three-by-three-foot hole in the loft floor and dropped the body through. They climbed down the wooden rungs, got another hold on the body, and, with the horses nickering their disdain for the smell of fresh blood, hauled the Rurale out the back door, past a wood pile and dilapidated privy and into the desert beyond.

Keeping an eye out for Mojaves, the bounty hunters carried the bloody Rurale's sagging carcass a good hundred yards from the barn. At the edge of a dry wash, they lay the body down.

Prophet stripped off the man's cartridge belt, which contained .44-40 shells for the Winchester carbine the man had carried, and looped the belt over his own shoulder. He hooked a boot over the dead man's bloody shoulder and rolled the man over the edge of the bank. The Rurale rolled, arms flopping, down the side of the bank to pile up at its base. Prophet stomped the overhanging earthen lip of the draw onto the body, then kicked a few rocks down, as well.

"That how you bury folks where you come from?" Louisa asked him, setting both hands on her pearl-gripped Colts as she looked around.

"If you wanna say a few words, go ahead." Prophet turned and had started back toward the barn.

Louisa touched his arm. "Hold on."

Prophet stopped and followed her gaze to the southwest. A lone, red-skinned rider sat an apron-sloped pedestal of red clay on the far side of another wash about a hundred yards away. Prophet couldn't see any details except the red flannel bandanna, quill choker, and the skewbald paint the big man was straddling. The Indian sat slightly forward on his blanket saddle, staring toward Prophet and Louisa. Slowly, he lifted the reins, turned the mount, and jogged down the far side of the knoll and out of sight.

"El Lightning?" Louisa said.

"Who else?"

"Menacing bastard, ain't he? What do you think he wants?"

Prophet studied on that for a time as he stared toward the clay pedestal where the Indian had sat his mustang. He looked around. Nothing out here but rocks and cactus and the occasional paloverde and mesquite clump. Good question. What did the Indian want here? Was it just white men's blood? Or something else?

Prophet raked a thumbnail down his beard stubble, adjusted his Colt thonged on his thigh, and tramped back toward the barn. He paused when he saw old Dad Conway standing behind the barn, staring suspiciously at Prophet and Louisa, fingering his grizzled chin whiskers. He had an old carbine hanging down his back by a rope lanyard, and a pistol strapped to his leg.

"What're you two doin' out there?" he asked.

"Lookin' around, Dad," Prophet said, narrowing his own suspicious eye. "That trouble you?"

The slouch-shouldered old man jerked his head back defensively. "Why should I be troubled if you're out lookin' to get yourselves perforated by Mojave arrows?"

"How you holdin' up, Dad?" Louisa asked the oldster. "This has been a lot of trouble for the old and feeble."

The old man bunched his lips and glared at the blond bounty hunter. "I'll show you old and feeble, you little — !"

"What's that sticking out of your pocket there?" Prophet interrupted him.

"Pocket where?"

"That pocket there!" Prophet walked up and shoved his hand toward the bone-handled knife sticking out of the man's patched duck trousers.

Dad jerked back, nearly stumbling, as he closed his hand over the pocket containing the knife. "Git away from me, damn ya!"

"Let me see the knife, Dad."

"No!"

Prophet towered over the pale, wizened oldster with long, coarse gray whiskers hanging from his knobby chin. "You ain't gonna make me throw you down and hogtie you, now, are you? Ain't you a little old for such silliness?"

Dad scowled up at Prophet, his eyes flicking across the bounty hunter's broad neck and rounded shoulders that drew his shirt taut across his muscular chest. He twitched a nostril and sucked his teeth, then reluctantly reached a gnarled, arthritic hand into the pocket and pulled out the folding barlow knife.

"So what?" The old man jutted his chin belligerently. "I see you carry a knife. Why can't I carry a knife?"

Prophet took the barlow knife out of the old man's hand and opened it. He inspected the blade, saw no blood even down around where the blade folded into the handle, and closed it. "I'm just wonderin' if it could have been you who slit the throat of the Rurale corporal manning the Gatling gun . . . oh, say, a half hour to an hour ago. Blood was still comin' out of him when me and Louisa found him."

"I didn't cut no Rurale's throat, and I'm hurt that you'd accuse me. Hell, I can't even climb up the veranda steps without gettin' all dizzy an' short of breath! How could I kill a young man?"

He stuffed the knife back down in his pocket, spat a wad of chew into a cholla clump, and grumbled as he ambled over to the dilapidated privy. He glanced once more at Prophet and Louisa as he jerked the door open. "Me? Cut a man's throat?"

He gave a shrill, caustic chuff, then stepped up into the privy with a grunt and pulled the door closed behind him. The locking nail clattered as he pushed it through its hasp.

"He's got a point, Lou," Louisa said.

"Yeah, I reckon. No blood on the blade, neither." Prophet turned around to stare south, doffing his hat and scratching the back of his head. "Throat cutters, Injuns, Rurales, curly wolves — I swear, I do believe the Devil's laughin' at me. My life ain't s'posed to be this hard."

"Life's always hard, Lou. You just prefer to ignore it and drink and diddle easy women."

Prophet glanced at her. She glanced away from him quickly, tightened her face and narrowed her eyes. "That ain't none of your business," he said, piqued.

"What ain't?"

"You know what I'm talkin' about, Miss Huffy Pants."

Prophet swung around and, deeply frustrated over everything that had happened over the past week, strode on back to the barn. He retrieved the Gatling gun as well as his rifle from the loft and hauled the machine gun across the street.

Several of the other men were standing at

different points along both sides of the main street and near the well, dusters or the bell bottoms of their charro slacks blowing in the endless wind. They eyed Prophet with mute interest as he climbed the veranda steps. He hauled the Gatling gun inside the saloon and looked around.

"What the hell you doing, Prophet?" Chacin said from a table in the room's shadows. He sat with a tequila bottle and a shot glass on the table beside him.

"Got more use for this thing over here, where we can keep a close eye on it," Prophet said, setting the Gatling down against the front wall and spreading the wooden legs of its tripod.

Chacin sipped from his shot glass and winced, his back wound grieving him. "I had a man keeping an eye on it."

"Found your man grinning through his throat. Buried him to keep predators out of the barn."

Chacin dipped his chin and glowered suspiciously at the bounty hunter, who turned the Gatling gun toward the blown-out front window right of the doors. Prophet sat down at a table near the gun and glanced at Ivy standing at the bar chopping a wild onion for stew.

She was looking at him between the wings

of her long, curly black hair jostling about her pretty, chocolate-colored face with its lustrous but fateful black eyes.

"Got any coffee over there?" Prophet asked her.

She set the knife and onion down on the chopping board and turned to fill a stone mug. She brought it over to Prophet, set it down on the table. Prophet took a whiff of the steam. As Ivy raked her intimate gaze across Prophet once quickly, then turned back to the bar, he said, "I sure would admire to know who's killin' the captain's men."

He said it nonchalantly, as though he were merely speaking to himself.

Chacin turned to the woman and curled his upper lip. *"Si."* His voice had a growl in it. "Perhaps an Indian."

"An Indian would have used the gun on us, or at least taken the ammo."

"How do you know it ain't the captain himself," Ivy said, returning to the cutting board. "How do you know it ain't your blond partner, or Red Snake or Kiljoy?"

"Well, I know it ain't Louisa," Prophet said, sipping his coffee and staring out the blown-out window with ragged bits of glass sticking out of its frame. Louisa herself was standing at the livery barn's right front corner, holding her carbine and looking around, the wind blowing her hair.

"She ain't that messy," Prophet continued. "As for Red Snake or Kiljoy — hell, I don't know. I reckon it could have been them. Don't know why they'd go about it so underhanded, though. Those rannies're cold-steel artists, not blade men. And I thought we were all gettin' along so good."

"Hawkins." Chacin threw back the last of his tequila shot, lifted his pistol from the table before him, and spun the cylinder across his forearm.

"Now, don't get owly, Captain," Prophet warned. "As long as them Injuns outnumber us, we're gonna need every gun we got."

"And let Hawkins and the other citizens of San Gezo knock us off one at a time?"

"Now, hold on!" Ivy said, holding her hands up — one holding the onion, the other the knife. She glanced at the knife, and her face turned darker. "I chop food, not men's throats. At least, I haven't had to cut a man's throat in several years now."

She continued chopping the onion, tossing it into a heavy iron stew pot and staring with wry bemusement across the room at Prophet.

Prophet snorted, sat back in his chair, sipped his coffee, then dug into his shirt pocket for his makings sack. Slowly, thoughtfully, he plucked his cigarette papers out of the sack and began rolling a smoke.

Who had killed Frieri?

Who had killed the corporal?

Why?

The afternoon drew on. Prophet sat in the chair near the Gatling gun, ready to fire at the first sign of an Indian attack. The others patrolled the streets, visiting the saloon now and then for coffee or a drink of something stiffer, or for the stew of canned meat and tomatoes that Ivy had bubbling on her range.

Chacin and Sugar Delphi were the only two who remained in the saloon, Sugar quietly playing a game of solitaire with marked cards. Chacin drank and walked to each window from time to time, holding his long-barreled pistol as he anxiously looked out at the street. The wound in his back made him lean slightly forward and wince.

The wind sawed and wheezed. It blew sand through the broken windows and moaned under the eaves. It was a hot, dry wind, and by mid-afternoon it had tattered Prophet's nerves the way lightning frays the limbs of a ponderosa pine.

He began to side with Louisa. Maybe he and the blond Vengeance Queen should pull foot out of San Gezo, after all. But even if they could bring themselves to abandon the money and the brigands, the Indians had them trapped here. First, they had to neutralize the Indian threat. Then they had to find the stolen loot and take down Red Snake, Kiljoy, and Sugar. And Lazzaro, if he was still alive.

The wind bounced tumbleweeds along the street and beneath the rotting hitchracks, sounding like the Devil having a tail-wagging good time on a Dodge City Friday night. The deal was that Prophet would have the good times between a modicum of relatively easy work stints, hunting outlaws. Ole Scratch appeared to be reneging on his deal, the bastard. This here job wasn't easy at all.

The big bounty hunter's chance of getting himself and Louisa out of this powder keg was very slim indeed, and he was still relatively young. If he cashed in his chips now, he'd be missing out on years of easy women and good times.

When Louisa came in for a drink, he said, "Take over here, will you, killer?"

"What're you gonna do?"

"Haven't seen Lazzaro or Senor Bocangel in a while," Prophet said, donning his hat and shouldering his rifle. "Gonna go up and see if there's anything I can do to make 'em more comfortable."

Sugar called as Prophet started up the stairs, "Best make sure my honey ain't grinnin' with his throat when you leave him, bounty hunter." She kept peeling cards off the deck in her left hand and arranging them on the table. "I'll be checking."

23

Prophet had just turned off the stairs and started down the second-story hall when he heard a man grunting and cursing farther down the dingy corridor that smelled of rotting wood, coal oil, and sweat. A woman was groaning and also cursing. Bedsprings were squawking raucously, rhythmically.

Prophet continued along the hall, walking on the balls of his feet. Ahead and on his right, a door stood cracked, showing a vertical line of gray light.

"Goddamnit!" the man shouted suddenly.

There was the loud *whump!* of a heavy body hitting the floor. Prophet felt the floor quake beneath his boots. The woman yelped, *"Ah-ohh . . . damn youuuu!"*

"Bitch!"

"You got no . . . you got no call to —" The woman broke herself off. Prophet stepped up to the crack in the door and peered into the room.

Just beyond the door, Miss Tulsa was on the floor, naked as a jaybird, her soft, pale back with a heavy roll of flesh around her middle facing Prophet. Her red hair was piled loosely atop her head. Cursing and crying, she crawled on hands and knees to a chair between a washstand and the bed upon which Tony Lazzaro was writhing naked amidst the mess of twisted sheets and a quilt. He was clutching his bloody side with one hand, the blood dribbling from between his fingers and staining the bed.

"I'll teach you to treat Miss Tulsa like she was dirt, you limp-dicked son of a bitch!"

The whore had grabbed an ivory-gripped pistol from Lazzaro's shell belt. She had it in both hands now, and she cursed again as she ratcheted back the hammer. Lazzaro stared at her fearfully, eyes widening as he rolled back against the wall and raised his hands palm out.

"I'll take that," Prophet said, reaching over the whore's head and closing his hands around the Smith & Wesson, wedging his left thumb between the gun and the cocked hammer.

The whore screamed as Prophet pulled the gun out of her hands, and depressed the hammer. She glared angrily up at Prophet. "Damn you — I'm gonna kill that lizard.

Miss Tulsa will *not* be treated this way! I'm tellin' Ivy!"

"Fair enough." Prophet flicked the Smithy's loading gate open and shook the gun as he rolled the cylinder, the shells clinking and rolling around the floor. "You best go downstairs, Miss Tulsa. Obviously, your services are wasted in here."

"She opened my wound!" Lazzaro said, wincing and pressing one of the bed's two pillows to his side. "Fetch Sugar for me, will you, Proph?"

Prophet looked at Miss Tulsa stumbling around heavy, naked, and breathless, gathering her clothes from the floor. "Send Sugar when you get downstairs, Tulsa."

"Fuck you!" Tulsa screeched at the bloody outlaw as she threw open the door, holding her clothes against her pillowy breasts and glaring over her shoulder at Prophet. "And *fuck you, too, bounty hunter!*"

As the whore stomped out of the room and headed down the hall toward her own digs, Prophet said, "Don't worry, Tony. I'll send Sugar." He grinned and winked. "Wanna make sure you're well taken care of."

"You better, damnit!"

"Feelin' all right, ain't ya? I mean besides a little lost blood an' all?"

Lazzaro squeezed his eyes closed, panting as he pressed the pillow against his side. "I'm feelin' just fine."

"If you think you'll be kickin' off soon," Prophet said, "you might as well go ahead and tell ole Lou where you had Sugar bury the loot. I mean, why let Red Snake and Kiljoy get it all? They'll just head on down to Mexico and blow it on cheap whores."

Lazzaro scowled at Prophet, hardening his jaws. "Just send Sugar."

"All right."

Prophet went out and yelled down the stairs, summoning Sugar to Lazzaro's room, then walked down the second-story hall once more. He knew that Senor Bocangel was in room 8, on the left side of the hall and one door down from where Lazzaro was groaning and making the bedsprings squawk.

He rapped two knuckles against the door panel. No response. He stared at the scarred panel, feeling a tightening of apprehension.

Could Senor Bocangel have met the same fate as Frieri and the corporal? Prophet released the keeper thong from over his pistol hammer and rapped on the door once more.

Still nothing.

Prophet turned the knob. There being no

locks on any of the saloon's doors, Prophet heard the latch click. He shoved the door wide, standing in the opening with his right hand on his Colt, his Winchester propped on his left shoulder. The door stopped before it would have struck the wall. Bocangel lay on the bed against the far wall, beneath a curtained window that the wind was battering.

Prophet walked forward.

Bocangel lay beneath a threadbare white sheet drawn up to his chin. His wool shirt was draped over the back of the room's sole chair angled near the bed. Bocangel was snoring softly through half-parted lips, eyes squeezed shut. Out cold. On the dresser against the left wall were several bloody cloths and a flat, corked bottle of liquid paregoric that the sawbones had left.

No wonder the Mexican was out cold. The tension knot in Prophet's belly eased, replaced with frustration.

He'd wanted to see if he could learn from Bocangel why'd he'd ambushed Prophet earlier. He had a sneaking suspicion that the cause of the Mexican's desperate move was also at the heart of the trouble here in San Gezo. At least the trouble that had been here when Prophet and his mismatched party had arrived ahead of the Indians.

Bocangel hadn't wanted Prophet to visit the mine. He had a feeling the others in the town didn't, either.

Prophet went out and gently closed the door, opening and closing his hand around the neck of the Winchester propped now on his right shoulder. He went over and looked out the window at the end of the hall on his left. The windblown grit gave the light an orangish, washed-out appearance. It ticked against the window and tossed the brittle desert shrubs this way and that.

From this angle, he could see the gap between the hotel and the next, smaller building to the east. He could also see the main street off to his far right. Red Snake Corbin was leaning up against a porch post on the street's far side, looking around warily for Indians and smoking a quirley, which he shielded with the palm of his hand. His long duster blew about his skinny legs clad in dusty black denim.

Marshal Bill Hawkins was just now walking up from between two buildings near Red Snake, holding a rifle up high across his chest, his black clawhammer coat blowing out like a giant bat's wing in the wind. Hawkins and the other townsmen would be sticking close to the saloon, since that seemed to be the Indians' target. If Prophet was careful, he could make his way out of the town without being seen by anyone.

Including the Mojaves, he hoped.

A foolish move, probably. But again he felt a strong pull toward the mine.

He walked back downstairs and slipped through the saloon's rear door without being seen. Kiljoy was outside, hunkered on one knee, smoking and looking ridiculous with the bandage around his face but appearing to be keeping a watchful eye out for Mojaves. He couldn't care less what Prophet was up to. The two glanced at each other coldly.

"Nice day for a walk," Kiljoy said.

"Yeah, ain't it."

Snugging his hat down tight on his head, Prophet made his way east of the hotel, walking along behind the other buildings until the rugged desert opened before him. Staying out of sight from the town, he retraced his earlier steps, cutting up the arroyo in which the Mojave brave had drilled his boot heel.

He moved carefully, every two or three steps swinging nearly completely around with his rifle aimed out from his hip, watching for bushwhacking braves. He saw nothing but a few spiders, jackrabbits, one coyote, and blowing weeds and dust as he made his way past where Senor Bocangel had tried to drill him.

Striding along the narrow wash, he moved around the bend, swinging east. Ahead, the canyon walls fell back on both sides, broadening the canyon floor. The walls rose higher.

The wagon trail leading from the town to the mine was on his left — deeply grooved from the heavy, double-shod wheels of the ore drays. But from his vantage in the brush and rocks along the trail, he could see no fresh tracks. The grooves were partly filled in with dust and sand and bits of weeds. Tumbleweeds littered the trail, and creosote, yucca, and jimsonweed had grown up between the ruts.

If the mine had been used recently, it hadn't been reached via the old road from San Gezo.

The wind moaned between the canyon's high walls. It was like a saw working on Prophet's nerves. He gritted his teeth and slitted his eyes against it, paused to look around carefully between the wind-buffeting witches' fingers of cholla stalks, then kept walking.

The mine lay two hundred yards inside the canyon, about a third of the way up the slope on his right. The trail wound up to it along a graded bed. There wasn't much to see of the mine but a portal that had obviously been caved in at the back of a small shelf carved out of the mountain.

Below the shelf lay a massive tailings pile and a jumble of iron and gray-weathered wood that was likely all that remained of the stamping mill, tipple, and tramway that had been used to crudely process the ore before it had been loaded onto drays and hauled across the desert to San Diego. Around the rubble were also the bleached white bones doubtlessly belonging to mules that had pulled the drays and that often dropped dead due to exhaustion or poor tending.

Prophet had been to many mines, and they were hard, merciless places for man and beast. This one, however, hadn't been worked in at least five years. He didn't have to climb the slope to see that. Not even a shod hoofprint marked the soft sand anywhere around the base of the tailings slope.

Hooves thudded behind Prophet. He whipped around. Three Indians on spotted ponies galloped around the bend in the canyon floor.

Prophet mumbled a curse and looked around for cover. There was nothing near that could conceal him.

Up the slope about fifteen yards was a wagon-sized boulder that angled out away from the ridge. He scrambled up the slope, breathing hard, hearing the hoof thuds growing louder, the Indians howling. Rifles cracked. Bullets spanged off rocks around Prophet's feet.

He threw himself behind the boulder.

Only, behind the boulder there was nothing but a ragged hole in the ground.

Prophet fell through it, knowing in the back of his mind he'd just thrown himself down an exploratory mine shaft. The shaft didn't plunge straight down. He bounced and rolled, losing his rifle and feeling rocks hammering him about the ribs, head, and shoulders. The angle was steep enough that he couldn't stop his momentum.

He hit the bottom of the shaft with a loud explosion of air from his hammered lungs.

He lay on his back, breathing hard, hearing spring robins chirping in his ears. His head spun. Fireworks flared behind his squeezed-shut eyelids.

When he finally opened his eyes and began to hear the chirping receding but feeling that every rib in his body was poking through his chest, he saw something angling up beside him. A root?

No.

Prophet grimaced, silently cursed, when he realized that what he was staring at was a human hand. The fingers formed a hideous, pale claw that was reaching for him.

24

"What the *hell*!"

Prophet got his heels and hands beneath him and scuttled a few feet away from the large, pale hand hovering over him, until the back of his head and his right shoulder smacked the hole's stone side wall. His right elbow pushed against something yielding, and he turned to see what appeared to be a tan wool vest.

The stench in the hole was nearly suffocating, and Prophet felt his eyes watering as he realized that the tan vest was worn by a dead man. The vest was blood-matted, and it was swollen over the bloated belly it covered.

Prophet looked to his left, saw the hand he'd seen before. It had a gold ring set with a square, brown stone. It protruded from a white shirt cuff. It belonged to another dead man who lay sideways against a rock, the arm and the clawlike hand sort of propped against it. The hand was no longer moving, and Prophet realized that he had made the hand move because his legs had been resting across the dead man's.

The sickly sweet stench of human decay made him suck a shallow breath and make a face as he rose onto his elbows, wincing against the burning aches in his ribs and hips and the back of his neck. He saw his rifle lying against the wall several feet away, beyond the legs of the body to his right.

His aching head swirled, unable yet to fully fathom his grim discovery. Dead men . . . here . . . ?

Had the mine collapsed, trapping miners?

The thought was snuffed by a sound from above. He looked toward the opening of the hole at the top of the steeply slanted shaft. He couldn't see the entire opening from his vantage, because of a lip of rock above him. He could make out about half of it, and the silhouette of a head staring down at him from the hole's lip, long hair hanging around the Indian's shoulders.

"Hey, white man!" a deep voice shouted. "Hey, you down there — you thieving bastard! You dead?"

The voice was so unlike what Prophet had expected from a Mojave that for a half a second he thought that someone other than the Indian staring down at him must have spoken. It was the voice of a white man with a slight Spanish accent.

Prophet stared skeptically up at the hole. He didn't think the Indian could see him down here in the darkness where little light probed. His eyes continuing to water, he held himself still, taking shallow breaths through his mouth.

"Where's the gold, gringo? Huh? Where'd you boys hide it?"

Still, Prophet said nothing as he frowned up at the ragged-edged hole and the head of the Indian — El Lightning? — staring down at him.

Gold?

Finally, the Indian gave a disgusted chuff. His head rose as he straightened. He angled a rifle down toward Prophet, and the bounty hunter jerked his head and knees back, rolling up against the wall behind him as orange flames lapped from the Indian's rifle.

Bam! Bam! Bam!

The reports echoed flatly, the slugs screeching off the rocks about six feet in front of Prophet. About ten seconds after the last echoing crash, he heard a fateful grunt. A stone and some gravel dropped into the pit, thudding and clattering on the rocks — as though it had been accidentally kicked there. Prophet looked up at the ragged mouth of the shaft he was in. The Indian was gone.

The wind moaned hollowly across the opening.

Prophet took a deep breath, shook his head at the fumes of putrefaction, and rose painfully to his hands and knees. He took quick stock of his condition, deciding that while he was badly battered, no bones were broken. Maybe a cracked rib or two, but he'd live.

Looking around at the two dead men, he lifted his bandanna across his nose and mouth, then crawled over to the man on his right — the one wearing a tan vest under a dark brown suit jacket. The body was badly bloated, including the face that had a yellow, gray-flecked mustached mantling its mouth. The man's pale blue eyes were open.

Prophet saw that he'd taken two bullets to the chest. He frowned at something poking out from beneath the man's left coat lapel, then reached down and with his gloved hand flipped the lapel back to reveal the sun-and-moon copper badge of a deputy United States marshal.

Prophet turned his startled gaze on the man with the upraised, clawlike hand, then saw that there was yet a third man lying beyond Clawhand. Prophet crawled the few feet over and saw, after he'd rolled the second body over, that Clawhand had an eye blown out. There was another bullet in his cheek, a third in his right hip over which a cheap, gold-washed timepiece dangled.

This man was older, grayer, his eyes a liquid gray blue, and he had a thick, dragoon-style mustache that hung down over the sides of his mouth. His lips were gray and wrinkled and stretched back from his long yellow teeth — a death snarl.

He, too, wore the copper badge of a deputy U.S. marshal.

As did the third man, Prophet saw a few seconds later. The third man — short and stocky, with thick, curly muttonchop whiskers — wore a long tan duster. One of the duster's torn pockets was bulging. What appeared to be papers peaked out of the top of the pocket.

Prophet reached down and pulled out the rolled sheaf of paper, removed a string and unrolled the papers. He felt his eyes bulge as he rocked back on his heels, sucking the bandanna in and out of his mouth as he breathed.

The face on the wanted circular staring up at him was that of Marshal Bill Hawkins, an evil leer on his lips; each etched eye seemed to be staring off in different directions. The name on the circular, just below the one thousand dollars being offered for bounty, was Hawk Johnson. He was wanted for "wanton thievery, cold-blooded murder, and the general harassment of law-abiding citizens" along the West Coast of the United States.

Prophet's heart thudded as he tossed the circular aside and stared down at the next one in the stack. His heart beat faster.

The face staring up at him now was none other than that of Ivy Miller, whom the lurid writing on the dodger called the "Negro murderess and common bank robber Thelma Knight." She also had one thousand dollars on her pretty head.

Prophet tossed Ivy's dodger aside and perused the rest of them one by one, reading off the names aloud to himself. Most of the others, maybe less well known than Johnson and Knight, were still using their actual names — Casey Blackwell, H. A. "Doc" Shackleford (who, indeed, had a doctor of medicine degree from King's College but who was also wanted for murder, bank robbery, "and other sundry barbarisms"), George Wentz (who called himself LeBeouf here in San Gezo), and Bernard "Dad" Conway, who had once ridden with Bloody Bill Anderson during the Civil War and who "had not lost the taste for savage violence in the years since Appomattox."

Prophet chuckled to himself when he saw the face on the last dodger — Tulsa St. James, who had a string of other aliases all listed on the circular offering seven hundred dollars "dead or alive." According to the dodger, she was a "dove du pave" and "throat-cutting murderess in cahoots with the notorious Negro murderess Thelma Knight."

Somewhere, for some reason, the various brigands from both sexes had thrown in together. Prophet remembered *El Lightning* asking about gold, obviously believing that Prophet was "in cahoots" with Johnson, Knight, Dad, Doc, and the others.

So, they'd stolen gold and, like he and his own ragtag bunch, were holed up here with it. Maybe the Indians had waylaid them or maybe they were waiting for their trail to grow cold before heading south, deeper into Mexico or maybe even to South America. These three dead lawmen had come after them and got themselves shot up and thrown in a hole.

Somehow, El Lightning and his bronco ilk had learned of the gold and wanted their share. Maybe all of it. Tulsa St. James had cut Frieri's and the corporal's throats to possibly further befuddle and frighten the others, maybe convincing them to ride on out of San Gezo. Thelma Knight had likely put the kill-crazy whore up to it, because it was easier, less risky than trying to kill the gang outright.

And Tulsa was so good at what she did. And a damn good actress, too, Prophet thought, remembering how frightened she'd looked when she'd seen Frieri lying dead beside her. She'd been about to drill Lazzaro with his own pistol, but who would have blamed her for that, after how nastily the wounded outlaw had treated her?

Eventually, the big redhead might have rid the town of all the newcomers, one by one.

Prophet chuckled.

Realization was like a cool, fresh breeze clearing the soot and coal dust from his battered, befuddled brain. On the heels of the realization, however, came a wintery chill prickling the hairs along his spine.

Johnson, Knight, and the others were holed up in the saloon with Louisa, who had no idea who in hell they were. Or what they were capable of. Prophet didn't much care about the others. But the idea that

Louisa was in that Devil's den sent Prophet reaching for his rifle, donning his battered hat, and starting up the steep wall of the shaft.

Holding his rifle with one hand, he climbed, hoisting himself with his free hand and his feet. He grunted and cursed his way up the side of the shaft. He was about fifteen feet from the dead men at the bottom when he grabbed a rock and started to pull.

The rock came out of the wall with a jerk.

"Ahhh, shi . . . !"

Prophet flew back off the wall, dropping his rifle.

He hit the bottom of the shaft, smacking his head on a rock. He lay on his back, belly rising and falling sharply as he breathed. He lifted his head, tried to put some weight on his elbows to push himself up, but his arms turned to water.

His eyes crossed. The hole became a watery blur.

He fell back against the ground, and his eyes closed. But in his brain he continued to spiral down, down into even deeper darkness.

Louisa cranked the Gatling gun's lever.

Bam-bam-bam-bam-bam!

The Indian that had just run out from the far side of the barbershop dove behind the well as Louisa's slug blew up dust at his moccasined heels. He poked the top of his head up above the edge of the well.

Bam-bam-bam-bam-bam!

His head jerked back as several of the Gatling's slugs tore through the bandanna, making a splash of color against his dark red face. The corner of the building behind him turned red as the bullets threw him back against it. He slumped to one side, jerked a foot, and lay still.

"Damn, you're good with that thing, Leona!" cried Kiljoy, who'd been relieved from his back-door guard duties by Red Snake.

Louisa stared out over the Gatling's smoking maws, perusing the street. "It's Louisa. And . . . thank you."

"Yeah, that's right," Kiljoy said, glowering as he remembered that she'd double-crossed him and the rest of his gang. "Louisa, not Leona. Gotta remember that."

Louisa swung a look at the man standing over her right shoulder, staring into the street from between the strips of bandage wrapped around his head and knotted beneath his chin, giving him the bizarre look of an ugly, overgrown toddler in a sun cap.

"Sit down, Kiljoy," she told the brigand. "You're making me nervous."

Kiljoy looked at her. "You oughta be nervous. 'Cause once we're finished with these Injuns —"

"Sit down, Roy!" This from Sugar, who'd resumed her quiet game of solitaire after she'd gone up to Lazzaro's room and re-wrapped his wound.

Doc Shackleford sat at the table with the blind woman, reading an old, yellowed newspaper on the table before him, round-rimmed glasses perched on his hawk-like nose. His carbine lay atop the table beside the paper. The doctor chuckled and shook his head, making no other comment.

Captain Chacin sat back against the wall opposite the bar, an arm hooked over the back of his chair, one black boot hiked on a knee. He leaned back against a pillow cushioning the arrow wound. He was look-ing around the room amusedly, taking it all in. His lone surviving Rurale cohort was out on patrol somewhere in the town.

When Kiljoy had retaken his own seat on the other side of the room from Louisa, the Vengeance Queen continued to swing the Gatling from left to right, appraising the street. Frowning thoughtfully, she looked at the Indian she'd just shot and the several others who lay where they'd fallen earlier and had been relieved of their ammunition.

"Persistent, aren't they?" She turned to Marshal Hawkins, who sat at a table near the bar with Ivy Miller, both of whom were nursing whiskies and keeping quiet counsel. The other townsmen — LeBeouf, Dad, and Blackwell — were stationed at various points around San Gezo, taking potshots at any Mojaves they ran across.

Tulsa St. James was in her room, still in a snit over Lazzaro's rough handling.

Hawkins returned Louisa's look. "Are they? I reckon I don't know a Mojave that ain't, when it comes to killin' white men."

"Besides," Ivy said, setting her shot glass on the table before her and regarding Louisa coolly. "You're the ones who brought them here, aren't you?"

"Are we?" Louisa said. "Or maybe they were already gathering out on the desert, planning a strike on San Gezo, and we just stumbled into their powwow."

"Now, that's a thought!" intoned Chacin.

The wind had covered the approach of someone behind Louisa on the other side of the blown-out window. She didn't hear a board squawk under a stealthy boot until it was too late.

Two arms wrapped around her, pinning

her arms to her sides, lifting her out of the chair and out the window.

She kicked and grunted through gritted teeth, losing her hat in the fray.

"Whoa, now, darlin'!" said the blond-haired townsman, Blackwell, with a laugh as he nuzzled Louisa's neck. "You're just too purty a little she-cat to be ignored any longer!" He laughed and gripped Louisa's writhing body tighter. "Hawk, you need me, we'll be upstairs!"

A gun thundered from inside the saloon.

Instantly, Blackwell's arms slackened.

Louisa heard the man gurgle in her ear. She glanced over her shoulder to see his eyes rolling back into his head as if to look at the quarter-sized hole in his right temple, just below his hairline.

He tried to clutch at Louisa, then fell to the veranda floor. Louisa stumbled forward and peered into the saloon, where Sugar Delphi stood behind her table, holding the stock of a smoking Winchester carbine against her shoulder.

25

Save for the moaning wind and the squawking of rusty shingle chains up and down the
dusty street, a heavy, nervous silence hung
over the Oasis.

Louisa stared at Sugar, who just now
lowered her carbine slightly, staring in
Louisa's general direction, and ejected the
spent shell from the Winchester's chamber.
As she seated a fresh one, Louisa looked
around the room — every man in the place
as well as Ivy Miller was staring at Sugar in
shock and extreme dismay. All the men
except Chacin, that was. The Rurale captain
smiled with one side of his mouth, twisting
an upswept curl of his mustache between
his thumb and index finger and showing a
yellow fang beneath it.

Kiljoy's eyes darted to each of the townsfolk. As short, broad, and ugly as he was, he
looked small and alone and badly outnumbered. The townsfolk shuttled their own

hostile glances from Sugar to Kiljoy and then to Louisa and Captain Chacin, both of whom they sort of lumped in with Lazzaro's bunch, since they'd ridden into town together.

"Guess what?" Doc Shackleford said, standing tall and dour and cold-eyed beside his table, taking one step from Sugar and raising an over-and-under, pearl-gripped derringer in each of his large, sun-leathered fists.

"Now, hold on," Chacin said cautiously, stiffening his wounded back and holding both hands up shoulder high, palms out.

"What's that, Doc? Spill it. Ain't no such thing as a stupid question." Kiljoy grinned though he sounded tense, holding both his hands over his holstered pistols — one on his thigh, another positioned for the cross draw on his left hip. He had a third one shoved down behind the waistband of his doeskin trousers. Even with both bandaged holes in his face, he looked eager to use the hoglegs.

"I do believe you and yours done wore out your welcome here in San Gezo — wouldn't you say, Hawk?" the sawbones said, shuttling his cold blue eyes toward the marshal.

"Hawk?" Sugar said. "Is that short for

321

Hawkins? Or could it be Hawk Johnson?"

Oh, shit, Louisa thought. *Here we go. . . .*

Another pregnant silence. Then Hawkins or Johnson or whoever in hell he was flared his nostrils and slapped leather, bringing up a long-barreled six-shooter.

Sugar triggered her carbine in the marshal's general direction then threw herself over a table to her left, turning the table over, which acted as a shield as the marshal and Doc Shackleford triggered lead into it. Behind her, Chacin cursed loudly in Spanish and tried to make himself small behind a ceiling support post.

Sugar hit the floor and rolled out of Louisa's sight as Kiljoy dropped to a knee, filling both his hands with blazing iron.

Louisa dropped below the window and extended her matched Colts over the bottom ledge into the saloon, seeing the marshal drop to a knee and begin triggering lead toward Sugar, Kiljoy, and Captain Chacin. Ivy pumped and triggered a carbine from behind the bar, her black eyes blazing as bright as her Winchester.

Louisa saw that Ivy was bearing down on Sugar, and fired two rounds that plunked into the bar top in front of Ivy. The black woman cursed shrilly and pulled her head down behind the bar as both Shackleford and Hawkins began firing at Louisa, who pulled her head down below the window. Bullets screeched through the air above her head and chewed slivers from the window ledge.

Louisa spied movement on the street to her left and turned to see Dad Conway and George LeBeouf running toward the saloon. They both looked anxious and fearful, holding rifles up high across their chests. Louisa was about to trigger shots to forestall them, but then suddenly Marshal Hawkins shouted, *"Hold on! Hold on, now! Beefin' each other ain't gonna do any of us a damn bit of good!"*

The shooting inside the saloon dwindled. Louisa remained crouched on the veranda, below the window, holding both her cocked Colts on Dad and LeBeouf, who'd stopped dead in their tracks when they'd seen the blond bounty hunter bearing down on them with her silver-chased six-shooters.

Inside, one more pistol popped. There was a short silence. Louisa could smell the rotten-egg odor of burned powder.

Kiljoy said, "Johnson, that you?"

"It's me," said the man formerly known as Bill Hawkins. He chuckled. "I reckon it's time to stop runnin' around the church privy. You in?"

"Hold on!" said Ivy in an indignant voice. "Shouldn't we talk this over, Hawk?"

"What's to talk over, Ivy? We're out-gunned by 'Paches. And I, for one, am damn tired of this town. With the help of Lazzaro's bunch, we might be able to make a run for Puerto Penasco."

"I'm for that," said a woman's voice.

Louisa lifted her eyes above the window, saw Tulsa St. James standing on the stairs at the back of the room. She held two pistols in her chubby fists. "A girl never quite feels clean in such a dirty place. And all these empty buildings give me the creeps! I say we bring 'em in and haul ass!"

A short silence. Louisa saw that Red Snake had entered via the room's back door and was hunkered on his haunches against the back wall, holding his Henry rifle's butt against his thigh. He'd entered the game late, and he looked confused but also wound up. Johnson lifted his head over a chair back, raking the room with his twitching eyes. Then he looked at Kiljoy. "Got any thoughts, Roy?"

"What you got, Johnson?"

"Gold," said Ivy Miller over the bar top. "Enough to set us all up high for the rest of our lives."

Kiljoy glanced at Chacin still hunkered

behind the ceiling support post. "What about the Rurale?"

Chacin turned to Kiljoy and then to Johnson. He smiled with half of his mouth again. "For the right price, amigos, I am a Rurale in uniform only." His grin grew wider, eyes brightening. "How much gold are we talking about, Senor Johnson?"

"You heard Ivy."

"All right," Kiljoy said. "What about Leona and Prophet?"

All eyes turned to Louisa, who knelt in the window, extending both cocked Colts into the saloon. She said nothing. No one did for a time. Then Sugar picked herself up off the floor and brushed broken glass and dust from her leather pants. "Don't worry about Leona." She turned her blind eyes toward Louisa. "She's one of us."

"And Prophet?" Louisa said, arching a dubious brow as she stared into the room over her cocked Colts.

"He could be a problem," Red Snake said from the shadows at the back of the room. "And you know what I've always said about problems."

Kiljoy said, "Refresh my memory, amigo."

"Shoot 'em down deader'n egg-stealin' Mescin muchachos." Red Snake gave a lopsided grin.

"Damn," Ivy said, rising from behind the bar. "I was just startin' to like the big man."

"No accountin' for taste," Red Snake said.

They all laughed.

At the bottom of the pit, the big man groaned.

He lifted his head, winced as a sharp stiletto of tooth-gnashing pain stabbed him from ear to ear. He opened his eyes and looked around, remembering where he was when the rancid smell of the dead men bit him.

He couldn't see much. Night had fallen. Staring up at the ragged circle of sky at the top of the hole, he saw stars. The night was silent, the wind having apparently died.

He took another breath, and the horrific stench was like a cold slap of water. Gaining his knees, he ran a hand across the back of his head, felt a tender goose egg at the crown. He felt a wetness there, as well. Blood. Most of it had dried, however. He'd had a good braining, and it was hard to remember all that had gone on for the past several days, but he felt the shadows of the troubling memories sliding around in his noggin.

He'd live. He wasn't sure he wanted it to all come back to him, but it would. He knew one thing, though — if he got out of the pit alive, he'd ride well around the next cursed town in his trail.

He grumbled to himself, felt around until he'd found his hat, rifle, and the gut shredder, then heaved himself to his feet. The bottom of the pit turned this way and that beneath his boots. Leaning forward, he steadied himself against a shelflike chunk of rock protruding from the side of the shaft.

"In Dixie Land where I was born, early on one frosty mornin'," he sang through gritted teeth, reaching up for a chunk of rock glistening in the starlight, beginning to climb.

He took it slower this time. Not so much because he wanted to but because every tug of his hand and push of his boots caused an invisible, angry giant to slam a sledgehammer against the crown of his skull. Sometimes not so hard but at other times so hard that he had to pause to keep from passing out.

"Look away!" he sang, his voice quavering with exertion, grabbing a rock above his head with his left hand, grinding his right boot into a slight cleft in the wall below him. He pulled, grinding his jaws, straining, singing, "Look away! Look away!"

He rose along the wall, raking his cheek

against it. "Look away! Dixie Land!"

His voice stopped echoing as he lifted his head from the hole and hauled his torso over the edge of the pit and rested against the cool, rocky ground, his legs hanging over the side. He drew refreshing draughts of air untainted by the horrific reek below though he could smell the death stench on his clothes.

Finally, he hoisted his legs out of the pit and rolled to the side, coming to rest on his back and staring up at the stars. The heavens blinked out for a time. When he regained consciousness, he could see a few stars but others appeared to be blocked by something between him and the sky.

He twitched his nose. Above the stench of death rising off his own body, he smelled sweat and bear grease. He heard a slight squawk, like that which hemp makes when it's stretched.

He jerked his head up, heart leaping in his chest.

It wasn't a straining rope he'd heard. It was the animal gut of the bows drawn taut before him by three braves standing over him, aiming the flint-tipped arrows at his face.

The brave standing farthest to his right showed his teeth as he shoved his dark face closer to Prophet's rasping, "Gold! Where . . . gold . . . is . . . or . . . you" — he raised his bow and lifted the arrow higher, drawing the missile back tighter against the gut string — *"die!"*

Prophet pulled his head back, staring at the pointed flint tips glaring at him with stony menace. He felt a muscle in his cheek twitch. He was about to open his mouth to speak when gravel crunched down the slope behind the three braves bearing down on him, and a man said in relatively clear English, "Hold it, brothers. Hold on, now. What you got there?"

He said something in the guttural grunts of the Mojave tongue, and the braves lowered their bows and stepped back, two parting to reveal the big Indian coming up behind them. Prophet didn't need to see the lightning bolt scar on his forehead to know he was looking at the tough nut himself, El Lightning. The man squatted in front of Prophet and grinned, showing his surprisingly white teeth in the darkness.

"Ah, amigo! You live!" El Lightning chuckled, his long, coarse black hair dancing around his shoulders. "I'll be damned. I thought you died down there. *Whew!*" He waved a hand in front of his head. "I don't mean to insult you, brother, but — *ay-heee*

329

— you smell bad!"

Prophet studied the big Mojave dubiously, trying to reconcile the man's savage appearance with his near-perfect albeit Spanish-accented English. The war chief held a Henry repeater in his hands; it hung by a braided strip of burlap from his neck and shoulder. The bounty hunter glanced at the three braves flanking El Lightning, then returned his gaze to the big man himself. "Wouldn't have a bar of soap on you, would you?"

"It is no laughing matter, brother. That stink. You need a bath." El Lightning glanced into the hole behind Prophet. "What's down there, anyway? Dead bobcat or something?"

"Three dead federals."

The chief drew his head back, ridging his heavy brows skeptically.

"Deputy United States marshals."

"Ahhhh!" El Lightning smiled. "I wondered what happened to them. We saw them from a distance two, three weeks ago, but I was more interested in your amigos."

"They're not my amigos."

One of the braves flanking El Lightning spat the hard consonants and clipped vowels of the Mojave tongue while glaring at Prophet over his leader's shoulder. El

330

Lightning grinned, his broad cheeks dimpling. "My brother, Sikasaw, is growing impatient. He says if you don't tell us where the gold is buried, he is going to scalp you and use your hair to clean his ass."

26

"That's a might personal, ain't it?" Prophet dryly quipped, meeting the gaze of the hatchet-faced brave who wanted to take his topknot. "I mean, since we just met, an' all."

"I think you're right. And after all you've been through, down there with those dead lawmen — whew, you stink, brother! — I think you could use a pull from my tiswin flask."

"Tiswin?" Prophet said, widening his eyes. If anything could clear the hammer out of his head and ease the misery of his battered bones and strained tendons, it was the extremely intoxicating Mojave tanglefoot brewed from sprouted corn.

"My Jicarilla squaw prepared me a batch special for this trip," El Lightning said. "Come. I am a most gracious host, brother."

The war chief straightened, said something to the braves in their mother tongue, then turned and strode down the gravelly hill. Two of the braves lunged toward Prophet, relieving him of his weapons, one giving special interest to the double-bore Greener, caressing the barrels fondly. The third kicked Prophet's ribs and grunted orders.

Cursing, Prophet hauled himself to his feet, taking his head in his hands when the giant resumed work with the massive sledgehammer. He wasn't allowed to linger and soothe his aches and pains, however. The three Mojaves kicked and prodded him down the hill where four horses stood. El Lightning galloped off atop his big skewbald steed, swinging up canyon beyond the mine, in the opposite direction of the town.

Prophet was ordered to climb onto one of the other three mustangs. Two of the braves rode double, leading Prophet's mount, and he lowered his head and pressed his fingers into his temples as the pony's fast, choppy gait kicked up the misery in his skull and a squealing in his ears.

If he'd been in better condition, he might have been able to leap off the mustang and escape into the brush. As it was, he couldn't have waved a fly from his face, much less tried to outrun Mojave arrows.

He was glad that he didn't have to endure the ride for long before a fire appeared at a confluence of two dry washes well concealed by thick brush, rocks, and organ pipe cactus. His horse was led into the wash. Around the fire were ten or so Mojaves hunkered on their butts, gear including saddle blankets and guns and bows and arrow quivers spread out around them.

The camp smelled wildly sweet, like a bobcat lair.

El Lightning stood a little to one side of the fire, his horse being led away by a short, humpbacked brave with a limp. As Prophet was ordered off his horse, he saw another brave rise from his position near the fire and walk over to El Lightning. Prophet blinked as the brave snaked a hand around the war chief's waist. But then he saw that El Lightning's companion was not a young man but a young woman, firelight glistening off her brown, well-turned legs.

She wore a strip of deerskin across her breasts and around her hips, with several strings of beads around her neck. Beaded rings dangled from her ears, partially concealed by her long, coarse black hair that hung nearly to her waist. Her breasts were large and firm and barely concealed by the deer hide. Even in Prophet's raggedy-heeled condition, he felt a manly reaction to the Mojave princess.

"Come and sit, senor." El Lightning beckoned to Prophet, then lowered his head to speak to the princess, who turned and trotted off in the direction of the horses. Turning back to Prophet, he said, "I would use your proper name if I knew what it was."

Prophet introduced himself as he looked warily around at the hard-faced braves all staring at him with open menace. They not only smelled like bobcats, they looked like them — cunning and savage. Some were cleaning rifles or greasing arrow shafts while others devoured small rabbits they'd cooked over the fire, grunting and groaning and breaking the small bones to suck out the marrow, scrubbing their hands on their arms and thighs.

They all kept firing quick, hungry, eager looks at Prophet, grinning at each other, as though at some private joke amongst them.

Prophet felt like a rabbit at a rattlesnake convention. He glanced at the three braves who'd slapped their horses away toward where the Indians' cavvy was gathered farther up the wash. They seemed to have divvied up his arsenal — one taking his Colt, one his Winchester, the last his shotgun. That brave was now showing it to another, older brave who was lounging back on his elbows and hiking a shoulder and pooching his lips with disinterest.

El Lightning barked orders and waved his arms in annoyance, and three braves who had been sitting around the fire scrambled to their feet, grabbed bows and arrow quivers or Spencer carbines, and scrambled off toward the horses. They'd been ordered to keep watch on San Gezo, Prophet thought. Maybe relieving other pickets. They were obviously keeping a close eye on the town. Watching for some indication of where the gold had been hidden.

El Lightning gestured for Prophet to sit down in the space opened up by the three dismissed braves. Then he sat down himself, pressing his moccasins together and resting his elbows on his raised knees. Two long-barreled Colt Army revolvers jutted from the red sash around his waist, and his brass-cased Henry dangled down his back.

The comely Mojave princess came out of the trees on the other side of the wash. She had an intoxicating walk — one which Prophet could have more fully appreciated in less threatening circumstances. She had a sheep's bladder flask dangling from her neck by a leather cord. The flask jostled atop her breasts that were also jostling behind their scanty deerskin covering.

As she approached the fire, the reflection

caressing her smooth, cherry-dark skin, El Lightning said something to her in their tongue. She continued past the war chief and knelt down so close to Prophet he could smell the girl's not unpleasantly gamey aroma.

She looked down at him, her eyes cold, one nostril flaring slightly. Her breasts rose and fell behind the flask. The fire shunted dark shadows across her round, pretty face. She sat so close to Prophet that he could see a couple of widely spaced freckles on her neck and along her jaw.

El Lightning chuckled, then lifted a hand to indicate the flask. "*Por favor*, amigo. Drink. Sno-So-Wey doesn't bite, though she looks like she could, huh?" He laughed.

Prophet saw that the girl wasn't going to extend the flask to him but instead sat there within two feet, silently taunting him. So he reached out and lifted the flask from her breasts. A .45 shell casing was shoved into the lip of the flask. Prophet removed it and, leaning close to the girl because the cord wasn't very long, took a tentative pull of the tiswin.

He'd prepared himself, but it still hit him like a loaded lumber dray, burning his throat as it went down and slammed against the bottom of his belly. He thought he heard it gurgle and steam down there. He'd drunk tiswin before and knew that if you drank too much you'd wake up later feeling like you'd been run over by a Baldwin locomotive screeching brakeless down a steep mountain.

El Lightning stared at him expectantly, the skin above the bridge of his nose wrinkled slightly. So as not to offend that war chief, Prophet took another, deeper pull from the flask.

He doubted the Indians intended to poison him. One, they hadn't gotten what they wanted from him yet, and, two, no Mojave would ruin good tiswin. He drew a sharp breath through his teeth, trying to quell the fire smoldering on his tonsils, then corked the flask with the .45 casing and set it back against the girl's lovely, jutting breasts. The tender nipples of both were outlined behind the deerskin swatch.

"Nothin' like tiswin," Prophet said, giving the girl a wink, which she totally ignored as she got up and went over to kneel before El Lightning.

"Not bad, huh, Lou? My squaw, I mean. She's Yuma. Stole her from Chief White Horn before I gutted him for allowing his sons to steal horses from my own band." El Lightning took a drink, then leaned over and kissed the girl full on the mouth. He set the flask against her breasts, fondled one of them, causing the girl to smile at him smolderingly, then waved her away.

When she was gone, El Lightning stared at Prophet for a long time. The bounty hunter held the war chief's gaze. He didn't have the information the man wanted, and for that he knew he might very soon be saddling a cloud or enduring excruciating torture. He wasn't sure how he was going to escape this wildcat lair, but he had to find a way or he'd die very slowly, Mojave style, screaming.

"Now, then," El Lightning said. "You've enjoyed my hospitality. Tell me where the gold is."

"How is it you have such a command of English, if you don't mind my askin'?" Prophet said, trying to buy time. But he was also genuinely curious.

El Lightning gave an indulgent smile. "I am only half of the blood. My mother was a Mejicana-Irish woman from Sonoita, captured by the Jicarilla and sold to the Mojave. She took me with her when she escaped. I was six. And all Mojave. I ran back when I was ten." The war chief smiled with satisfaction. "And became the greatest warrior the Mojave people have ever known."

"Modest, too."

"Huh?"

"Never mind," Prophet said. "You didn't care for the reservation, I take it."

"I wouldn't know. I never went. A select few of my people and I — braves who vowed to follow me and to fight the white men to do the death — hid in the Sierra Madre. We will take our land back. It will require time as well as arms and ammunition." El Lightning bored holes in Prophet with his eyes. "And gold. It will take much gold for all the arms and ammunition we will need for the final revolution."

"I doubt Johnson has that much gold. Probably just robbed a bank along the border. They don't grow banks very big along the border."

El Lightning shook his head. "I saw the strongbox through the spyglass I stole from an American cavalry officer I gutted and left to die howling in the desert."

He paused, making sure the threat struck home. It did. Prophet felt his intestines sort of coil and uncoil like disturbed snakes.

"It was a large box and a heavy one, lashed to a big mule. Much gold. I will ask you only once more, my friend Prophet. Where is it? Buried out here? Or hidden in the saloon?"

340

Prophet sighed, made a fateful expression. "I don't suppose it would do any good to tell you I'm not a member of that gang. I'm a bounty hunter. I rode in here with some curly wolves I was tracking. We threw in together on account of you slingin' lead and arrows at us. Ran into Johnson in San Gezo. Wouldn't know him from Adam's off ox. Never even heard of the man. West Coast brigand, it seems."

El Lightning merely arched a brow. The story had fallen on deaf ears.

"Well, shit," Prophet said, glancing at the three braves behind him, armed with his own guns and staring at him like a pack of hungry wolves. "I'm not sure what to tell you."

"Don't bullshit me, Prophet. Where is the gold? Buried out here? Surely, they don't have it with them in the saloon!"

"I do believe that's where they have it," Prophet said, not knowing what else to say, merely trying to buy as much time as he could.

He had no satisfactory answer to El Lightning's question. All he could do was hem and haw and hope maybe one of the braves moved up close enough that he could go for a gun. If he was going to die, he'd die at some cost to the Mojaves. He also wanted to make it a fast death. Being slow roasted over an Mojave fire wasn't how he wanted to be sent off to his pal, Ole Scratch.

"You lie like a coyote, Lou."

"Now, hold on, El Light—"

"They would have hid it or buried it outside where flames could not reach it if we burned the saloon." The war chief grinned. "Have you ever seen a flaming Mojave arrow, Lou?"

Prophet let his gaze flick toward the two long-barreled Colts protruding from El Lightning's sash. "I'm gettin' damn tired of all this palaver." He gave a ragged sigh. "All right — here's the information you're wantin'. You know that little pink adobe at the far end of town?"

"*Si.*"

"We buried it in there —" Prophet cut the sentence off as he bolted off his heels, dove over the fire, and smashed his head and shoulders into El Lightning's chest.

The war chief gave a startled grunt and hit the ground on his back. Prophet wrapped his hands around both Colts' walnut handles and rammed one of the guns into the war chief's belly. El Lightning slashed that hand away before Prophet could cock the weapon. On the ground around him, shadows moved.

Something hard slammed against his head. It felt as though his skull had been cleaved in two.

The area around the fire pitched and bobbed around him, slowing blurring before turning completely, mercifully black.

27

The fires of hell were finally consuming Lou
Prophet. He hadn't counted on the heat being this intense. He also hadn't counted on
the fact that Ole Scratch would have laid
him out on a rough stone slab when he
should have been working.

Where were the planet-sized coal piles?

Where was the stove?

Where was his shovel?

There was only darkness and heat. A
fierce, burning heat and the savage smash-
ing of a giant sledgehammer against his
exposed brain.

He tried to squirm his way off the slab
but he couldn't move. His hands and feet
were secure. He shook his head from side
to side as the flames licked around his face,
at times more intense on one area than
another. He struggled. He groaned. His
mouth was as dry as a swatch of old leather
left out in the desert, his tongue so thick he

had trouble keeping it in his mouth and out of the flames.

Something sharp dug into his chest. He felt a warm draft, heard a guttural chortling.

Finally, to his own surprise, he was able to open his eyes. The light was like razor-edged javelins impaling the orbs. He squeezed them shut, slitted them, the light slithering like burning kerosene under the lids. Inside the light, he saw the bird — a large, bald-headed bird with flat, BB-like eyes and a wretchedly hooked beak.

The bird's head suddenly turned red. The body jerked and sort of leaped in the air. A rifle barked somewhere in the distance as the bird flew off Prophet's chest and landed in the red gravel to his left. Prophet's head pounded. The back of his neck was stiff and sore. He lay his head back against the ground.

Shortly, he heard the thuds of an approaching horse. He turned his head to the right, saw Mean and Ugly galloping toward him down a low rise. A small man with a straw sombrero and wearing flannel shirt and ragged denims sat in the saddle, holding a Spencer carbine in his right hand. Mean snorted and blew and for a second Prophet thought the horse would trample him before coming to a skidding halt, spraying sand and gravel over the bounty hunter's bare arms and chest.

"Senor," a man's low voice lamented. "Ah, senor . . ."

Prophet couldn't see the man's face against the brassy sky, but he recognized the voice of Senor Bocangel. Through one squinted eye he watched the short, wiry little Mexican swing awkwardly down from Mean's back, a canteen in his hand. The horse snorted and stomped.

As Bocangel dropped to one knee beside Prophet, the bounty hunter looked around, trying to get a better fix on his circumstances, his condition.

Looking down his chest, he saw that he was naked. Not wearing a stitch. The skin across his long, broad body was blistered, brassy and mottled red. His ankles were strapped to stakes buried in the gravely ground. Same with his wrists.

"Oh, senor," Bocangel lamented again, popping the cork on the canteen, then cradling and lifting Prophet's head with his left arm. "Here . . . fresh water from the well. Drink."

Prophet let some of the cool liquid dribble into his mouth. It was instantly refreshing. He could have drunk the entire canteen but just a few sips made him feel queasy, so he stopped.

"How long I been out here?" he asked the Mexican.

"The Mojaves pulled out day before yesterday. In the morning. They staked you out here just before they left, I think." Bocangel shook his head. "You are very lucky. They must have seen Johnson pull out with the others and decided to follow them rather than torture you, as only Relampago can torture."

"I got all my parts?"

"As far as I can tell, amigo."

"Untie me, will you?"

"*Si.*" Bocangel set the canteen aside, slipped a folding knife from his right boot, and began sawing through the leather strap tying Prophet's left wrist to its corresponding stake.

When his last limb was free, Prophet rolled onto his side. His head did not hurt as bad as it had sometime over the past day and a half. It was mostly a dull ache in his jaws and behind his eyes. His face and the top half of his body — every inch of it — felt as though someone had raked him hard with coarse sandpaper.

He looked around, ran the tip of his tongue across his lips. They were cracked and bloody from the burn, tasted like rock salt. The sun blasted down on him and Bocangel, who had stepped away to retrieve Prophet's hat from where the Indians had scattered his clothes and his boots.

"Put this on, amigo. Till we get you out of the sun, uh?"

Prophet looked at the hat. For a second, it didn't look like his. Nothing seemed right at the moment. He supposed the multiple brainings and being staked out to dry like a buffalo hide in the sun would do that to a fellow. Giving a ragged chuckle, he took the hat and snugged it down tight on his head.

Mean and Ugly regarded him skeptically, twitching his ears. "Yeah, it's me, hoss." Prophet looked at Bocangel, who was limping tenderly around in the sand, his leg and arm wounds wrapped with strips of blood-spotted cloth. "Pull out . . ." Prophet frowned, squinting both eyes. "That what you said? Johnson pulled out?"

"*Si.*"

"And the Injuns?"

"*Si*, senor. They followed the desperadoes. I saw them skirting the town a little after Johnson and the others left with the gold."

Prophet grabbed the chinstrap of Mean's bridle and heaved himself to his feet, grunting and groaning and shifting his weight from one sunburned foot to the other.

"What about my partner?"

"La rubia?" Senor Bocangel shrugged. "She rode out, too, Lou. Musta thought you were dead, huh? As did I. I rode out here to hunt rabbits. I just thank God they left me in one piece. I thought they would kill me as I thought they had killed you."

Prophet didn't hear that last. He was leaning against Mean and Ugly's neck, trying to get his land legs back and working the information Bocangel had imparted through his sluggish brain. Louisa had gone with the outlaws.

"Where was the gold?" he asked Bocangel.

"In the cellar of the saloon."

"The storeroom . . ." Prophet remembered that he'd been vaguely puzzled that there had been no food stored in the room behind the main saloon hall, as there would have been if ten or so folks had actually been living in San Gezo. They'd have had to store a lot of food, making maybe two or three supply runs to San Diego every year.

Only gold had been stored in that room. In the cellar beneath the wooden door in the floor.

The naked bounty hunter turned to Bocangel standing beside him, holding his clothes like an offering. Prophet was badly sunburned, and he knew that raking clothes across his tender, throbbing flesh would aggravate the torment, but he couldn't go after those killers naked. They had to have forced Louisa to join them. No way she would have gone willingly.

He grabbed his summer-weight long-handles off the pile in Bocangel's hands. Leaning back against his horse, he steeled himself, shook the underwear out, and raking air through his gritted teeth, began pulling the garment on. Witches' fingers tricked out with razor-edged nails raked his tender skin, enflaming the fire.

"You need some medicine, Lou."

"I need a bottle of tanglefoot's what I need."

Grinding his molars, he finished dressing, even wrapped his holster and shell belt around his waist though his Colt was gone, as were his Winchester and gut shredder. First things first, he thought, swinging up onto Mean's back, his denims feeling like hot irons against the insides of his thighs. Whiskey, guns, and ammunition.

Then he'd fog Louisa's trail, try to pull her out of the gang before she got whip-sawed between them and El Lightning. He had no idea what was going through her head. It was most often impossible to know.

Had they taken her, or had she gone willingly? Was Johnson's gold too enticing for her?

No. Prophet was ashamed for thinking it.

He extended his hand to Bocangel, wincing. The Mexican shook his head and offered a wan smile. "No need, senor." He led Mean by the horse's bridle over to a rock. He stepped onto the rock, giving a wince of his own and sort of hoisted himself over Mean's hindquarters.

"Thanks," Prophet said tightly.

"De nada."

Prophet looked around. "Where are we?"

"Town is that way, amigo."

Prophet touched spurs to Mean's flanks, and the horse trotted southwest along the edge of a shallow, brush-lined wash. Fifteen minutes later, he and Bocangel entered town from its east end. Prophet checked the horse down and sat staring down the broad, main street littered with several dead Indians, twisted where they'd fallen in the battle that had been waging for the past couple of days.

There was one dead horse. Prophet clucked Mean ahead, reined up near the dead mustang. Bocangel dismounted first and then Prophet swung tenderly down from Mean's back.

The butt of a carbine rifle stuck out from beneath the dead horse. Prophet knew that all the Indians' rifles and pistols had been confiscated earlier by his own party, for the weapons themselves and also for the ammo they carried. He'd seen this carbine before, sticking out from beneath the horse, but he'd been too busy for bothering with a gun pinned beneath four hundred pounds of dead horse.

He bothered with it now, grabbing the gun by its stock, planting one boot against the horse's hip, and pulling. The gun slid free. Prophet worked the cocking lever until the gun was empty. He scowled at the five cartridges in the palm of his left hand.

Bocangel extended his own carbine to the bounty hunter. "You may take my gun, Lou."

"No." Prophet reloaded the Indian's carbine, the stock of which had been decorated with brass rivets forming a wolf's head. "I may not be back."

He slipped a goatskin water flask from around the horse's neck, shook the flask to judge how much water was in it, and turned to Bocangel. "What's your part in all this?"

Bocangel shrugged. "My son and I guided Johnson and Senorita Knight south of the border. We lived here in San Gezo, Joaquin and I. We had gone to San Diego for supplies. We prospected these mountains, you see, Lou. In exchange for our help, Johnson's gang offered us a sackful of gold dust each, and . . . our lives."

The old Mexican turned his mouth corners down and stared out over the desert stretching off beyond the mountains. "Joaquin . . . he became greedy and stole a bar of the gold, and set off across the desert. I chased after him, to bring him back before Johnson realized he was gone. The Indians got to him first. They found the bar."

"And realized how much gold Johnson's bunch must have been hauling." Prophet stepped as lightly as he could to keep his burned skin from screaming.

He slung the goatskin flask around his neck, slid the rifle into his saddle boot, and led Mean over to the covered stone well standing in the center of the main street. Bocangel walked across the street to the livery barn and disappeared inside. Prophet winched up a bucket of water, filled the goatskin flask as well as his own canteen, hung both from his saddle horn, and swung into the leather.

Bocangel walked out of the livery barn carrying Prophet's saddlebags and bedroll. "You will need these."

Prophet waited until the Mexican had strapped the bedroll behind his saddle cantle and set the saddlebags over the horse's rump.

"Which way'd they head?"

"West across the mountains. There is a spring there, the last one for a hundred miles."

"Will they know where it is?"

"They will follow the only trail."

He cast a backward glance at the Oasis Saloon and Dance Hall. Bocangel stood in the street behind him. Dust licked up around his boots in the rising breeze. A bad-luck wind in a cursed town.

Prophet said, "Much obliged, senor."

"Go with God, Lou."

Prophet turned his head forward, put spurs to Mean's flanks, and trotted for several yards along the street before galloping on out of San Gezo, following the trail snaking west.

28

One day earlier, the outlaw gang comprised of Hawk Johnson's gang, Lazzaro's gang, Captain Chacin and his one surviving Rurale, and Louisa Bonaventure reined up at the base of the Montanas Muertas, where the canyon spilled into the waterless desert.

Louisa reined her pinto up beside Sugar's black and looked around the dozen riders through the dust kicked up by their horses and the mule that the black woman led and which had a Wells Fargo strongbox strapped to the stout pack frame on its back.

Lazzaro was riding lead with Hawk Johnson, the man with the constantly nervously twitching eyes who'd pretended to be the San Gezo town marshal. Lazzaro looked around, grinning to cover his wariness.

"Well, you gonna sit there all day, grinnin'?" said Johnson. "Or you gonna get your loot. We got ours, don't we? Intend to share it with you, don't we?" He gave an oblique smile. "As long as we all make it across the desert to Puerto Penasco together."

One corner of his mouth rose with faint menace.

"That's right," Lazzaro said. "That was the deal. I reckon we gotta trust each other, don't we?"

Lazzaro glowered at his unlikely accomplice. His face was gaunt, pale, and hollow-cheeked. He rode with one hand clamped over his wounded side. A while ago, as they'd ridden down the canyon from San Gezo, Louisa had spied blood leaking from the wound behind the gang leader's long cream duster.

Lazzaro glanced at Kiljoy sitting his roan beside him. Both men rode out away from the canyon mouth and into the desert beyond. As Louisa watched, sitting beside Sugar, the two riders grew small behind their rising tan dust tails. They disappeared into the ravine about a half a mile away, reappearing a half hour later.

Lazzaro had ridden into the ravine with one set of saddlebags on his horse. As he galloped back to the group, Louisa saw that he had a second set of saddlebags — the ones containing the stolen Nogales bank money — flapping over the first set.

"How much you got?" asked Doc Shackleford, sitting a rangy strawberry mare near the black woman, Thelma Knight, and the mule hauling the strongbox. Tulsa St. James sat a big cream to Shackleford's left, wearing a long duster, stylish black gloves, and a white silk scarf on her coifed red head. She had a surly, impatient expression on her pudgy, brown-eyed face. The whore carried a sawed-off shotgun in each of the two sheaths she wore on her saddle, one on each side of her mount.

"Sixteen thousand," Lazzaro said a tad defensively.

"Not much compared to what we got," said George LeBeouf, pulling his horse's head up away from a clump of jimsonweed. "But I reckon it'll buy us a few *putas* in Monterrey." He and several of the other men chuckled before the burly outlaw glanced at Louisa, Ivy, and Sugar, and drawled, "Pardon, ladies."

"We got the money," Sugar said, pulling her horse up to where Lazzaro, Kiljoy, and Johnson sat clumped at the head of the pack. The blind woman slid her pistol from the holster on her right thigh and shot Lazzaro through his forehead.

The shot spooked the horses and evoked two indignant brays from the mule.

Guns came up with loud snicks of iron

against leather. All eyes swung to the blind woman, who, stony-faced, holstered her own smoking pistol as Lazzaro rolled down the side of his pitching horse to hit the ground with a thud. Sugar swung her left arm out a couple of times before grabbing Lazzaro's reins.

She turned to Johnson, who stared skeptically, both eyes twitching, over the long barrel of his own Colt leveled at the blind woman's belly. "He was my man," she said, staring straight ahead. "And he'd come to the end of his trail. I wasn't going to give you the satisfaction of doing it yourself, Johnson. Now, let's ride before those savages catch up to us."

Louisa had also palmed one of her Colts. Now she couldn't help curling her upper lip approvingly, suppressing the Colt's hammer, and returning the gun to its holster. The others in the group laughed nervously as they regarded the blind woman. Even Roy Kiljoy and Red Snake laughed, though with a little less genuine humor as the others, staring down at their dead leader, who lay on his back, both eyes open, blood dribbling from the gaping hole in his forehead, just above the bridge of his nose.

Johnson, Thelma Knight, and the others moved out. Louisa stayed back with Sugar, who turned to her as the hoof thuds of the others dwindled into the distance.

"You're still here," Sugar said. She turned her head toward Lazzaro and stared off over the outlaw leader's body. "I'm glad. I need you now, Leona."

"Maybe we need each other, Sugar."

Sugar turned toward Louisa. "Why do you need me?"

"I don't know." Louisa turned to stare back up the canyon in the direction of San Gezo, where she'd left so much — not the least of which was her lover and partner, Lou Prophet — behind. "Maybe to show me another way."

What way was that? she wondered all that day as they rode a winding trail through the heart of the Montanas Muertas, at the tail end of the outlaw pack.

What way was that?

Maybe the way she'd always been looking for to leave her grief behind. If killing thieves and killers hadn't done it, maybe joining them, becoming them, would.

Lou was likely dead. The night before, she'd scoured the town and the desert for him, but the wind had blown all his sign away and he hadn't answered her calls. Killed by the Mojaves, most likely, though it was impossible for her to imagine the big, rugged man dead. The idea was incomprehensible to her. It left her feeling hollow and numb.

With him gone, what else did she have left but to try to make life sufferable?

It was a long, hard ride without water except that which they had filled their canteens with before leaving San Gezo. Louisa looked around carefully as she followed the winding trail but saw no sign that the Indians were following them. But they had to be. Johnson had confessed to her and the others that El Lightning wanted the gold. With as much gold as Louisa suspected was in the strongbox — enough to arm every Mojave in the Southwest and Mexico, no doubt — the Mojaves would chase the desperadoes to the ends of the Earth.

They came to the barranca's southern edge just after dark. Hawk Johnson and Red Snake had scouted ahead and found the spring. The group set up a dry camp in a broad niche in the rocks along the side of a steep ridge. The spring lay in a stone bowl just below the camp, only forty yards away.

There was little cover around the spring, so the group decided to remain in the niche for the night, keeping an eye on the rock tank and scouting the area under cover of darkness. They were all wily enough to know that the Mojaves could have the tank covered and be waiting to pick the gang off one by one when they went down for water.

The horses were picketed together at the edge of the camp, where they could be easily watched. Louisa spread her bedroll near Sugar's, under mesquite branches overhanging the bank. The group was silent, the rocks and brush around the camp dark with purple starlight mottling the open areas.

No one smoked. The stars hung down. There was no breeze to speak of, and coyotes howling a mile away sounded near enough to throw a stone at.

Kiljoy, Johnson, and Thelma Knight stole off to scout around the group's bivouac in search of stalking Indians. Doc Shackleford took the first watch on the shelf overlooking the spring.

There was nothing to do but eat jerky and biscuits, drink water, and doze. Louisa couldn't sleep, however. Razor-edged thoughts raced through her skull. She did not feel so much sad about Prophet. Or she didn't think it was sadness that made her chest feel as though she'd been impaled with a war lance. She felt only numb, as though she'd awakened after a long sleep and couldn't get her bearings.

Her closest ally now was Sugar. How odd

that she'd find herself so tied to a blind outlaw woman. But then, nothing ever made sense.

"Why'd you do it?" she said sometime after midnight, when she'd taken a turn scouting the water tank.

Louisa leaned back against the bank under the arching branches. Sugar lay back with her hat down over her eyes, but Louisa sensed the redhead was awake. Her shoulders were rigid under her leather jacket, as though her senses were in full play.

Sugar poked her hat brim back off her forehead. "Because he thought I couldn't live without him, and I was beginning to believe it myself."

"What changed?"

Sugar lifted a shoulder. "I realized I had to live without him." She turned to Louisa, looking past her in Sugar's mysterious way. "You're my eyes now, when I can't see for myself."

"How can you see for yourself? I don't understand that."

"I can't see much, just shifting shadows. They have more definition when they're dangerous. And I can smell things, hear things you can't hear, sense danger in places you'd never dream."

"Do you sense it here?"

Sugar chuckled under her breath and settled her head back against the bank. "The Mojaves are all over. We'll be ambushed tomorrow, probably after first light."

Louisa looked around at the dark bank rising on the other side of a long strip of purple light marking the floor of the wash. She pricked her ears, hearing little but a soft, ticking silence, the low snores of one of the men on her left.

Turning to Sugar, who had her hands laced together on her belly, she said, "Shouldn't we tell the others?"

"Why would we want to do that?" The outlaw woman's lips stretched wide, showing the ends of her white teeth. "When the bullets and arrows start flying, I'm thinking me and you and the mule and Tony's saddlebags'll just slip off together."

Louisa considered this as she shuttled her gaze to her left, where the others were gathered on both sides of the niche, most of them sleeping. "That's quite a plan, Sugar. Likely won't work, you know."

"No." Sugar dropped her voice an octave. Her hands rose and fell slowly atop her belly. "But is there really anything here you're gonna miss all that much, Leona? Besides him, I mean."

Louisa rested her head back against the

bank and tugged her hat down over her eyes. "Nope."

The gang rose at dawn and quietly saddled their horses. They drew straws to decide who would carry the canteens down to the spring, fill them, and bring them back to the group.

With all the canteens filled, the group would then meander down the ridge through thick cover and out onto the open desert and on the trail that would, after a three-day ride, bring them to the Sea of Cortez and much reveling in Puerto Penasco.

Red Snake Corbin drew the short straw. Cursing under his breath and checking the loads in his pistols, he let the others hang their canteens over his saddle horn. Tulsa gave him a mocking kiss, and Thelma Knight told him to "go with God."

"Thanks very much. That means a lot, comin' from you, bitch."

"I love it when you call me names, amigo."

"Fuck you, Ivy. Or whoever the hell you are."

"It would have to be really late and I really drunk."

The black woman and the others chuckled.

Keeping a cocked Remington in his right hand while holding his horse's reins in the other, Red Snake led the mount up and over the shelf and down the other side.

Slowly, he moved amongst the rocks, swinging his head from left to right, watching for flying arrows. The canteens clattered softly against each other as they hung down both sides of his horse. The horse sensed Red Snake's tension and jerked his head high, so that Red Snake had to keep jerking down on the reins.

The spring lay ahead in a broad open area in which green tufts of grass grew. Someone had mortared stone around it, and roofed it, so that it looked like any well. There was no cover for fifteen yards around it.

Slowly, his heart thudding, his hand sweating against the gun handle, he led the horse up to within six feet of the coping. A bucket sat on the edge of the stonework, a rope attached to it. Red Snake looked around once more, then grabbed two canteens off his saddle horn.

He depressed the Schofield's hammer, holstered the pistol, and with both canteens slung over his shoulder, walked over to the well. He set the canteens down at the base of the stonework, grabbed the wooden bucket, and glanced into the gaping hole.

His eyes widened and his lower jaw dropped when he saw the Indian staring up at him from just below the lip of the well.

The brave's short, stocky body was wedged across the opening about four feet down from the top, his feet grinding into one side of the stonework, his shoulders into the other.

He had an arrow nocked to his bow. The Mojave's presence had just started to register in Red Snake's brain before the outlaw's heart stopped beating. The stroke alone would have killed him had the Indian not loosed the arrow with a sharp twang that echoed inside the well and sent the wooden missile slamming into Red Snake's skull through his left eye with a liquid thunk.

29

Mean and Ugly snorted.

Prophet, who'd been dozing against the side of a boulder, jerked his head and rifle up.

The rifle was already cocked. He saw the hatchet turning end over end toward his head, and he twisted sideways, hearing the hatchet whistle past his right ear and slam into the boulder behind him. The hatchet tumbled onto his shoulder as Prophet squeezed the Winchester's trigger.

The Indian standing crouched and wide-eyed a few feet up a rocky grade before him flew straight up and backward as Prophet's .44 round blew his throat out the back of his neck before leaving him thrashing on the uneven ground, bleeding over both hands clamped to his neck.

Prophet grabbed Mean's reins as the horse curveted and whinnied his disdain for the Indian's sudden appearance. Hearing guns begin popping in the distance, Prophet heaved himself to his feet, his denims mercilessly raking him, and swung into the leather. He did not wait to see if any other Mojaves were stalking him, but crouched forward over Mean's neck and rammed his spurs against the gelding's flanks.

Horse and rider leaped the still-spasming Mojave and headed on down a meandering wild-horse trail and up a grade toward a low saddle. He spied movement on his right, saw a brave with a carbine scrambling amongst the rocks. The brave was caught off guard by the galloping rider and managed to snap off only one wild round before Mean gained the saddle and lunged down the other side.

The sun was not yet up, and the terrain was mostly shadows, but Prophet could see smoke rising from amongst the rocks and brush a hundred yards beyond. He could see the shooters scrambling around on the lip of a rise, shooting away from Prophet and into a depression beyond, in which other shooters scrambled around, returning fire.

Beyond both sets of shooters the mountain tapered down toward open desert stretching off toward the Sea of Cortez unseen in the south.

Prophet sawed back on Mean's reins and looked around quickly. An escarpment jutted from a sandy, aproned hill on his right. He reined Mean around, booted him up the rise and around to the backside of the scarp, dismounted, and tied Mean to a spindly mesquite.

Shucking the Indian rifle from his saddle boot, he cocked it one-handed and ran into a notch in the scarp, suppressing the pain in his sunburned hide as he climbed up the notch. He found a niche amongst the rocks near the top of the scarp and found a comfortable perch.

"Four rounds," he told himself.

From his vantage, he could see several Mojaves shooting into the broad, shallow gully beyond. He couldn't see much of them because of the brush and jumbled rocks, but he could see enough to place a couple of well-aimed shots. He didn't think that any of the Mojaves before him had seen him, and he hoped they wouldn't until he could get his hands on more ammo.

Smoke puffed from the brush and rocks about sixty yards in front of him. It also puffed from about a hundred yards beyond the Indians, the crackle of reports rising and flatting hollowly around the mountain. Bullets fired by the desperadoes blew up dust and gravel and rock shards around the Mojaves, who were not shooting from stationary positions but scrambling around the rocks, moving in on their prey.

Prophet took aim, fired.

The Indian had moved as he'd pulled the trigger, and the bounty hunter's bullet blew a branch off a pipe-stem cactus to the right of the brave.

The brave whipped around, wide eyed with anger and surprise, and Prophet's second shot made the brave jerk back against a boulder. The brave dropped his rifle as he fell to his knees and, clutching his belly with both hands, fell forward on his face.

Prophet ducked down behind the rocks, waited a few seconds, then edged another look toward the Mojaves, shuttling his gaze from left to right along their flank. None, it appeared, had realized the shot that had killed the brave had come from behind them. The Indian closest to the dead brave was fifteen yards away and flinging arrows at the outlaws as he darted amongst the rocks.

"Two shots," Prophet muttered, pulling his head back down. "Not bad. Not half bad at all."

He climbed tenderly down the scarp the

way he'd climbed it, stole around from behind the rocky thumb, and ran crouching in the direction of the dead brave, weaving amongst the dry shrubs and boulders. He'd just run out from behind one such boulder when an arrow snicked nap from his right pant leg.

Wheeling, he saw that he hadn't been as covert as he'd thought he'd been. A brave was running toward him, wildly leaping rocks while he nocked another arrow. Prophet threw himself to his left as the Indian sent another shaft missiling toward him.

Prophet fired from his backside too quickly. The brave yowled as Prophet's bullet drilled his left knee.

Cursing at the wasted bullet, Prophet fired again, aiming more carefully and punching a slug through the middle of the brave's calico shirt. The brave flew back over a rock, one leg hanging up on the rock, his foot bobbing as he died.

Like several of the other braves, including the first one he'd shot, this brave was wearing a single bandolier on his chest. Prophet looked around — no other Indians, or desperadoes for that matter, were bearing down on him — then ran over and pulled the bandolier from the brave's chest and slung it over his own head and shoulder. He stepped behind a barrel cactus and slipped .44 rounds from the belt and thumbed them into the Winchester's breech.

With the gun loaded, he walked out from behind the boulder, rested a shoulder against it as he surveyed the field of battle before him.

He could see several dead Indians, including the two he'd killed, and two dead desperadoes farther down the draw. The shooting continued, an angry fusillade accompanied by the Indians' war whoops and the desperadoes' angry shouts. He squinted his eyes against the brassy sun but could not see Louisa amidst the rocks and cactus and occasional humps of clay-colored earth.

The Indians were moving away from Prophet, running and leaping as they triggered lead or flung arrows toward the desperadoes. They had the desperadoes on the run now, and Johnson, Knight, and the others were shouting and running away, swinging around now and then to fling lead behind them.

Prophet dropped to a knee and ran his wrist across his chin. Where was Louisa? She might already be dead. In that case, he was wasting his time. Let the Indians and the desperadoes kill each other. He'd be left with the gold and stolen Nogales bank money to head north with.

But he had to know of Louisa's fate. He had to know if she was here of her own free will, or if they'd forced her to come. He had to know if she was dead or alive.

He rose and ran crouching forward, tracing a circuitous route, pausing occasionally to fire at the Indians.

It wasn't long before most of the Mojaves were aware that they'd been flanked. He dispatched three. Surprised, the others scrambled up a long, rocky jog of hills on his left and out of the field of fire. Not many remained. He counted only five or so. His own bullets and those of the desperadoes had dispatched most of El Lightning's band of devoted warriors.

Prophet turned left to walk around a boulder and tripped over a dead man. Kiljoy. The outlaw had two Mojave arrows in his chest, about two inches apart and straight through his heart. He stared up at Prophet, and he seemed to be smiling.

Prophet ran crouching forward, toward where the gunfire was dwindling. The desperadoes had turned on each other now. As he watched, Thelma Knight shouted angrily and triggered a rifle from her shoulder. Her shot blew up dust behind a string of horses galloping about fifty yards beyond her — a pinto, a black, and a pack mule. Louisa stopped her brown-and-white pinto and turned, lifting a carbine to her shoulder.

Knight fired again. The second rider, Sugar Delphi, jerked sideways and almost fell from her saddle.

Prophet stopped beside a cactus and stared as Louisa fired her own carbine. The black woman took the bullet as she ran. The shot jerked her to one side, and she dove awkwardly into a patch of cactus on her left and lay unmoving.

Louisa, leading the beefy pack mule and being followed by the blind redhead, who sagged over her saddle horn, kicked her pinto into a gallop through the rocks and cactus and spindly brown shrubs, dust lifting behind hers and the other mounts. They were heading for the open desert to the south, Louisa glancing back at the wounded Sugar.

Prophet stared, lower jaw hanging. His mouth was dry. His guts were knotted.

Movement ahead jerked him out of his trance. A Mojave was running through the brush. He gave a yowl as he leaped a boulder and disappeared behind a large, flat-topped boulder twenty yards ahead of Prophet.

El Lightning was holding a rifle — Prophet's own Winchester '73 — in one hand, a bloody war hatchet in the other. Prophet heard the rifle crack. A man screamed. There were two more blasting reports on the heels of El Lightning's victorious yowls.

Prophet ran forward, leaped atop the boulder, and stopped, crouching and raising his rifle to his shoulder. El Lightning stood over Hawk Johnson's bloody body. Johnson was on his back, hands raised to his shoulders, palms out, shaking. His mouth formed a horrific *O* as he stared up at the big Indian straddling him.

El Lightning casually lowered the Winchester's barrel and blew a slug through Johnson's face. The outlaw's body relaxed, and his head turned to one side.

The Indian lifted his head slightly, widening his eyes. He did not look at Prophet, but he smiled.

"I left you to the buzzards, Lou."

"And you left one man alive in San Gezo."

El Lightning winced and shook his head at his own folly. "I should have tortured you slow and killed you. It would have given me great pleasure . . . to hear such a big gringo begging for his life."

"I'd make you beg for yours," Prophet said, "but —"

Just then El Lightning whipped around

and turned Prophet's own rifle on him. Prophet's Indian carbine roared twice, blowing the Mojave war chief up off his feet and into the rocks beyond, blood spurting from the two holes in his chest.

"— I don't have time," Prophet finished.

He ejected the last spent cartridge, heard it clatter onto the boulder, and seated a fresh round in the chamber. Guardedly, he leaped off the boulder and retrieved his Winchester, also confiscating the war chief's two crisscrossed bandoliers, so that he now had three draped over his neck and shoulders.

El Lightning lay with his body twisted, head turned to one side, the blue and ochre lines across his nose and the savage lightning bolt glistening in the harsh desert sunlight.

Holding the rifle barrel out from his hip, Prophet looked around. No one else was moving out here. No one except a few buzzards tracing lazy circles about a hundred yards over the charnel ground.

Prophet walked forward. Strewn amongst the rocks, he found the bloody, dusty, battered bodies of Tulsa St. James and Dad Conway lying ten yards apart. He found Doc Shackleford piled up at the base of an organ pipe cactus, dead, his bloody guts in his hands. A buzzard was perched proudly atop his head, giving Prophet the evil eye.

Prophet looked south. Louisa and Sugar were just now reaching the base of the mountains and heading off into the desert, their shadows short in the late morning light, copper dust rising. Sugar sagged lower in her saddle.

Prophet turned and tramped back toward where he'd left his horse behind the scarp. Halfway there, he stopped and frowned down at one of the dead Indians. Stooping, he picked his Colt .45 out of the dust, wiped it clean on his shirt, holstered it, clicked the keeper thong over the hammer, and continued to where Mean and Ugly stood waiting anxiously behind the scarp.

A half hour later, he was galloping across the desert, following Louisa's faint sign.

He rose up and over a low rise and reined up suddenly, curveting his horse. Fifty yards away, Louisa knelt on the ground with Sugar sagging faceup in her arms. The mule hauling the strongbox stood between Louisa's pinto and Sugar's black, all three cropping idly at weed tufts.

Louisa stared down at the blind woman. Sugar was not moving. She didn't seem to be breathing.

After a long time, the Vengeance Queen lifted her blond head and stared at Prophet.

Her hazel eyes were at first stony beneath her tan hat. Then they acquired a shocked, stricken cast. Her face crumpled, and she lowered her head again, shoulders shaking.

Prophet heard her sobbing. Or was it the Devil laughing?

He sat his horse, staring at her. After a long time, he clucked to Mean and rode toward her.

The employees of Thorndike Press hope you have enjoyed this Large Print book. All our Thorndike, Wheeler, and Kennebec Large Print titles are designed for easy reading, and all our books are made to last. Other Thorndike Press Large Print books are available at your library, through selected bookstores, or directly from us.

For information about titles, please call:
 (800) 223-1244

or visit our Web site at:
 http://gale.cengage.com/thorndike

To share your comments, please write:
 Publisher
 Thorndike Press
 10 Water St., Suite 310
 Waterville, ME 04901